THE CAGED GIRL

MONICA ARYA

DEDICATION

To my son, Ari. My brave, little lion. It is a huge honor raising a son that I know will be the change. You are brilliant and kind. I'm proud to know that you'll use your *privilege* of being a man to do big, beautiful and good things in the world.
I love you so much, my sunshine.
XO

And to the girls who have always had to fight for everything they have. I know you're tired, but the life you've always dreamt of is so worth chasing. I promise you'll get there, just rest a moment and keep going.
This is our now.

AUTHOR'S NOTE

Dear reader,

I am honored that you chose one of my books to read. The Caged Girl is the **sequel** to The Favorite Girl. Although Demi is on a completely new adventure, it is best to read The Favorite Girl first to understand many characters and the overall plot.

The first book in this series :
THE FAVORITE GIRL

Some of the trigger warnings include : human trafficking, kidnapping, violence against women, sexual assault and rape, graphic scenes, necrophilia, and much more.

No animal abuse. Beyond that, there are detailed lists available on my website.

SECOND AUTHOR'S NOTE

Hello, my precious little birds, I just wanted to double check that you know this book is very dark, violent, twisted and graphic.

Early readers have called it the darkest book they have ever read and it is probably the darkest I'll ever write.

Please check out those trigger warnings on my website if you are triggered by *anything*. There are triggers in The Caged Girl that weren't seen in The Favorite Girl. Please, please proceed with caution.

AUTHOR'S THIRD WARNING

Sign here if you understand how dark, disturbing, and graphic this novel is :

_____

(I'm kidding. Maybe? Maybe not. But please check out that list and take my warnings seriously.)

If you're truly ready, let's walk into the Ivory world, together once again…

PROLOGUE

"MOP THE BLOOD UP, NOW!" Alister shouted at me. I stood there, staring down at the shiny white marble floors. The blood continued to spread as the woman with her head fractured open laid there with her eyes widened, but no life left in them.

Sighing, I feel annoyed. She's made my work all that much harder. I've heard people say that life isn't black or white, but in my humble opinion, it is, in fact, one or the other, tinged with red. Droplets of blood splattered against both good and evil. Alister said girls should have structured time in the darkness to stay pure and calm. He said girls should be obedient, refer- encing dated religious material. He believed that women could threaten humanity with hysterical behavior triggered by menstruation and needed to be tamed by men.

Alister Ivory is the owner of the stunning, exclusive resort, La Gabbia. He also happens to be my new boss, and my former boss's estranged brother. Dr. Ian Ivory was a renowned and demented surgeon who enjoyed keeping girls in cages at his lavish estate with an all-white aesthetic back in America. I didn't think I'd survive the hell I was in. I was the housekeeper and was forced to marry their son in another one of the Ivory family ploys. They called me, 'the favorite girl'.

I did not want to be the favorite ever again in my lifetime.

After barely escaping, I found myself on a small, private island. Alister happened to know the people who "saved" me when I was stranded in the middle of the ocean. I knew better. Nothing was a coincidence. The Ivory family had my entire life mapped out for me, even when they were dead. But here I was, knowing I could either be the cat or the mouse, and I had to be the cat this time. I had to hunt them slowly. This would take endless time to map out a plan of perfection and execution.

Dropping to my knees, I swirled my finger into the pool of blood.

"What on earth are you doing, stupid girl!" Alister's high-pitched voice rang in my ears as he kicked me in the ribcage with his hideous thick, black shoe.

Sucking in a breath of air, I clenched my eyes shut as I stood. I didn't feel pain. Not anymore. Between being sold into trafficking at a young age by my own parents, and then working for a family who sold brides for a living, I was fortunately now a rock. But even rocks have cracks, and the unknown can seep in.

Grabbing the mop, I began sloshing the blood around while staring at the woman. She'd probably drank too many Miami Vices after eating at the all-you-can-eat buffet. The on-site doctor loved taking his time. Granted, he had his work cut out for him, with the guests ending up sick with food or alcohol poisoning. But I wasn't a fool. I knew he was tied up in something else—something worse and gruesome. I knew he was just another one of Alister Ivory's pawns and helped with the alternate business he had hidden away at this resort. I just haven't found it yet, but I will. Even if that means I must be the favorite girl.

"Did you read the fucking manual yet?" Alister shoved it at me aggressively as I held the mop between my hands.

"You must choose something and be good at it. I think for now we will keep you as a dove." He shook his head as I opened the booklet and looked at my options.

Dove Training 101
Nightingale Training 101
Breeder Training 101
Disposal of Products
Distribution of Products
Cadaver Maintenance
La Gabbia Skincare

"What are the products?" I raised my eyebrow as I ignored the dead woman on the floor.

Alister snickered as he licked his lips. "You are a dove. You need not to worry about anything beyond serving our female clientele."

CHAPTER
ONE

THE ROPES around my ankles tighten as the chirping grows louder. Sweat beads drop down my temple and I'm terrified. I'm frozen in place, wishing I could run. The window is open, and the salty ocean air is swirling around me, yet I can't breathe.

"Hello, my precious little bird…" he rasped into my ear as my heart pounded so hard I was convinced my chest cavity would crack. His hand trailed up my leg as I remained paralyzed in fear. His fingertips padded against my inner thigh just before he brushed them under my panties and pushed them inside me.

Jolting upward, I screamed and dared to open my eyes.

"Shh…Demi, it's just a dream. You've got to stay quiet." Marcie, my roommate, rushed over to me.

Blinking into the darkness, I reached down to my ankles, checking for the rope I so vividly felt.

"Demi, you're a sweaty mess," Marcie whispered as she pressed a cool washcloth against my head. Her long, bleach-blond hair was tousled over her shoulders, gently brushing against me.

She had a small, battery-operated desk lamp turned on, which I knew was a risk of its own. Alister loved darkness, and La Gabbia, the luxurious wellness resort, had strict hours where the lights at the entire resort were powered off, even though we were 'doves' and on the light floor.

I looked around our room. Everything was still white, including the brick walls surrounding us, but I could tell his preference was black. The way he only dressed in all black, the way he hated the light, and had white and black tiling scattered like a chessboard. Alister was Ian Ivory's younger brother, and something told me he was trying to be a shadow of him, but at the same time, had his own unique sickness that just begged to come out.

"Marcie," I started, but quickly pause, not knowing how to formulate the many things I've been dying to tell her. She seemed trustworthy—*seemed* being the key word.

She looked at me with her head tilted and a tiny, sleepy grin grew on her face.

"Yes, Demi?"

"How long have you worked here?" I asked instead of the original question.

"Hm…it's been five years." She shrugged and tiptoed over to the little basin in our room and hung the washcloth above it.

When I first moved into the room with Marcie, she hardly spoke to me. Then, when she finally decided to acknowledge me, the only thing we talked about was work. She'd always been extra kind to me when the night terrors happened, though.

"Why did you choose to work for La Gabbia?" I hoped she was in a chatting mood.

She smiled at me. "The same reason you did, silly."

I shook my head. "I never gave you a reason why I was working here…"

She flashed her pearly white teeth at me. "Money. A home. A life of luxury?" She stretched her hands over her head and laid back down in her bed.

"You call this a life of luxury?"

"Yes, Demi. I call this a life of luxury compared to the…"

My heart raced as she stared at me for a moment and the smile across her lips was washed away.

"Compared to the what?" I choke out.

Marcie reached for the string hanging from the lamp and let out a long sigh. "Let's hope you never find out." The light went out, and we were plunged back into complete darkness.

I laid down with my eyes opened. Marcie didn't know this, but I had to find out. That's why I was here.

I had to end it all.

CHAPTER
TWO

"I CAN'T BELIEVE he let your hair stay like this." Kandi was trimming my hair that had, apparently, grown out too long. "We will have to dye it." She shook her head as she snipped at it meticulously. "It's so dull." Kandi's hair was a stark, shiny blonde, neatly cut into a bob. All the girls here had the same hair except for one difference—some had bright blonde and the others had shiny black.

"What color?" I swallowed the lump in my throat.

"Blonde." My heart raced as Kandi's hands moved quickly.

"Why do some of the girls have black hair, and the others have white?" I scratched around my shoulder. The tattoo Alister made us all get—a small raven—was causing some kind of reaction, but he didn't care. My heart constricted knowing it was the way he marked us. Marcie had a dove on her shoulder, and so did Kandi.

Kandi looked behind her and then spun the small chair around. "Where did you come from, Demi?" She slanted her eyes at me and leaned in. Her hands pressed down against both of mine and squeezed them tightly against the handles.

"New York," I lied.

"Mm-hmm...everyone's from New York." She spun me back around and aggressively brushed out my hair.

"I don't want to dye it. I'll do the wigs."

"Fine. I guess we can try that. If there ever comes a day that Alister Ivory tells you to wear your hair black, then you should know life as you know it will be over. Anything left in that heart of yours will be gone, because you will go down into the darkness and never return," Kandi said calmly as I stared at the girl in the reflection in front of me.

Closing my eyes, I took a deep breath in and out. Today was my orientation day for the new position Alister had placed me in. I could do this. I could stay strong and play another one of the Ivory games.

A loud knock echoed against Kandi's door. She stopped whatever she was doing, including aggressively tugging at my hair.

"Mr. Ivory," she stammered as my eyes flung open and I saw Alister coming through the door. He was taller than his brother, and far better looking. *Much* better looking. His hair was black, and he always wore a three-piece fitted suit. He stared at me through the mirror and smiled as he fidgeted with his cufflink.

"You'd be gorgeous with black hair, my beautiful Demi." My original hair was long and black before the Ivory family bleached and cut it. Now here we were, doing the same thing.

Alister dismissed Kandi from the room before he approached me. I looked at her as her bright green eyes widened as she shut the door behind her.

Alister had to be in his early forties at most, and the only reason I even knew for sure he was related to Ian was because of Bradley telling me about him, and seeing the photos in the abandoned album on the boat I barely survived.

Brushing his fingers against my cheek, he smiled at me. "I'm sorry."

I swallowed as I turned to face him, and he licked his lips.

"For what?" I asked, hoping the shake in my voice wasn't noticeable.

Opening a drawer from the vanity in front of me, he pulled out a tube. Unscrewing the top, he squeezed some of the clear cream out. My shoulders tightened as I watched him rub it between his fingers and dropped down on his knees in front of me. Leaning back into my chair, I held my breath as he began gently brushing the cream against my neck where the rash from my necklace had grown larger and itchier.

Why is he being...kind?

"I'll have the doctor start you on some kind of healing antibiotic. The tattoos are done when you are sleeping, so it may be done a bit hurried." This was the same man who kicked me in my ribs for not cleaning up a pool of blood fast enough.

"It's fine," I answered as he finished up and stood.

"Demi, the people who found you stranded in the ocean knew who you were. There was a tracking device on the boat that you and Bradley were on, and...well, I figured if you could survive my brother, then you'd be the perfect person to work here." Alister reached his hand out. I looked at his palm, not sure what he wanted me to do.

None of what he was saying shocked me, because I always knew there were no coincidences in this family. I knew when I was instantly transported to Ivory Island—the privately owned island—that I was there for a reason. Even if they didn't find me first, I'd have found them.

"Ian and Daphne were monsters. They crafted

brides to marry wealthy men and suffer for the rest of their lives. I, on the other hand, believe in pleasure and then…" He paused and folded his hands together.

"Well, you don't need to know all this right now. Why don't you let Kandi fix you right up, and then you'll need to head to orientation with the rest of our new team members."

Tracing my lips with his finger, he leaned back down and locked his lips against mine. Gasping, I pulled back.

But he pushed forward and bit into my lower lip, letting out a soft chuckle.

"Shh… You can never say no to pleasure here, Demi. This wasn't our first kiss but rather a first taste." Clenching my eyes shut, he bit into my bottom lip so hard that I tasted blood.

Releasing me, Alister left the room and I refused to open my eyes until Kandi shook my shoulders.

"Demi, here." Shoving a handkerchief at me, I could see pity in her eyes. She was Marcie's roommate before me, and I wondered what happened between the two of them. All I knew was that I couldn't trust anyone.

I looked into the mirror and watched the blood drip down my chin and onto the white dress Marcie told me I needed to wear, along with the white shoes that had a thick padding in order to not emit any sound. I've already seen the rest of the girls wearing them. "I have something else for you to change into, don't worry." Kandi instructed me to tilt my head and let her do my hair. Orientation would start in a few hours, and I had to look my best. I needed to be the submissive, perfect woman in another Ivory world.

CHAPTER
THREE

"HELLO EVERYONE. My name is Suzanne. Today, we gather to learn how to welcome, care for, and appreciate our guests at La Gabbia. This resort was built from the ground up by Alister Ivory, and is invite-only to guests who need an escape from reality." The woman standing on stage had straight, black hair and was wearing a black ball gown. Her thin fingers were covered in gorgeous rings with various diamonds.

"Your group is known as the doves, and your counterpart colleagues, who are in orientation after this, are known as nightingales."

I brushed my finger against the raven tattoo on my shoulder. Looking around the room, I was surrounded by women in all white, with their hair chopped into a stark blonde bob that matched the wig on my head.

Every single girl had a tattoo of a dove in the exact same place.

The difference between the Ivory estate back in Charlotte and here was that I was no longer alone. Part of me also rationalized that this was safer somehow. This was a resort, with actual guests who were here for vacation. There had to be some kind of regulation by the island, but then again, my former boss, Dr. Ian Ivory, was running a deranged human experiment and 'business' from the comforts of a Charlotte, North Carolina suburb.

"Hey." A light tap against my legs shook me from my thoughts and I looked at the woman next to me. "This is weird, right?" She brushed her hand against her blonde hair and then reached to touch mine. "Why do we all have to match? I—"

Clearing her throat, Suzanne was looking straight at us.

"It is crucial that you all listen carefully to what your assignments and roles at La Gabbia are, my precious little doves."

My heartbeat grew erratic as chills splattered against my arms, and I locked eyes with Suzanne.

A small, sinister smile grew across her bright red

lips. Dropping my eyes down, I focused on my breathing.

"Your role is to serve and entertain our guests. Our female guests primarily are drawn to this resort as they heal and recover during their married phase of life, while their partners are brought here to learn to displace any resentment or anger they may feel as the attention is shifted from them to the demanding roles that being a wife entails. That's not our only focus, as we've recently added and expanded to any couple who is on the brink of demise in their relationship. Ultimately, we separate the couples and then bring them back together when it's time to depart. Mr. Alister Ivory has always been an advocate of a healthy marriage and family dynamic because of his own quite damaging upbringing. He believes divorce could be significantly reduced if couples go through this program, which is very much disguised as a fun, all-inclusive, but also an exclusive resort vacation." I found myself completely taken aback. This was different... This was...strange. Alister wanted to help couples?

"There are countless success stories as seen here." Suzanne clicked the remote and on the large screens behind her, images of smiling couples and quotes from them appeared.

"La Gabbia saved my marriage, but also allowed

me time to rest and pour back into my cup as a mother and wife before going back home with our baby, which we were also able to have made possible thanks to La Gabbia. My husband and I have never been as close. Thank you, Mr. Ivory and team!" A woman's voice played through a video clip, and then was seen rocking her baby as her husband looked on lovingly.

Suzanne clasped her hands together and looked at us before opening her arms wide. "My beautiful doves, you will each be assigned a section of La Gabbia and begin working with new guests today. Remember to smile and speak quietly. The guest is always, always right. However, I must add that no one, and I mean no one, is allowed to depart from La Gabbia under any circumstance unless they go through our check-out process. This is simply to maintain the utmost safety and security of our guests." Suzanne took a sip of a pink liquid from a champagne flute and lifted it into the air. Within seconds, an entire group of women dressed exactly like me swiftly moved through each row and gave us all a champagne flute as well.

"Cheers to the most amazing experience of your life, and a job you'll never retire from or leave..." Thea tipped her flute gently as the girls around me did the same, and I mimicked them.

I didn't actually drink the champagne because, as

soon as I inhaled the fragrance, nausea pooled in my belly.

The scent of peonies made my head feel light.

"Do you smell that?" I turned to the girl next to me, who was licking her bottom lip after she finished drinking.

"Smell what?" She shrugged.

"Floral? Peonies, maybe?" I whispered.

Her forehead crinkled as she eyed me with confusion. "No?"

I nodded and looked away, swallowing the saliva in my mouth to coat the dryness of my throat, which felt like it was closing in on me.

"I'm Taylor, by the way." She reached her hand out and I looked down at it.

"The music industry didn't work out?" I added with an awkward laugh.

Taylor looked at me with annoyance. "You are the strangest person I've ever met. I don't understand what you are talking about."

"Like Taylor Swift?" I had just recently learned about Taylor Swift from Marcie, who loved to quietly hum her songs before bed.

"Oh, yeah. Okay. Ha." Taylor let out a fake laugh and then looked at the girl on her other side.

I felt embarrassed. I was trying to be this normal girl talking to someone, but I made a fool of myself.

Maybe the truth was, I'd never be normal or even able to pretend to be.

"Time to stand and shuffle out quietly, little doves. Someone will be there to guide you to your stations and guests as soon as you exit."

Taylor stood excitedly as I stared at Suzanne. She was looking right back at me without blinking. Tilting her head, she lifted her hand and wiggled her fingers at me.

I wasn't going to depict weakness or fear, so I forced a smile on my face. Suzanne knew something about me already—maybe everything—and now I needed to know everything about her and this so-called family and marriage saving resort.

CHAPTER
FOUR

I WAS ASSIGNED to shadow my roommate Marcie for half of the day, and then I'd take over and jump right in to helping guests get situated with their stay. "Essentially, the couples come through and check in. The bell boys will collect their luggage and put it in their separate rooms." Marcie was walking rapidly, and I was jogging to keep up. Her blonde hair shook with every turn as she pointed at buildings. "This is for our female guests. Do you want to peek into the room to familiarize yourself with it?" I shrugged and nodded as she scanned her badge and a door slid open. Repulsion grew in my body as it resembled the doors at the Ivory estate back in Charlotte.

Except there was no small all-white twin bed or white brick walls. Instead, it was a beautiful room with ocean views and a large bed. A towel crafted into a bird was sitting on the end of the bed, while a bottle filled with blush-pink liquid, along with a unique set of products, sat on the nightstand.

"What is that?" I pointed, knowing it was the same 'champagne' we had toasted with just a mere hour ago.

"Infused-sparkling water, and the Ivory-exclusive skincare." Marcie walked to the balcony and slid the door open. Something buzzed in her pocket.

Marcie lifted a phone-like device in the air. "This will warn you anytime your assigned guests open their doors."

"Why would we need to know that they opened their door?" I walked over and joined her on the balcony. The scent of sea salt as the sunshine warmed my skin was comforting.

"So they don't escape." Marcie was staring straight at the ocean without a hint of humor on her face.

"Are you..." I started, but she jerked her body toward me, and I walked backward into the white brick wall.

"Oh, Demi. Sweet, sweet Demi...stop asking questions. If you're so concerned, why did you choose to work here?"

I exhaled as Marcie's warm breath brushed against my face. "I didn't choose, per se. The couple who helped me when I was stranded in the ocean brought me to this island, and Alister allowed me to stay and recover in one of the rooms, and then he offered me a job."

"The couple that so-called rescued you knew exactly where you and Bradley were. Alister always wanted you to work here, especially after your brilliant performance." Marcie brushed her finger against my neck.

I knew the boat had to have been tracked. I knew there was no easy way out of this life from the Ivory family. I was going to end them all, one way or another.

"I want to know what this resort is really doing, Marcie. You might as well tell me."

Marcie squinted at me and then looked away before turning and walking to the balcony railing. "Do you know what happens to your body when you drown?" She turned and gripped the railing from behind her. Her collarbone protruded as her eyes glossed over.

"No," I whispered.

"Your body first goes into fight-or-flight mode. Then, your airway begins to close. Afterward, you lose consciousness, and then...cerebral hypoxia, which is the final stage before death. All this happens mostly when you are aware that death is right there waiting."

"Okay, why are you telling me this?" I crossed my arms and watched as the waves crashed into the shoreline.

"You survived in the ocean once, Demi. Stop asking questions and doing whatever you think you are planning, because I can guarantee you won't survive again." Marcie began walking back into the hotel room with no sound coming from her footsteps. The damn shoes would haunt me forever.

"The main thing is to not discuss their husbands. These couples are in a fragile state of their marriage, and your goal is to let the wife focus on herself, her needs, and feel free..." Marcie guided me down the hallway until we reached the in-house spa. "Many of our guests are eager to become new mothers or simply women who have been neglected in their marriage. Our goal is to let them heal, rest, rejuvenate, and then reunite with their spouse for two days. I'll be honest, many of these couples haven't had sex in months, some even years. They want to have sex; they want to be loved and wanted by their spouse. These are couples fighting for their marriage and families, and La Gabbia is that bridge to turn that dream into a reality." Marcie pointed to one entrance of the spa. "Nails, massages, and facials are that way, and then the other side is buia sessions. Got it?" She tugged out a stack of papers and handed them to me.

"It's a required minimum seven-day stay. No one leaves at any cost without checking out properly." Marcie was speaking so quickly that my heart was racing.

Putting my hand up, I blew out a breath of air and asked, "What are buia sessions?"

Marcie shook her head and swiftly turned on her heels. "Demi, buia sessions are dark sessions. That's all you need to know as a dove; you aren't a nightingale."

Crossing my arms, I continued following Marcie to the front of the resort where I could see couples being welcomed by other women wearing all white with their perfectly cut blonde hair.

The same blush-pink sparkling water was being served and fresh peonies decorated the trays. Death was here. Now, I knew it was here. Those peonies only thrived and grew on mortality.

"What if I want to be a nightingale instead of a dove?" I whispered quickly before we approached the front desk.

Marcie's eyes widened and her hand dropped to mine. Digging her nails into my flesh, she whispered, "Don't ever wish that on yourself, Demi." Wincing, I tugged her hand off me.

"Jamie, the girl at the front desk, will help you find your first couple. Have a good day, and hopefully I'll see you back in the room tonight."

"Hopefully?" I looked down at the crescent shapes embedded into my skin from Marcie's nails.

"If you survive and don't mess this up. Alister Ivory doesn't allow room for mistakes, Dem." She shrugged before reaching into her small pocket. Tugging out a tube of nude lipstick, she swiped it against her lips. "Just don't do something stupid where you'll wish you were dead... I've heard it's a common issue around here."

CHAPTER
FIVE

JAMIE, the woman at the front desk, assigned me to a couple who looked like they came out of a J. Crew catalogue.

"Straighten your shoulders and fix your face!" Jamie said aggressively, and I instantly straightened my spine and plastered a smile on.

"Hello, Mr. and Mrs. Rothschild. I am Demi, and I'll be your personal guide to the resort. Welcome to La Gabbia, where your dreams become your reality." I clasped my fingers together as the beautiful couple in front of me looked toward each other.

"It's nice to meet you, Demi. I'm Sage, and this is my husband, Declan." Declan just stared at me without any hint of emotion. He was easily over six-feet-tall with light brown hair that was meticulously gelled and combed to the side. Sage Rothschild had a Louis

Vuitton purse slung over her shoulder and was stunning. Her long, blonde hair was tousled over her shoulders, and her icy, light green eyes had an eager sparkle to them. She was wearing a blush-pink sheath dress and cream-colored heels.

"Mr. and Mrs. Rothschild, I am here to take your bags to your designated spaces." I was startled by the voice behind me and turned around.

My jaw dropped. "Bradley," I rasped as I stumbled back into Sage and Declan.

The man in front of me had short blonde hair and pale skin. But he was the man I thought I had loved. The man I thought would save me.

Bradley Ivory was Ian Ivory's son—and had never let me in on that little secret until we were on a boat in the middle of the ocean together.

"I'm sorry, you must have me mistaken with someone else," he said as he pulled me away from the couple.

"Brad…"

Declan cleared his throat behind me, but my body was trembling with fear. Should I scream? Run? What…

"Demi, we can have a chat later, but I must get our valued guests, Mr. and Mrs. Rothschild's, luggage to their room."

My head was light, and I could see little specks in my vision as my hands went cold.

Bradley smirked at me before rolling the designer luggage away.

"Demi, I hope you aren't making our wonderful guests linger in the front of the resort?" Alister Ivory appeared in a three-piece suit, his eyes low and dark as he looked at me.

He brushed his hand across my face before using his index finger to tilt my chin upward. "Demi?" His voice shifted from threatening to concerned.

"Bradley," I whispered and lifted my eyes to meet Alister's. His dark brows knitted together as he looked at me with an expression I had hardly seen someone show toward me.

Worry. Alister Ivory was worried about me.

"Mr. and Mrs. Rothschild, I'll have another one of my precious doves assist you. My Demi is a bit new to the job and will be right back to serving you as soon as she takes a moment to recuperate." Alister laced his fingers with mine and led me away just before snapping his fingers three times toward Jamie, who immediately lifted a phone to call whom I assumed was my replacement.

I felt as if I were walking through a tunnel. As soon as we turned down a few hallways, Alister led me into an elevator that was painted all black, except for the gold trimming and buttons.

Looking up at the ceiling, I saw it was mirrored and Alister's eyes caught mine.

"Bradley," I repeated, as if it were the only word I knew.

"That was not my nephew, Bradley Ivory, Demi." Alister adjusted the gold rings that he always wore. I didn't think I'd ever paid attention to the many tattoos that covered his hands.

He was such a stark contrast to Dr. Ian Ivory, who was obsessed with the color white. Here I was, already seeing black and white splattered throughout. It had to mean something...

"Yes, it was." I stared down at the white-padded shoes I had on my feet. Why did Alister want some of the girls in white when, clearly, he favored black and dark tones?

"Bradley Ivory was my brother's bastard. He died with you in the middle of the ocean."

My head turned to Alister as the elevator stopped and the doors opened. I tilted my head in confusion. "Died...with me?"

Alister took my hand and tugged me out of the elevator.

Cornering me against the wall, he stared at my lips. Brushing his thumb against them, he leaned in close, and I pushed my head further into the wall.

His minty breath blew against my mouth. "My brother's precious little bird died there in the ocean, but was reincarnated as my perfect raven." My breathing stilled as he leaned in close enough for our lips to almost touch, but he didn't kiss me.

"Don't you dare think about touching me," I murmured, looking straight into his dark eyes.

A devious smile grew on his face as he lifted his hand and wrapped it around my neck. Instantly, I grabbed his hand and tried to pry it off, to no avail. Choking, I tried to plead with him as the smile stayed on his face and he tightened his grip.

Digging my nails into his hands, tears streamed down my face.

"Don't you dare think about speaking to me like that, Demi. I will cut you up into pieces, fry you, and serve you as an appetizer to our guests. Do you understand me, my beautiful little raven? They do love a good piece of brown meat."

Nodding, he released his grip and cracked his neck from side to side as I doubled over and gasped for air.

Drool dribbled out of my mouth as my eyes burned, but I didn't dare look up at him.

"When you're ready, you can join me in the library."

His shiny black dress shoes clicked against the all-black marble flooring as my back slid against the wall and I sank downward. Sucking in breaths of air, I lifted my head when I knew he'd turned away. This was a penthouse in the resort. Breathtaking panoramic views of the crystal-clear ocean was all around me, but the rest of the house was decorated in nothing but black with gold accents.

"Demi...don't keep me waiting," Alister crooned out. Pressing my palms against the cold floors, I forced myself up and began walking.

It was the most beautiful home I'd ever seen. The Ivory estate back in Charlotte was sterile, but this...this was evil. This was living in the shadows. Part of me felt safer in the dark than in the light.

Passing a gold-encrusted mirror, I caught a glimpse of the girl in the reflection. I stood out against the décor with my bright blonde hair and white sheath dress.

I missed my long black hair that was tucked under this itchy wig, I missed wearing anything but white, but I didn't miss myself. I didn't know who I even was. *I'd always been an idea or a thought of what someone else wanted me to be.* Perhaps that's why I was called to the darkness so much more. I could hide the various versions of myself I was forced to be.

"Turn right," Alister's voice called out. I froze in my spot, knowing that he was watching me. Glancing around, I could see cameras, in each corner, and I knew there were hidden ones everywhere.

I wrapped my arms around myself as I made my way into another hallway with small lanterns lighting the way.

My eyes widened as I walked into the library space. But it wasn't a library filled with classic novels; it was a room filled with black-and-white paintings of naked women and leather-bound books, all with tiny lettering I couldn't make out.

Alister was sitting in an oversized chair by a fireplace. The fire crackled as he lit a cigar and looked at me carefully. Waving his hand to the empty chair across from him, he motioned for me to sit down.

"Demi, do you know what the most underrated, yet lucrative, business in the world is?"

I was staring at an image of a woman who had the same short bob-styled hair cut I had, and I could tell by the light contrast, she was blonde. Her eyes were smudged with makeup as she looked over her shoulder. Her spine and thin waist protruded while her body was bare.

"No," I answered while crossing my legs and staring at Alister, who had now spread his legs apart with his elbows resting on his knees.

"Fantasies." He leaned back into his chair and snapped his fingers.

Not even a moment later, Kandi, the woman who did my hair, showed up in a white gown, pushing in a clothing rack. Her lips were in a tight line as she looked at me with concern.

"Smile, baby. *Smile.*" Alister chuckled before standing. I sat there frozen as I stared at the rack of dresses. They weren't white...they were all black.

Kandi's lips quivered as Alister approached her. "Turn around." Alister leaned into the side of her face, brushing his cheek against her hair.

"Please, Mr. Ivory, I'm begging you." A small tear rolled down her cheek as she looked at me pleadingly.

Alister sighed loudly before snapping his fingers again. Within seconds, another young woman appeared in an identical gown to Kandi's. "Turn around, Megan." Biting her bottom lip, she glanced at Kandi with envy.

"Unzip her," Alister barked at Kandi as Megan winced and slowly rotated.

"Please, I can bring you an ashtray," Kandi pleaded.

"Demi, stand up," Alister ordered as my stomach flipped.

"Stand up!" he shouted at me. I gripped the armrests and pushed myself up.

This is it. This is the moment, the pivotal moment when

I'm about to be sunken into Alister Ivory's sick and twisted games.

I stood next to Alister as he towered over me. Running his hand through his shiny black hair, he grinned at me before taking another puff of his cigar and then pulled my lips apart with his thumb. Blowing the cigar smoke into my mouth, I immediately started to cough at the repulsive taste.

Kandi and Megan were trembling as they watched.

"I'm going to save kissing you for the day I spread your legs apart and feel you everywhere." He smirked as he took my hand and placed his cigar in it.

"I need you to put this out for me, my beautiful raven." Tucking a loose strand of my hair behind my ear, Alister whispered, "Put the cigar out on the ashtray."

Looking around, I didn't see an ashtray. Kandi began unzipping Megan's dress and allowed the material to fall outward on both sides.

"Oh my God," I gasped as I saw Megan's shriveled and bruised skin, with hundreds of burn marks all over her back.

"She's one of our nightingales. It's strange seeing her in white, but she was promoted when too many doves turned up dead…"

"Now put out the cigar, Demi," Alister snapped at me as I stood there.

"I won't do it." My voice cracked as I shook my head.

"You'll do it, or I'll kill her." He grabbed my wrist and shoved it closer to her skin.

"No!" I shoved his hand from mine and stumbled backward.

Alister laughed before he walked over to one of his shelves. "Why didn't you do as you were told?" Megan peered at me over her shoulder, tears streaming down her face.

Alister walked back with a sharp machete in his hand.

"Alister, you cannot be serious!" I ran in between the girls and Alister.

"On your knees." Alister pushed me to the side and tapped the machete blade on Megan's shoulder.

The cigar was burning in between my fingers.

"Okay! Alister, please!" I screamed as I lifted the cigar. Megan was already on her knees, sobbing as Alister lifted the blade into the air.

"Alister! I'm begging you!" I shrieked as memories of the girls I couldn't save back in Charlotte flooded my mind.

Alister turned to me and squinted. "Put the cigar out,

Demi. This is your one and only second-chance. I promise you that, my raven."

"One…two…burn." Alister sang out while swinging the machete. I wanted to cry, but I couldn't. I wanted to take the cigar and burn Alister's eyes, but I couldn't. I knew the only outcome for disobedience with an Ivory was death.

"I'm so sorry," I whimpered as I lifted the cigar and smashed it into Megan's flesh. The cry that left her lips seared through my heart as the flesh around the cigar melted.

Alister wrapped his hand around mine and pressed it harder as I realized that, in some sick way, I was happy it wasn't me.

Alister pulled my hand away from her back and dropped the cigar to the ground. "Clean it up, Megan, and then get the hell out of my space. Both of you leave." He bellowed while wrapping his hand around my waist and tugging me away. Grabbing a dress from the clothing rack, Alister guided me down a hall with flickering lanterns hung.

"That was absolutely beautiful, my raven. I knew there was evil inside of you."

Looking up at him, I hated myself for what I did next.

I smiled proudly.

CHAPTER
SIX

ALISTER IVORY WAS POURING himself a glass of whiskey as I awkwardly stood in his bedroom. His bed was massive, covered in silk and black sheets. My breathing slowed as I eyed the mirrored ceiling, staring back at my reflection. "Would you like anything to drink?" Alister asked me, his voice low.

I turned to him and walked to the built-in bar he was at. Taking the glass from his hand, my fingers brushed against his thick gold rings. I took a sip of the strong liquor and shuddered. Alister scoffed.

"I had heard of you from my brother, Ian. He told me they'd finally found you. He was thrilled you'd be marrying Conrad." Alister poured another glass and joined me on the balcony. The sky was bright blue and melted into the stunning ocean.

"Ian and I had a tumultuous relationship, to say the

least." Alister winced, then tossed the whiskey back. "But you killed them all. My heroine."

"Bradley. Clearly, I didn't kill him." I hated how I still had positive emotions for Bradley. How memories of him gifting me a pair of Nikes or of him giving me a reason to fight, flooded over the fact that he had lied to me. He was just as evil as all of them. He wanted to come here and take over this…empire.

"It's not Bradley. The man you saw is Warren, who is Bradley's twin brother. Ian and I had an agreement to separate them. It was Ian's way of voiding Bradley of any emotion and Warren has become my well, just as Bradley was to Ian. A man who is willing to do anything for this family and business because he has nothing outside of these walls."

I looked at Alister, shaking my head. "You are all liars. I know it's him."

Alister filled the space between us and brushed his thumb against my bottom lip once more. "Bradley had a small birthmark on his lower cheek, did you know that?"

Swallowing, I knew exactly what he was talking about. "Warren does not have that." Alister moved away and opened a drawer, pulling out a photo album.

"Here." He tapped his finger against a black-and-white image of two young boys.

They were identical beyond the birthmark.

How could Bradley have never mentioned a twin brother, and why was he not in any of the photos he had shown me on the boat?

"Demi, take your clothes off." Alister took the album and flung it to a corner of the room.

My hand tightened around the glass as the ice melted from the warmth of my palm. "Alister…"

"You're the first and only woman who has dared to call me by my name." He drew his finger against my collarbone.

I rolled my shoulders back. "I'm not taking my clothes off."

Gripping my wrist aggressively, he pulled me toward the fireplace. "Look up there. Do you see it?"

I followed his finger to the strangely crafted painting. It was textured and red. Squinting, I couldn't understand what I was looking at.

"The lips of women who spoke back to me. Luckily, our in-house florist knew just how to preserve and dry them after I sliced them off their pretty little faces." Alister sighed and crossed his arms.

I felt my throat close as he dropped his eyes back to mine. "I'd like to start work today."

Taking my hand, he placed it on his crotch, and I could feel him becoming aroused. "Then who will tend to this and my other needs?"

I tugged my hand away and knew that I had to tread carefully with defiance.

The lips on the wall had my stomach tumble, even though my former boss had decorated with bones. Something about the way Alister had probably raped and kissed those same lips before ripping them off those innocent girls' faces had my eyes watering. I knew those lips trembled in fear as he stole their lives away from them.

"Mr. Ivory, I kindly request that you allow me to do the job I was assigned to do here. As you know, I've always just wanted a place to live and a job. I know there are new guests checking in today, and I'd hate to upset the other...girls by disappearing and having fun." I smiled.

Alister's eyebrow lifted as he cupped my face. "My brother and nephews were right about you. You are worthy enough to be the favorite girl." He tucked a straggling piece of hair behind my ear before snapping his fingers.

"Yes, sir?" I was startled by the woman in a flowy white gown.

"Take Demi to meet with the couple she's been assigned to." Alister waved me away.

Turning over my shoulder, I mustered the confidence to ask. "What are the black dresses for?" Referring to the cart he had a woman roll in, filled with various dresses.

Alister grinned. "You'll see soon, my raven. So very soon. Off you go with my dear Sarah." All these women looked so similar, I couldn't tell if they were different girls or the same, and Alister was simply changing their name.

The woman beside me guided me out. She didn't blink, her lips were thin with nude lipstick streaked across. Her hair was slicked back in a perfect blonde ballerina bun.

I silently followed her into the elevator.

"He's not a bad man," Sarah whispered with her fingers laced together.

I looked at her reflection through the glass in the elevator.

Letting out a small laugh, I grabbed her arm and took her by surprise. "You silly little girl... Don't you know all men are bad."

. . .

The elevator doors slid open, and we both stepped out. The resort was truly beautiful. It was pristine in every way. "Come quickly." Sarah picked up her pace, but as I tried to do the same, I tripped over something. Not something…rather, someone.

"Oh my god." It was Taylor from the orientation. She was on her hands and knees, sweeping with a hand-sized broom and tiny dustpan.

Tiny specks of sand were in it. Was she seriously being told to sweep sand?

"Sorry," I mumbled and patted her shoulder.

Her eyes shot opened as she looked at me. "No, you're not. You don't even recognize me. You left us behind to die." Her voice was raspy as she stared at me.

"Wh—" Memories of the caged girls from the Ivory estate flooded me. No, there was no way. She wasn't there. Those girls… Those girls were meant to become brides.

"You left us all behind." Multiple voices echoed around me as I was surrounded by a sea of white and green eyes.

"No, please no!" I screamed and slapped my hands against my ears.

A moment later, I felt a sharp sting against my cheek. "Shut your mouth." It was my roommate,

Marcie. She was standing there, staring at me with agitation.

"Kandi, fix her face. Mr. and Mrs. Rothschild have been checked into their rooms and then taken to the separate pools. You need to meet with Mrs. Rothschild first before going down to..." Marcie flicked her eyes to Kandi, who was brushing my face with makeup.

"Demi, don't screw this up. If you do, you won't be the only one dying. Alister kills all the girls who are assigned to the new girl. That's me, Kandi, Taylor, Sarah...basically anyone you've interacted with here."

This was it. This was how they had their iron chokehold around our necks.

"I promise, I won't." I had to pull it together. I needed to focus on the bigger picture. Why was I here?

CHAPTER
SEVEN

"MRS. ROTHSCHILD, I apologize for my absence earlier. I attended additional training. I'm a bit new here." I smiled with a glass of pink champagne on a white- and gold-encrusted platter.

"Why is everything so white here?" Mrs. Rothschild pointed out as she adjusted her hat. "Even the dress code is so strange. Did you know women can only wear white, and my husband had to pack all black? Why is that?" She took a piece of fruit covered in white chocolate. "I finally tried a little color in my life, and then back to the rules." She sighed as she touched the seam of her dress.

"The Ivory aesthetic." I pursed my lips and began folding a towel before adjusting her bag neatly.

"My husband, Declan, got a referral from a guy at work. Apparently, their marriage was just as shitty as

ours. You know we haven't had sex in two years?"
Mrs. Rothschild stared at her giant diamond ring. "So,
this is it. This is the last chance. Not that either of us
can get a divorce. I wouldn't know how to survive out
there...I've never been alone."

I don't think she was talking to me exactly, but more so
herself.

"Thank you for sharing that with me, ma'am."

Mrs. Rothchild looked at me while sipping the
champagne. "Do you have sex? I mean, you're
gorgeous. I'm sure men just fawn all over you."

"I'm not allowed to." I glanced around and saw
other girls wearing the same dress as me, with the
same exact blonde bob. They were serving each guest
with plastered, fake smiles.

"What do you mean, you're not allowed to?"

I shouldn't have said that. I thought back to the
contract I had signed with Alister Ivory the day I
walked into the resort and was offered the job of my
nightmares. I had envisioned drowning myself in the
beautiful ocean or maybe even jumping off the highest
floor, but the girls I left behind, the ones I had
abandoned...

Closing my eyes, I saw her face. My sister, Layla.

The one who betrayed me, yet the one I loved more than anything.

I could have saved her and saved us. Maybe she wouldn't have had to make the decisions she did, which, essentially, was to serve me up to Ian Ivory in exchange for her own freedom. She died a painful death, which was the easy way out; meanwhile I was dying every single day.

The contract Alister Ivory had me sign stated the *Great Eight* as he called them:

1. No sex for pleasure, unless told otherwise.
2. Doves wear white, and only white.
3. Nightingales wear black, and only black.
4. You will obtain an IUD, along with potential removal of organs as we see fit.
5. You must obey and adhere to all rules.
6. You must never speak up, speak out, and speak loudly.
7. Accept that men are superior. Women are inferior.
8. Accept that marriage is the most sacred bond, and we will save them.

"I just choose to be celibate and focus on my guests," I quickly answered and reached for Mrs. Rothschild's plate. "Can I bring you anything else?" Clearing my throat, I stepped back as she lifted a book.

"I smuggled this in." She shrugged.

I glanced at the cover. "What's it about?" I looked over my shoulder. I wanted to read, but they wouldn't let us have any books here beyond strange manuals I hadn't looked at yet.

"Three teenage girls go missing in this small town, and the main character, Mila, has to find out how to cover up the dark secrets of her family before her fiancé finds out the connection between her and the serial killer. But honestly, that's just me trying to make it sound light. It's really twisted. This author, Monica something...she writes dark stuff. Sick, really. I can give it to you after I'm done." Mrs. Rothschild lifted her hand to shield her eyes from the bright sun.

Shaking my head, I remembered the small white apron wrapped around my waist. "Here." I tugged out the Gucci sunglasses each of us were told to give our guests.

"I guess this place was worth the cost." She put them on after looking at the brand symbol.

"What do the men do here? All I've done is get a

massage and a facial, then sat out here baking in the sun."

"I'm not sure. I don't work down there," I answered and saw one of the other girls looking at me.

"Down there? They have my husband in a dungeon?" She laughed. I laughed with her, knowing there was a possibility they did.

"Here." She handed me a wad of cash. "Find out, and I'll double it."

"I can't take that."

Mrs. Rothschild smiled. "You work for me while I'm here. Take it, and find out."

Quickly grabbing the cash, I shoved it into my apron before turning away.

"I'll go grab your lunch, ma'am."

CHAPTER
EIGHT

STANDING IN THE KITCHEN, my mouth parted. The kitchen staff, all women, were wearing white lingerie. They were giggling and cooking while smiling at the mirrored wall.

"What..." I saw Jamie from earlier. "What are they doing?" My eyes widened.

Jamie shushed me and shoved a tray in my hand before cornering me.

"Are you crazy? You go to the side door and do not cut through the view." She looked up in the corner of the room.

Fuck. A camera.

"What are they doing?" I repeated as she nodded for me to go back outside.

"Demi, right? Demi?" She knew my name but was trying to act like she didn't.

I clenched the tray of food in frustration.

"I don't know, because I've never been down there." Her voice shifted from annoyance to fear.

I couldn't do this. This dove title wasn't going to get me anywhere. I had to find a way down to where the men were sent.

I have to become a nightingale.

———

Mrs. Rothschild spent her day being pampered, and all I did was walk her around to each area and waited on her hand and foot. When she went to her services, I was expected to clean. I thought about the woman who bled out in front of the resort and how I was forced to clean her blood up.

Was she one of the guests? She was removed and had disappeared from the resort. I never saw a man with her. The first few weeks I was here, I wasn't even allowed to leave the reception area. I was just mopping and cleaning until I was finally assigned this job.

"You can leave." Mrs. Rothschild lifted her fifth glass of champagne. She and a few other women were sitting together for cocktail hour.

I clutched my hands together. "No, it's fine."

"They are having some themed ball for the ladies tonight, and I don't want you there. I want you to find out what my husband is doing, and why he was so excited to come here."

"Mrs. Rothschild—" I started.

"Please stop calling me that. Call me Sage. Declan is my third husband. I married him for his money, unlike the rest of these women who actually love their husbands for their receding hairlines, saggy balls, and two-thrust fucks."

I pinched my lips to the side and suppressed my laughter. This was the first time in a long time that I found something funny. "Tonight is the best night for you to find out what the men get to do. And if I find out it's more fun than this pussy party they have me tied down to, then I'm going to slap a mustache on and go there." She winked at me.

"Okay." I took her emptied glass. "Have a good-night, Sage." I spun around on my heels. This was the perfect option. The ladies would be busy, and the resort would be tied up hosting. I looked at Sage. "You would have fit in really well in the Ivory family." She had the shiniest blonde hair, the softest green eyes with specks of gold, and flawless pale skin.

"I don't know what that means, but I think you're calling me a basic white woman." She lifted a brow.

I smiled before leaving her. "Never. Goodnight, Sage."

I couldn't go down like this in all white. Marcie said it was dark down there and that the nightingales wore all black.

I walked to the elevators and the doors opened. It was Bradley. No, it was Warren—at least, according to Alister. I stumbled back as he looked at me. There was no birthmark on his face. Alister was right.

He was Bradley's twin? I saw Bradley die in the ocean; I fed him a poisonous pill.

"Demi, I know I startled you. Alister informed me that you assumed I was…someone else?" He waved his hand toward the elevator. "What floor would you like to go to?"

"I'd like to go alone," I whispered as my shoulder brushed the wall of the elevator as I cowered away in fear.

"I'm sorry, I cannot let you do that." He patted his belt. Squinting, I saw it. There was a needle.

He'd drug me if I didn't listen?

"My room. The sixth floor." I walked into the elevator and stood to the side. "Bradley," I called out, but he didn't even flinch. He just stood there like a statue with no emotion.

The elevator arrived at my floor, and I ran out. Turning around, I watched the gold doors slowly shut as his green eyes disappeared behind, and just as they began to close, a smile grew on his face. "Bye bye, Demilion."

Gasping, I slapped my hands across my mouth. It was him. I knew these liars tried to fool me.

But how was Bradley alive?

Walking backward, I was trembling as I reached into my apron and tugged my badge out. Sliding against the scanner, I began to sob as I raced to my room.

Just as I turned the corner, I slammed into Kandi. I screamed as she slapped her hand across my mouth.

"Demi!" Streaks of mascara were running down her cheeks. "Shh...it's okay. It's okay."

She was crying, too.

"What's wrong?" I stammered and kept looking behind me out of paranoia.

"Nothing. Aren't you supposed to be working?"

I scanned into my room and watched the white doors slide open.

I had to find out what this was. I couldn't save the girls in Charlotte, and I couldn't save my sister. But I could find out what this was. I could end the entire Ivory family once and for all.

"Kandi, wait… I need your help."

She wiped her tears away and smiled. "How can I assist you, Demi? Do you want me to help you get ready for the ball?"

"I need you to take this wig that you glued onto my hairline off. I need my black hair back," I whispered as I saw the small camera blinking in the hallway.

"No, sweet Demi, you are to have blonde or white hair. I can lighten it for you? We are doves, after all."

"Kandi, please. I'm going to rip my hairline off if I do it myself."

Kandi shoved me into my room and waited for the door to close before looking at me. "What is this?" she hissed at me. "Only nightingales have black hair."

"Are we being watched?" I cradled myself.

"You and Marcie have the one room on the entire floor that isn't laced with cameras."

Parting my lips, I found that shocking. "What makes me so special?"

"Not you, it's Marcie. She's…she's… Just forget it."

My heart sank. "Kandi, I know something is happening here. I'm sure you all were told about me and my past. I'm sure all of this is some sick web, but I will die trying to end this."

"End what?" Kandi gritted her teeth as I opened Marcie's closet. All white gowns, shirts, pants.

"Fuck!" I shouted.

Nothing black. But then I saw it, a small box off to the side.

Tugging it out, it was all black clothing.

"Was Marcie a nightingale?" I looked at Kandi.

She nodded slowly. "Yes. She was the only nightingale that got to..."

"Got to what?" I lifted a short, black tulle dress.

"Be set free from the cages."

CHAPTER
NINE

BEGRUDGINGLY, Kandi took the blonde wig off. A realization hit me as I ran my fingers through the natural texture and waves.

"Was this…" Chills grew on my arms.

"The hair belonged to the woman you replaced. "Most of the hair that is turned into wigs come from…" Kandi gripped her stomach as her cheeks flushed red and her entire body language shifted. "No. Never mind, I can't be any part of this, Demi. You're going to get killed, and I don't want to be killed. I have…"

"You have what?" I asked as I slipped into the black tulle dress I had taken from Marcie.

"I have a daughter waiting for me." Kandi wiped away a tear. "Taylor, Jamie, and Suzanne do, too."

"Demi, you don't have a reason to live, but we do.

It was either we work here and never leak any secrets of La Gabbia, or our daughters would get trafficked into becoming a nightingale. You have no idea what it's like to have no options."

Grief and sadness plagued me as I realized how sick it was that Alister preyed on a mother's love for a child. But Kandi didn't realize that my life was one I had to live to save all the others; I was the only one who could try to end them all. I knew I'd find out what was on the bottom floor of this posh resort tonight. I knew I'd find out why those girls were called nightingales.

I quickly put darker eye makeup on and swiped bright red lipstick onto my lips. "You're going to need someone to get you there. Let me see what I can do." Kandi shuddered as she lifted the phone and made a very confusing request.

"Hello, this is Kandi calling from upstairs. I was requesting a nightingale to come to the doves' residential floor to collect a box of black gowns we found." She ended the conversation before hesitating and finishing my hair.

"Wow." A voice startled me a few moments later. A woman wearing a black gown stared at me.

"You're going to need someone to sneak you in." She tilted my chin up and swiped the lipstick that smudged.

"I'm Anu, a nightingale. Say goodbye to life as you know it, my dear. Once you go down into the pits of hell, you'll never be the same."

I couldn't help but let out a small laugh. "I'm already dead. I don't think you understand what kind of hell I'm coming from."

Anu smiled at me. "The Ivory estate back in America, where there are actual laws, is nothing compared to what you're about to witness. The women down there are only living because they are scared of what will happen to their bodies if they die. And the women up here are only living so their loved ones don't die."

"What happens to their bodies when they die?" I asked as I slipped the black heels on.

"Hopefully, you'll never have to know."

———

Opening the door, Anu waved me over to the cart she had outside the door. "Get under."

I looked at the cart and nodded. Sliding my leg in first, I glanced at Kandi, who was shaking her head.

"You're really going to do this?"

Shrugging, I cracked a small smile. "No one else is. Remember, you all have something worth living for. I'm living for this."

Anu tugged the black sheet over the cart and began

rolling it down the hall. There was a pull in my chest where I knew this may be the last time I'd ever see Kandi or this floor of La Gabbia. I knew that once I ascended into the darkness, there was no hope in ever finding the light. This time, it would kill me.

"What are you doing up here?" a masculine voice called out. I clutched my knees to my chest and bit my lower lip.

It sounded like Bradley. There was a long pause from Anu, and I could see a sliver of the white platform shoes making its way around toward me.

I sucked in a breath before Anu's black ballet flats quickly slid in front of his. "Sir, I'm going back to the cag—"

"Stupid woman." Bradley hushed her immediately. "If I ever catch you up here again, I'll slit your throat and drink your blood."

I was trembling as his footsteps wavered away and Anu quickly pushed the cart until we got to the elevator. I knew the elevator could take you to any floor in the resort, but there were different badges. My badge only allowed me access to specific places in La Gabbia. Peeling the sheet back a bit, I looked and watched as Anu bent forward and had her eyes in front of the panel.

It pinged before the doors shut and swiftly slammed downward. "Anu," I hissed.

She kept looking forward with her arms crossed as she nervously tapped her foot.

The doors opened and I sat back, hiding myself under the cart. Her shoes clicked against the black marble floor as she pushed me into the darkness.

What was I thinking? This was too soon for me to come down here and do this. I didn't even know what I was going to do yet.

"Get out," Anu whispered as she parked the cart in a corner. I sat for an extra minute before dipping my leg out first and then sliding toward the edge.

As soon as I pushed upward, my jaw dropped.

It was all dark. Complete darkness besides one thing…

A giant gilded cage in the center of a stage with black brick walls surrounding it.

One small light shined at the cage in which the door was open. Squinting, I could make out the theater-style chairs that were crafted into a semi-circle around the stage.

"Anu…" My voice shook. "What is this?"

"Welcome to hell, Demi. I guess you're a nightingale now."

CHAPTER
TEN

ANU HAD DISAPPEARED, leaving me standing in the corner. I glanced around but couldn't see any small red lights flickering, which were always attached to the cameras in La Gabbia.

Sliding against the wall, I looked around the space until I was directly in front of the cage.

The enormous, rustic gold cage sat in the middle of a massive, all black stage. A light shone directly onto a small golden swing, which hung from the center. My heart raced as the silence of the space intimidated me.

"Why are you standing around? The show is about to start!" I spun around and my eyes locked onto piercing green eyes and shiny black hair that was matted down with gel. "Who are you?"

• • •

"I'm…"

Shaking his head, he grabbed my arm and tugged me away. "Alister will slit your throat, and mine, if we mess this up." My ankle almost twisted as I picked up my pace in the slightly too large black heels.

"What…" I started, but the man pulled me through thick drapery. There were girls everywhere, yet it was pin-drop silent.

They were all sitting quietly in front of the wall-to-wall vanities. It was incredibly dark beyond the small flicker of light from the small lamp perched on each girl's table. They were painting their eyes in black shadow, their hair was slicked back in a neat bun, and they all wore the same black tulle dress I was wearing.

It resembled what I always envisioned a dressing room for a ballet to look like.

"I'm Carlo." The man who dragged me in pointed to an empty vanity. "Go, slick your hair back and fix your makeup." He paused and studied my expression. "Fuck, you've never done training, have you?"

Placing my hand on my chest, I hoped I could steady my breath and rapidly beating heart. "Training for what?" I swallowed.

• • •

Carlo shook his head and slapped his hand that had one of the same rings as Alister—a thick gold band, encrusted with two birds.

A dove and a nightingale.

"Training for the nightingales."

"No." I shook my head.

"I thought you were the new recruit after Harley died." Carlo's eyes were lined in thick black liner and smudged out.

"Come on, I can't have any of you girls messing this up for me." He shoved me toward the empty vanity and sat me down in the plush seat.

Looking at the girl next to me, I slumped over the neatly lined makeup and hair products.

"Karina," she whispered and stuck her hand out.

Forcing a small smile, I laced my fingers with hers. Her hands were frigid as she stared at my lips.

"Wipe that off." She sighed.

I was confused as I let go of her hand and looked into the mirror.

I reached for a tissue and questioned, "The nude lipstick?"

"The smile." She turned away and added more gel to her hair.

Breathing out, I knew what was coming next would be something I'd never unsee. But I had experienced this with Ian Ivory and his family. How could Alister Ivory or a fancy resort be worse?

"Did they put the IUD in?" Karina rubbed her lips together.

Nodding, I blew out a breath of air. "Yes. As soon as I got here."

"Oh, so you're a pure nightingale, not a breeder. Lucky you."

My stomach flipped. "What is…"

Karina spun around on her stool and looked around before leaning toward me with a makeup brush. She began adding blush to my cheeks. "I'm a nightingale, too. Thank God. I'd rather drown myself than be a breeder."

"I don't understand the difference."

Karina pursed her neatly nude-painted lips. "The Ivory family loves their birds. But you already know that, don't you, beautiful Demi." Karina winked at me before pulling my stool closer to hers.

"Doves are the girls upstairs; they take care of the

wives who come here. It's the best job you can have at La Gabbia, because it's the lowest risk. You just serve the rich bitches who are neglected by their asshole husbands and make sure they want to come back. I know they say the wives earned their spots with everything, but I think they are just spoiled women. The doves go through sensory deprivation and are kept in all white cages until they are trained to be submissive people-pleasers. Next up is us...the nightingales. We are trained in the darkness." Karina shuddered. "I'm guessing you just skipped through, being the favorite girl and all..." She licked her thumb and brushed it against my hairline.

"How did you know about..." I trailed off as light music began to play all around us.

"Shit, it's almost time to go." Karina cupped my cheek.

"We had to live in pitch-black cages for six months. This entire part of La Gabbia is a fantasy—it's called the euphoria floor or sometimes the euphoria program. Their wildest fantasies are only what they see in their dreams. In the darkest depths of their imaginations. But the reason there's so many of us is because we don't all survive. At the end of each guest's stay, a girl is killed." Karina's eyes grew moist.

"Russian roulette." She shrugged. "They need to stock the fridge and all."

The other girls started to line up after neatly tucking in their stools.

"What do you mean, Russian roulette? And why does a girl die at the end of each guest's stay? The fridge? Stocking it with what?"

Karina stood and brushed her hands down the tulle skirt. "Demi, this is all a fantasy for them and for him." She pointed at a framed image I would have otherwise missed.

Alister Ivory.

"The men who come to La Gabbia are invited because they are pre-screened. They are the richest men—the ones who own, control, and are used to having everything their way. Their marriages are in shambles, yet they need it for an image. So, La Gabbia was built on the false notion that couples come here and find solace. These men all know what it really is. They know they get to descend into the darkness, doing anything and everything they've ever wanted to. Things you'd be too embarrassed to say out loud. They want to feel powerful and masculine. They are gifted a nightingale. We are here to serve and obey and to make their fantasies come to life. But at the end...Alister has them do one thing that seals the fact that he is the most powerful man in the world. He controls everyone, including all these men."

"Showtime, ladies!"

One by one, the girls all stopped in front of the massive image of Alister Ivory, bowing their head and clasping their hands together.

He is their god.

Karina looked at me as a straggling tear fell down her cheek. "I'm only here again because my previous client couldn't do it."

"Do what?" My legs shook as I stood and watched how void of any emotion, they all were.

"He couldn't kill me. So, they killed him. Then they hung him upside down on stage and let him bleed out as a warning to the other guests. Kill or be killed."

CHAPTER ELEVEN

ONE BY ONE, we stood in meticulous lines. Everyone looked the exact same, with neatly pinned hair and black tulle dresses paired with black heels. I didn't understand. There was no white anywhere like the top floors of the resort or at the Ivory house I was accustomed to. This was absolute darkness. I always thought I'd never be able to look at white the same way—that I'd be ruined and scared. But here I was, surrounded by darkness, and I realized there was more to hide here. There was more to fear here.

"Let's go, nightingales." Carlo straightened his shoulders and looked grim. As each girl walked past him, he tapped their shoulder.

Karina glanced back at me once more. "I hope the bullet doesn't land on you." She walked out the door, and I stood next to Carlo. I was the last girl.

"You're in cage eight after the show." He tapped my shoulder, and as I put one foot in front of the other, Carlo's cold hand gripped my arm.

"Demi, they know who you are and what you've done to their family. I... It was nice knowing you." Carlo's brows knitted together as he sighed. My entire plan had always been to figure out what was here on this private island. I thought it was a place of solace for Bradley and me to finally start living. My heart ached every time I thought about him. I loved him. Maybe I still did. Knowing he was here after we both tried to kill each other in some way made me feel safer. It felt like we were both supposed to live and had a purpose.

The tulle was itchy on my legs as I stepped forward and left the dressing room. We were all ushered into seats in front of the stage where the empty cage sat. My heart began racing as I noticed the rest of the girls legs shook in fear. Suddenly, the screen behind the cage turned on and began showing black-and-white images of women in aprons, serving men. I looked behind us and my eyes widened. The male resort guests were trickling into the movie theater-styled seating with popcorn buckets in their hands. "Hey, what is this?" I looked at the girl beside me, wishing I was sitting next to Karina or someone I had already spoken to.

The girl looked at me with zero emotion and smiled. "Euphoria," she whispered.

"What does that mean?" I hated this. I hated feeling like I was the mouse when I had sworn I'd be the cat this time.

Alister Ivory took the stage and stood in front of the cage. He brushed his fingers against it. Oh no, I couldn't afford for him to see me. He'd have me killed. Glancing side to side, I dug my nails into the fishnet tights. I had on significantly more makeup and my hair was black. Alister had only known me as the blonde, bare-faced Demi in all white.

"Gentlemen, you have been meticulously selected to join us at La Gabbia's Euphoria collection. This aspect of our all-inclusive resort is built on the belief that men must have an outlet. This program has been devised and revised for over a century, composed of the three Rs.

1. Rage
2. Release
3. Relaxation

"You see, in today's day and age, men and women have become equals—too much of equals. It's disruptive to the balance of our world. Women have always been created to be our submissive while men are dominants. The basis of human origin is sex. Sex is what men need to thrive and show status. As a strong believer in marriage, I do think the two don't always run parallel to one another. Marriage is a bond between a couple that depicts more of an emotional care versus physical. It's unfortunate, but true." Peeking over my shoulder, I watch the men eat their popcorn and nod in agreement.

Meanwhile, all I wanted to do was run on stage and knee Alister in his crotch, so he'd never feel pleasure again. How could he love and appreciate marriage so much, but he was a perpetual bachelor?

"This program was designed for the men who build our society into the habitable, adaptable, and advanced civilization. Without the powerful, intelligent, and talented men, this world would be nothing. I know you don't feel appreciated or desired after a long day of work. I know your wives nag you and taunt your masculinity. The laws that are put into place are toxic. You should be able to release your inner rage and urges in peace."

Alister paused and looked in my direction. I dropped my eyes quickly and hoped under my breath that he didn't see me.

Clearing his throat, he continued, "You see, my friends, ultimately when we allow a woman to have the privilege of being our wife, they alter and change who they are. They feel cherished and loved. They begin to stop taking care of themselves and us. Here at La Gabbia-Euphoria, I have built a program where you can release the natural urges all men have."

"Tonight, we won't have our usual performance. My star-performer is not feeling well enough to go into her cage." Alister pointed behind him.

There were some whispers filled with annoyance by the men in the seating behind us.

"But fear not, you each have your very own fantasy assigned to you. The gorgeous nightingales in front of you are here to serve you and your wildest dreams. Please remember, at the end, one guest will be selected to participate in my favorite part of the experience. Until then, enjoy your release. Your wives are all sipping champagne poolside, thinking their husbands are in resort group therapy." Alister and the rest of the men laughed.

I was gritting my teeth while clenching my fists.

The girls were all so thin and under their eyes were deepened bags, probably from malnourishment.

The room was too dark. Only the glimmers from the one light that shined on Alister allowed me to see the others. I wanted to be a coward and run; I wanted to go back upstairs to the main resort and find Bradley and beg him to explain everything to me.

Alister sat on the black stool and placed his elbows

on his knees while leaning forward. "We call the girls in Euphoria my precious little nightingales. There is a reason for this, gentlemen."

"In ancient Greek mythology, there was a goddess called Philomela. She was raped and mutilated by her sister's husband, Tereus. She eventually got revenge and was transformed into a nightingale, a bird renowned for its song. But there's more to this story that will be uncovered as we create our own journey with my gorgeous nightingales, that I'm sharing with you thirsty bastards. Ultimately, the only nightingales that can sing are males, and that is how it should be. Women need to be silenced; we are too tired to listen to their nonsense. They don't need a voice and there is only one good use for their pretty little mouths."

Laughter echoed around us as the men clapped. My head was light as I recalled Ian Ivory's obsession with Greek mythology and the story about the peonies. The story Alister Ivory was fixated on was about a woman who was mutilated and raped? I looked around at the girls, who were stoic. I could see tears streaming down some of their cheeks, while others looked as if they were void of all emotion.

"Nightingales, it is time for you to report to your cages and remember to make daddy happy." I officially wanted to vomit. The girls stood around me and began walking in sync.

"Get up." Karina was in the row in front of me. She cut her eyes and shook her head as I looked behind me and the line I was holding up because I was frozen. I didn't want to go and see what was next. I didn't want to save these girls. I wanted to run away and let them die the same way I did to the girls back in Charlotte.

How could I single-handedly end this without getting myself killed? I also knew that day in the ocean when another boat appeared to save me wasn't a coincidence. Bradley and I were being followed and watched. The Ivory family had eyes and ears everywhere. *They only let you die if they want you dead. They know the greater torture is being alive and under their control.*

CHAPTER
TWELVE

I STOOD in front of the door that was engraved in gold lettering, Cage Eight. The others had already gone into their designated rooms.

My chest was rising and falling rapidly as I pressed my hand against the door, and it slid open.

It was Declan Rothschild, the man I had welcomed to the resort with his wife, Sage earlier. But it wasn't the man who startled me; it was the room. The room was mostly dark beyond a red light flickering in the corner, and there was a black cage. There was also a table of items: leather whips, handcuffs, knives, and other items I had no idea what they were.

Declan was dressed in a suit, but his button-down was removed. His face flushed red as soon as the door closed behind me, and I pressed my back against the cold metal.

"I...I didn't request," he stammered as he began tugging at the hem of his suit jacket.

"You didn't request what?" I cleared my throat and tried to stop looking at the cage that had a small swing and chains in it. The room was too warm, unlike the rest of the floor.

Declan blew out a breath of air and stood. "Not what...who. I didn't know it would be you."

A red light switched to green, and Declan's eyes widened. "They told us we'd be financially penalized if we didn't use this time for what it is allocated for." He slid his jacket off and I pressed my palms on the door behind me. Looking behind, I noticed there was no lock or doorknob. I was trapped.

"Mr. Rothschild, there's actually been a mistake."

"She doesn't let me choke her." He slowly walked toward me.

I was trembling as his gaze fell all over my body. I hated how dark the room was, and how the whites of his eyes stood out more. I hated how I couldn't run.

"Mrs. Rothschild seems like such a wonderful wife." My voice shook as he placed his hands around my waist.

"You're gorgeous. I've never been with a woman who wasn't White. I've always wanted to try someone exotic like you." He smiled. "I think they didn't read through my application as carefully."

Declan let out a laugh as he raised his hands up my body.

"Application?" I questioned.

He squinted at me, and I shuddered when he touched me.

"I don't think I paid all this money to hear another woman fucking yap. Honestly, that's why I asked for her to be gagged and bound before I entered." His hand slammed around my neck and my lips parted in shock as I gasped for air.

"Please," I screeched as his grip tightened and shock flooded through me.

He moaned as he continued to squeeze my throat. I wanted to fight back harder, but my mind wasn't processing this quickly enough. I slapped my hands around his forearms and dug my nails into his skin, which only caused him to laugh.

"Yes, baby. I love it rough, too." He slammed my head against the door before dragging my body by my neck toward the bed cornered in the room.

Slamming me on the bed, he wouldn't let go, even as my eyes rolled. "Dec—" I rasped, but then everything pieced together as he pressed his body weight against mine, completely aroused.

This was Alister's Euphoria program for the men. *Rage, release, and relaxation.* This was what the nightingales were being used for.

I was too lightheaded and dizzy as one hand slid down my body and his fingers clawed at the thin, lace panty.

"No," I whispered as I choked on my saliva and could feel him tug and finally, rip my underwear from my body.

"No," I said once more. What a simple, yet normally powerful, word, but it didn't have any meaning in this world. An Ivory world. Declan lifted his hand and swung at me.

The crack of his palm against my already sweating face had my eyes fill with tears as he continued to hit me.

Screaming out, he called me Sage—his wife's name. "I've dreamt of doing this to you! All the times you ignored my needs. I've given you everything, you selfish bitch! I paid so much for the life we have and yet, you failed me!"

Everything started to darken around me.

I'm nothing more than his fantasy. His disgusting, vile and terrifying fantasy.

A fantasy where he could violently hurt his wife and do whatever he wanted to with no repercussions. A fantasy he could live out to nurse his fragile male ego.

Just as my eyes started to close, I heard loud footsteps and suddenly saw him.

Alister Ivory was towering over Declan Rothschild, and the glimmer of his gold rings caught my eye.

He was going to hit me, too.

But then, just as he lifted his arm, the gold rings met Declan's jaw and a crack echoed. He repeated action as I clenched my eyes shut.

"How dare you touch what is mine?" he boomed.

I slowly looked up at Alister as he lifted me into his arms and carried me out.

"Demi, my beautiful, precious little bird." He kissed my forehead, and just like that, everything around me went completely dark.

CHAPTER
THIRTEEN

SOMETHING COLD WAS BRUSHING against my face as I slowly opened my eyes. There were no lights on beyond a television screen in front of me.

My entire body ached as I turned my head slightly. Alister Ivory was caressing my face with his fingers.

I was in his bed. His forehead creased as he stared at me. "I want to leave." My voice was scratchy as a tear slowly rolled down my cheek. My throat was aching from my screams and cries as Declan attacked me.

A trivial smile grew on his face. "My beautiful Demi, you know the only way you can leave the resort is in a casket."

"Declan is being taken care of. He's going to have a penalty fee to stay. But why, my sweet dove, did you come down to La Gabbia's Euphoria?"

"I wanted to see you," I lied. Although I felt weak and terrified, I knew Alister didn't lie. I'd never leave the Ivory family unless I was dead.

"Demi, I knew there was a reason I had to have you, too." Alister brushed his fingers through my hair.

My body tightened as I could feel his breath against my face. "Let's watch this movie I had made especially for you." He turned over and sat up in the bed. Reaching over, he handed me a tub of popcorn.

My stomach churned. Dr. Ian Ivory had a popcorn cart in his home office, where he'd watch the girls he held hostage.

Pushing myself up, I realized I wasn't in the tulle skirt anymore. I was wearing a thin, black nightgown. Glancing over at Alister, I didn't understand why he saved me from Declan.

Focusing on the massive screen in front of me, I realized it was the same room I was trapped in with Declan.

Declan was pacing around the space, shouting at the cameras to let him out.

I glanced over at Alister and saw him eat his popcorn with a large grin on his face. He looked like he was just a normal man enjoying a movie.

Suddenly, Declan's door opened and two girls in black gowns and masks came in, rolling a steel table that had something concealed under a white sheet.

"This is my favorite part," Alister whispered. "He had specifically checked off on his form that he did not want this exploration. He was too scared." Alister let out a laugh.

The two girls began explaining something to Declan, who dropped to his knees and screamed.

"No! This isn't what I agreed to," he screeched. The girls backed out of the room as the door slid shut.

Declan stayed on the floor for a while, and Alister pressed a button on his nightstand. "Get the fuck off the ground and do what you need to do, Declan. You know you want to. She's put you through hell. Didn't you say she laughed when you couldn't give her an orgasm? Didn't she compare you to your older brother? Didn't she..." Declan rose as Alister taunted him. "You'll never be man enough for your wife unless you heal here. It's this or death. You should be so lucky that I'm allowing you to breathe."

Declan's fists clenched as he stood and peeled the sheet off the table.

"Oh my God." I slapped my hands across my mouth as I slammed my eyes shut.

It was a woman in all white with blonde hair.

But she was pale in a way that I knew she didn't have life in her.

"Alister, no," I cried out and tugged the blanket higher.

Alister pulled the blanket down as my breathing grew shallow.

"Keep your eyes open and watch the screen, Demi." I knew it wasn't a suggestion, but rather a threat.

Declan swung his fists at the dead woman in front of him.

"No!" I screamed and slammed my eyes shut.

"Open them or I'll peel your eyes out." Alister shook me.

"Demi, the Euphoria program saves marriages. It saves these men from doing something detrimental to their wives and wrecking their families—the families that our society and world need. Look what he did to you, my raven. We've got to heal him." Alister spoke calmly as tears ran down my face.

"Sage! I fucking hate how you don't see what I do for us. I paid so much money for you!" Declan was choking the pale corpse.

"This is sick. Alister, I'm begging you to stop."

Alister looked over at me, then leaned over, wiping my tears away before licking his fingers. "Mmm, delicious. Your pain tastes so delicious. My brother was right." Alister sighed.

"The man and woman on the boat saved me from the ocean. They saved Bradley, too. That's why they brought me here. You had me followed?" I shuddered as I averted my eyes from the screen.

. . .

Alister put his popcorn on the nightstand, turned, and leaned in on his palm. "I had heard of you. My nephew Bradley hated his father, and I couldn't blame him. Ian was always an entitled asshole. We grew up in the same home and were told by our father to leave a lasting impression on the world. Ian took it too far." Alister yawned.

I let out a dry laugh and shook my head. "*Ian* took it too far? What is this?" I pointed at the screen but froze.

Declan was naked and laying on top of the dead woman. My body instantly folded over as I grabbed the popcorn bucket and vomited into it. "No," I cried. My stomach churned at the pleasure written all over his face as he dug his nails into her body and pushed inside her, at the satisfied moans as he called her by his wife's name.

"He's going to go home a better man, Demi. Have you seen the news recently? There are suburban husbands and fathers killing their families. There are men who are abusing the woman they swore in front of our Lord and Savior to protect."

"Alister."

He stood and wiped my mouth with a tissue. "The issue is you can't see the bigger problem I'm fixing."

Clenching my teeth, I took a step back from him. "This is not a solution. Aren't the nightingales someone's daughter, sister, wife?"

Alister tilted his head. "No. Some are the caged girls you chose to leave behind. I saved them. I brought them here and turned them into my beautiful doves. They are caretakers; they see sunlight and interact with guests. The nightingales are women from our society who have done nothing but hurt us. They are mostly the drug addicts I've collected and saved. And then, there are the breeders." Alister took the bucket from my hands and placed it down before taking my hand and walking me to the luxurious bathroom.

"The breeders?" My voice trembled.

"Demi, we are an all-inclusive, exclusive resort for the wealthy. We are full-service. Sometimes we have unique couples coming to us with their marriage in shambles because they cannot reproduce, so we have options for that, too."

"I don't understand what you mean by that. Who are the breeders? These girls aren't birds or animals, Alister." My head turned as his palm cracked against my cheek.

Gasping, I clenched my eyes shut as he aggressively took me to the bathtub. My skin stung as I slowly opened my eyes and looked at the monster in front of me. "I wanted you to be a nightingale. I wanted you to be in my own Russian roulette. You don't even know what happens every time a guest checks out. You don't even know about my fun little game to ensure no man or woman leaves this establishment with the intent to ruin all my hard work."

Ripping my lace nightgown off, he smiled as he looked at my naked body. "Then I saw you... I saw the chocolate eyes that enticed my brother and nephews. I knew I always had to have more than him. Look at me now, Demi." He turned the bathtub on and demanded that I get in.

"Please, I don't want to," I whispered.

He snapped his fingers and just like that, a woman appeared. It was Marcie, wearing her usual all-white outfit. "Marcie, darling, will you clean up the favorite girl of La Gabbia, please? She vomited earlier, and I can't bear the smell of her."

Marcie's eyes met mine, but she quickly looked away. I could tell she was forcing herself not to say what she wanted to. Alister left the bathroom and shut the door behind him.

"You look just like her, you know..." Marcie said quietly as she lifted my hand and guided me into the tub.

"Marcie, I went down to..."

"Hell?" she answered as my body sank into the warm bath.

"They call it the Euphoria program." I was scared to close my eyes and see the scenes of Declan raping a dead woman or beating her lifeless body.

"It's uncanny how much you both are alike." Marcie squeezed a sponge and began lathering soap onto it.

"Who?" I paused.

Marcie sighed. "Your sister, Layla, of course."

My heart pounded against my chest but suddenly, everything felt still."

"Marcie…" I trailed as my head ached with confusion.

"My sister died in Nashville, Tennessee. She was the reason I went to Charlotte and ended up in Ian Ivory's torture chamber. She betrayed me. She fell for that monster—the man who trafficked girls into Ian's arms."

Marcie slapped her hand over my mouth, but I hit her hand off me. "Don't you dare touch me." I seethed as hot tears stung my eyes.

"Demi, your sister didn't betray you. She saved you."

CHAPTER
FOURTEEN

AFTER MARCIE BATHED ME, I was given a silk nightgown to wear. "This is what he wants you in." Marcie pinched her lips to the side.

"I need you to tell me how you know my sister when I saw her die in front of my eyes. I need you to tell me how Bradley is walking around this resort when I killed him. I killed them both." My body was shaking as Marcie pulled the gown over my head and my hair dripped down my back.

"Demi, when Mac and Tini saw you in the ocean that day, they said you asked for plain white rice and yogurt."

I nodded as I remembered that moment, thinking someone was saving me but quickly realized there was no way my life hadn't already been meticulously planned out for me by deranged monsters.

"You said that to show them compliance and that you were brainwashed by Ian. You said that because you're a brilliant girl and want to live." Marcie grabbed a hairbrush and began brushing through my sopping wet hair. It was all true. I saw their green eyes and blonde hair and knew they were all just the same. I knew I had to pretend I was consumed by the Ivory family.

"Marcie, please tell me, is my sister alive?"

"Not the sister you knew. Best you just let her stay dead." Marcie tapped my shoulder and walked away.

Looking over her shoulder, she smiled at me. "Alister Ivory is an even sicker bastard that Ian ever was. Just be careful. I know you want to burn it all down, but he'll never let you go unscathed."

I stood there and watched her leave before turning to the vanity and leaning into it. Staring at myself in the mirror, I knew she was right. But more than anything, I couldn't calm my nerves, thinking my sister was potentially alive. Glancing up at the ceiling, I also knew I was being watched. What did the girls mean when they said one gets chosen at the end of each guest's visit? Chosen for what?

"Demi..." His voice echoed in the minimalistic space as my racing thoughts combated the peace in his tone.

Clearing my throat, I replied, "Yes?"

"Come to bed," he said calmly.

I wanted to go back to my room, but I knew better, so I obeyed. I walked through the door and saw Alister Ivory standing in front of the oversized window. I couldn't see the ocean since the darkened skies met with the water, blending into an abyss of nothingness.

He was wearing a matching black silk pajama set with his hair brushed neatly.

"I'd like to go back to my room with Marcie, please. I sleep well there, and I'm sure I need to tend to Mrs. Rothschild. She's probably wondering where I had gone. I truly apologize about leaving my position and coming to the Euphoria floor, Mr. Ivory." I had my arms behind my back and my fingers laced together.

Alister stared out of the windows, and the small clock on his end table taunted me with its ticking.

"Do you know what I've always dreamt of, Demi?" He spoke softly before turning around, his dark eyes such a contrast from his brother's.

"No," I replied almost inaudibly.

"I've always wanted a family. A wife and a few children. Children I could raise into happy and productive humans. A wife who looked at me with pride and knew I did what I had to do."

"I'm sure you have plenty of inventory here for a

bride." As fast as I said the snarky statement, I regretted it. Alister's hand curled into a fist. Stumbling back, I put my hands in front of my face. "I didn't..." I stammered as he filled the space between us.

Peeling my hands down, he looked at me carefully. "You're right, Demi. I could fuck, marry, or kill any girl I want to." He brushed his hands against my cheek. "But you see, since I was a young boy, Ian has always won in every single way. Our father's love and adoration, our mother's care and comfort. I was always the...well, the black sheep of the family." He ran his hand through his hair and smirked at me.

"Then I found out about you—the one person who successfully took my brother down. And a woman, nonetheless." He let out a dry laugh. "My nephews, Conrad and Bradley, were fighting over you the way my brother and I did over who'd get to help Papa kill his next victim."

My heart sank. Ian and Alister's father was just like them... Was this why they were natural killers? This family business ran on for generations.

"You know, I've always been lonely. But I've also been more fearful if I choose the wrong woman and feel some kind of emotion to her, she'll then betray me.

I'd have to kill her, and then our children would forever be upset with me." He brushed his fingers against my eyelashes, causing me to flinch.

"Please," I whispered. I didn't know what I was pleading for. "Ouch!" I cried out. Alister had ripped out some of my eyelashes and held them in between his fingers. My eye watered as I covered it.

"Did you know if you make a wish on an eyelash, it comes true?" Alister smiled. "My mother would let us do that." He placed my eyelashes in his palm and lifted one near my lips.

"Make a wish, Demi," he crooned.

My nostrils fluttered as fear coursed through me. "I don't have one," I breathed out.

"Of course, you do. Everyone has a wish." Alister closed his eyes and mouthed words silently. "There, I've made it for you. You're welcome."

Blowing some of my eyelashes away, he opened his eyes. "Let's go to sleep." He tugged at my hand and pointed at the bed.

He walked over to a jar displayed on his dresser and lifted the glass top off.

Sprinkling the rest of my eyelashes into it before shutting and placing the jar back on the dresser, he sighed proudly. I immediately climbed into bed as my chest rose and fell rapidly.

"Sweet dreams, Demi." He kissed my cheek, and the lights all turned off.

I waited until his breathing shifted to slide out of the bed. The moonlight provided just enough light for me to make my way to the jar.

Leaning over, I lifted the glass top and squinted. Sticking my fingers into the jar, I felt the soft little hairs.

Slapping my hand over my mouth, I realized something.

It was a jar full of eyelashes. Cringing, I shut it quickly, but the glass clinked too loudly.

"You've thought of a wish, my darling raven?" I shot around and saw Alister sitting up in bed, watching me. The whites of his teeth and eyes stood out in the darkness.

"I'm so sorry," I stammered and raced back to the bed. Climbing in, I laid flat, praying he wouldn't be upset.

He turned toward me, putting half his body over mine. "It's alright to be curious, my beautiful bird." I kept my eyes closed as he brushed his fingers through my hair.

"What did you wish for?" I quietly asked.

"I wished that I'd find the strength to not slit your

throat, drink your blood, and make one of the nightingales wear your face whenever I missed you." A sob left my mouth as stomach acid rose in my throat.

He placed his finger against my lips. "Shh, now we must sleep."

CHAPTER
FIFTEEN

ALISTER – *Ten years ago*

"Papa, why must she wear only white?" My brother Ian and I were watching our father bleach the unconscious woman's hair. Her head was balancing in the bathroom sink as her pale lips parted.

"Speak quietly, Alister!" he hissed at me. Papa was wearing white surgical scrubs. His hair—a bright blonde that matched Ian's—was combed over neatly. Our whole home was all white. We all were forced to wear the green-colored contact lenses as well. My hair was black like Mother's, and no matter how much Papa would try to bleach it, it'd never look like theirs.

Mother's hair was long and beautiful. She chose to keep it tied in a neat bun and wore a blonde wig, instead. When Papa wasn't home, she'd take it off and dance with us outside, letting her long, raven-like locks fly around her. She didn't choose to marry Papa; she was forced to when she was trafficked from India as a teenager. Papa said it was his one piece of color in his life.

She wasn't meant for this life, and neither was I. But Papa had saved Mother in some ways. She was trafficked into Papa's business of death, but he fell in love with her. She was the favorite girl for him. She knew that defying him would land her in one of the all-white cages where the girls were deprived of their senses. I preferred darkness—I thought it did a far better job at sensory deprivation. There was nothing more fear-inducing than obscurity. There was nothing more peaceful and depriving than total loss of control of your environment. But Papa never listened to me. He thought white was superior—which was another reason he wanted to marry Mother. He said the color of their skin also depicted the social class difference. He was more worthy than her because of his skin tone. Ian was oddly fair compared to me. I had seen Papa bleach his skin once and take him somewhere anytime he had any kind of tan on his skin. We were forced to wear long sleeves even when it was painfully hot.

I once offered Papa this brilliant advice of changing the white therapy to dark, but he slapped me and told me to let Ian learn the family business properly. He told me I would never be man enough to withhold the Ivory name because I was my mother's softened shadow.

"Frederick." My mother walked in on all of us cleaning the woman in the bathtub after Papa had bleached her hair and attached an IV to her vein.

"Lana, please prepare for the welcoming ceremony of the caged girl." Papa smiled as Ian and I scrubbed her naked body with soap.

Papa turned to us. "Make sure to get under the fingernails." My mother and I looked at one another in a way that I knew she was trying to comfort me.

"Of course, my love." She glanced over at my brother, who never once stopped cleaning the woman. Papa waited until Mother left, then exhaled slowly before speaking.

"My sons, you must marry a woman with a broken wing, because once you repair it and help her fly, then you have all the power. You hold the key to the gilded cage that she will stay and serve you from. She thinks she's the favorite girl in your world, but really, she's nothing more than the caged girl, born to serve and obey you."

Ian's jaw ticked slightly as he nodded and absorbed our father's evil. I didn't want to keep a woman in a cage and do this. I looked at the nearly dead woman lying in the bathtub.

"Did you hear me, Alister? Ian already has the family business mapped out. He's going to carry on my legacy of submissive brides for the wealthy men who need an obedient counterpart. He's going to carry on all of what I have poured my blood, sweat, and tears into." Papa stood and grabbed a towel to dry his hands. "And what are you going to do, son?"

The entire bathroom smelled like bleach and soap.

"I don't...I don't know," I murmured as Ian laughed and mimicked my words.

"A real man finds a problem and solves it. Are you a real man?" I could tell Papa was becoming irate.

"Yes, Papa." I stood quickly and straightened my shoulders. "I was thinking I should create an escape."

I licked my bottom lip as Papa's face lit up with curiosity. "An escape?"

Really, I just wanted to escape this house. The all white, sterile environment. "Yes, an all-inclusive and exclusive resort for those who are looking to release their inner demons, urges, and desires." My heart was racing as my father waved me out of the bathroom, leaving his golden son behind. For the first time in my life, I felt seen by him.

"Tell me more." His hands were crossed behind his back as we walked down the stark hallways that were only lined with black-and-white images of strange features. Features of women who were kept captive on the other side of the estate.

"Papa, sometimes I feel anger and rage, and I want to hurt someone. I want to feel powerful and be in control of their life." My cheeks warmed as I confessed this to my father.

He stopped at the end of the hallway and swiftly pushed me against the wall. His hand wrapped around my neck as my eyes shot wide open, and I began to choke on the lack of air.

His face was emotionless as he continued squeezing and saliva trickled down my lips as I tried to pry his fingers off.

"Please," I pleaded. But he didn't stop until I began to see stars and tunnel vision set in.

Finally, as my eyes began to close, he let go. I hunched over and began coughing violently as he took a step back in his platform white shoes.

"Papa," I cried as the pain penetrated through my throat.

"I feel like the most powerful man in the world. I *am* the most powerful man in the world. Your life was in my hands, and there is nothing more masculine that that." Papa began walking away and stopped.

"Come. Come now, son." Following him, we began walking toward the side of the estate I'd never been to. "Shoes." He pointed at the basket full of the same platform white sandals we were forced to wear whenever we were anywhere in the house close to this side.

Papa swiped his badge over the keypad, and the door silently slid open. I stared down the hallway. Everything was white and excessively clean, and there were small fluorescent lights above each door.

I walked closely behind Papa before we turned to a room that didn't quite match the others.

He opened the doors and together, we went in. It was a conference room with marble floors, and there was a glass window on one side that had another room with a small cot and a young girl inside.

Papa continued over to the popcorn machine. "My favorite snack to eat while watching her." He smiled at me. I looked at her as she stood and made her way to the glass. Her thin frame was covered with an almost translucent white gown. Her long blonde hair looked tangled and the bags under her eyes were deep and dark.

"When I was a boy, I wished for a hamster." Papa handed me a bucket of popcorn. "But my father said, 'Why would you cage an animal when you can cage a woman?' Women don't realize they are, in fact, more powerful than men. They carry life, they can comfort and weaken a man through lust and desire. It's our job, Alister, to make sure we hold the power. An Ivory man doesn't just hold the power above women, but also above all other men. You must always have something over their heads to be successful and powerful."

Papa started to eat the popcorn before leaning back in a chair. "You're eighteen now. I've waited longer than my father did."

"For what, Papa?" I asked as I watched him stare at the young woman with tears streaming down her face.

"To watch you become a man."

I wanted to die. Ian told me what Papa made him do when he was eighteen. He was gloating about it while I knew it may kill me.

"There's a concealed door through the side." He handed me his badge. "Swipe my badge and then go in the cage and show us you are a man."

"Papa, I don't...I don't want to do this. Please," I pleaded with him as I looked down at the floor.

Not even ten seconds later, he lifted his hand and slapped me across the face. "You are a fucking pathetic little boy." He stood and threw the popcorn to the side. I gripped my cheek as my flesh burned and my father went into the stark white room.

He swung his fists at the girl before he slammed her into the small cot and strangled her. He looked straight at me as he choked her.

My lips parted and I didn't know what to do. If I tried to help her, he'd kill us both. Papa slid his pants off and forced himself over her. The room was sound-proofed so I couldn't hear her screams, but I could feel them in my soul as her mouth opened. Then she looked over at me and mouthed, "You did this," before closing her eyes and laying there as my father raped her.

"You coward." I could see her lips form into the cruel words. How dare she? Father was right; women had no right to do this. But the reason Papa didn't hurt Mother was because he was using the caged girls to get his desires and rage out. This was the reason we were a happy family. I could do this for others; I could become powerful in my own way.

CHAPTER
SIXTEEN

I WOKE up feeling groggy and mostly surprised I had even fallen asleep. My arm was aching.

"Madam, I'm here to remove your IV," a soothing voice called out. Turning my head, I saw a girl in a short white apron dress donning a pixie blonde haircut. Her pale green eyes looked strangely calming.

"IV?" I rasped as I looked down at my arm and saw a needle taped down to my vein. "What is this?" Lifting the blanket off my body, I still had the nightgown on, which didn't mean much at all.

"You were unsettled at night, my darling raven." Alister walked into the bedroom, adjusting his cufflinks. He was wearing another entirely black ensemble.

"What did you do?" I sat up and ripped the IV out as the woman—Taylor, I remembered from orientation —stood by the bed and immediately tried to intervene and settle me down as if I were some toddler throwing a tantrum.

Alister came over to me and brushed his fingers against my jawline. "My darling, if I wanted to do something to you, I wouldn't have drugged you. I'd have made sure you were wide awake, enjoying every moment of it." He dragged his index finger against my neck.

"You must get back to work today. Except, I've decided to make you a floater between heaven and hell." Alister smirked at Taylor, who was standing in all white. It occurred to me that he had designed this entire resort to encapsulate quite literally heaven and hell.

"I don't understand what that means?" I slid out of bed.

"Mrs. Rothschild's husband, Declan. He's…well, a bit shaken up after last night. Clearly, he isn't man enough. You'll need to ensure she is enjoying her stay here while we have Declan complete the Euphoria program."

"The dead woman he…" I crossed my arms.

"At the end of each guest's checkout, we have a ceremony where they are to take the life of a nightingale. Those nightingales get to continue serving men, even in death."

My stomach flipped. He was killing these women, then letting men rape them.

"Taylor, take Demi upstairs, and make sure she's in her proper uniform upstairs. We can't have our resort looking like some trashy standard all-you-can-eat bull-shit." Alister laughed as he waved us away.

Grabbing my hand, Taylor picked up her pace and turned toward a small elevator. "What were you think-ing," she shook her head and whispered as we both stepped in. Waving her badge against the pad, the golden elevator doors slammed shut and went up to the floor where our rooms were.

"Taylor, we have to help those girls," I breathed out as my body shook with how frigid the space was.

"Why?" She shot a look of disgust at me. "Demi, the problem with women like you is that you're trying so hard to find something wrong. It's this whole 'woe is me' production that I am so tired of." Taylor grabbed my hand as soon as the doors opened and quickly led me to the wing of the resort we resided in. Swiping her badge against the keypad, the door slid open, and I was once again blinded by the all-white aesthetic. "Kandi is waiting for you. Your hair is a mess, and you look like you just did the walk of shame." She clicked her tongue and shoved me inside the open door of Kandi's makeup and hair room.

But just as we walked in, I took a step back and screamed. Kandi was already brushing another woman's hair. Taylor covered my mouth with her hand and quickly slid her badge to have the door slide shut behind us.

"No, I'm done. I can't do this anymore." Sweat beads began to form across my hairline as Taylor tugged me to the small sofa cornered against the wall. Kandi was completely unbothered as she began spreading makeup across the other girl's face.

"This is sick. You all are so sick," I cried out as I watched Kandi squint and bend over to meticulously line the woman's eyes.

Turning to a binder, she flipped through it and nodded. "He wanted red lips." Grabbing a tube of bright red lipstick, she looked over at me. "Do it."

I was still wearing the black nightgown Alister gave me to wear. My mind was spinning from everything that had just happened in the past twenty-four hours. In some pathetic way, I was hoping this was just a regular resort with maybe a secret gambling lair for the men. I didn't think I could survive another Ivory game.

"It's crazy that you're their daughter-in-law, and here you are, working with us. If you would just obey and accept this all, then I bet you anything Alister would make sure you were the queen of this entire legacy," Kandi said.

"Now put the lipstick on her." She raised her brow as Taylor shoved me off the couch and I stood. Kandi's eyes flicked to the corner where a small camera was.

"Do it with a smile," she whispered so quietly I almost missed her words.

My hand shook as I took the tube of lipstick from her and walked around to face the woman in the chair.

Rolling the lipstick up, I leaned forward and swallowed the lump in my throat.

But just as I was about to press the lipstick on her mouth, her head fell forward.

Sucking in a breath, I gasped.

"It's fine. Rigor mortis and whatnot is wearing off or whatever." Kandi sighed and aggressively pushed her head back.

"How did she…" I began as I slowly lined her lips in red. Brushing my finger against the hole in her head, I started to cry. "Russian roulette," I whispered.

"Smile!" Kandi poked me and cleared her throat.

I forced myself to smile as I covered her thin lips and looked at the dead woman wearing lingerie in front of me.

"She was a nightingale and served the Euphoria program for an entire year. We are so proud of her.

Most girls only hang around for a month before they get…" Kandi looked over at Taylor.

"How can you both support this? I don't even understand." I looked at the dead woman in front of me and stepped back. Her lips were now a bright red, which stood out against her lifeless, pale skin.

"Do you realize that men with money are what makes the world go round, Demi?" Taylor opened a closet and tugged out a short white dress. "Here, change. We've got to go tend to the wives soon."

I walked to the binder laying on Kandi's vanity and sniffled as I flipped through page after page. Each image was a dead woman laying in her own blood. I froze. "Oh no." It was an image of the woman from the lobby who I had mopped up her blood.

"That one tried to run." Kandi shook her head. "That's why the best shot is in the head. But the guy shot her in her neck, so she was still able to run." She shrugged.

"Are you putting makeup on them for their funeral?" I asked, even though I already knew the answer.

Taylor let out a laugh. "Oh, Demi, you're silly. Alister likes to recycle here. He's very environmentally friendly."

"You see, Alister Ivory craves power the way an alcoholic craves another drink. Rumor has it, as a boy, he was always the black sheep of the family. Ian had created this incredible business and carried on their deranged father's legacy. But then, Alister wanted to be even bigger and more dominant, so he created La Gabbia. The world's first and finest exclusive resort for the wealthy to live their wildest and most obscure fantasies. Fantasies that would otherwise have you arrested if done on American soil, which is where most of our guests come from."

I slid into the tight dress in a state of shock, and Taylor helped me zip the back. "There's a dead woman sitting with us right now." I looked between the four of us.

"Where are these girls even coming from?" I knew for a fact that Ian was trafficking girls through the man who my parents had sold my sister and I to. But this... this seemed far more detailed, far more complicated.

"These girls are addicts." The door behind us slid open and I turned around to face a gorgeous woman with long black hair and a black lace gown. "I'm Marisha. Alister has asked me to make sure you head to Mrs. Rothschild immediately before returning to Euphoria."

I looked at Kandi and Taylor. "What are you going to do with her?"

Marisha tapped her foot impatiently as I stood there, waiting for an explanation.

The silence taunted me.

"Did you know that Marilyn Monroe's corpse went missing for ten hours?" Marisha stared at me as my forehead crinkled with confusion.

"No. I...I don't really know much about her in general, let alone facts about her death." I knew the agitation was clear in my tone, and I swore I could smell death circulating around me.

"A group of men...wealthy men were said to have taken their turn with her." Marisha opened her hand to me.

Looking at her palm, I shrugged. "They raped her dead body?" Placing my hand in hers, she wiggled her free hand at Taylor and Kandi, who were whispering and working on curling the dead girl's hair.

I watched the door shut behind us as Marisha glided and stood out against all the white.

She smiled at me. "You really do look just like her."

"My sister was here, wasn't she?" I fought the violent rage in my body where I dreamt of killing everyone, one by one, until they told me what had happened to her.

"I guess you could say that." Marisha quickly turned before swiping her badge.

"I thought only white was allowed up here?" I tugged at the white dress I was wearing.

"You're right, Demi. I'm just your shadow, and shadows are usually dark, aren't they?"

"Marisha, I'm begging you to tell me about my sister."

"I thought you'd want me to finish the story about Marilyn Monroe so you could better understand this business?"

I nodded, knowing no one would tell me about Layla. I hated even picturing my sister's face because the last image I had of her branded into my mind was when she pleaded with me to end her life with the rust-tinged knife after our trafficker had brutally beaten and attacked her.

"There's a large group of wealthy men who have fantasies, Demi. Disturbing to some, but empowering to others. They are untouchable in the world, and having their fantasies come true is how Alister Ivory has made billions of dollars. Do you know how much money men will pay to be able to have judgment-free sex with…"

"A corpse?" I swallowed and fought back the nausea that was coursing through me.

Marisha sucked in a breath as we walked out into the lobby. "Yes. Now go, Demi. I must leave." Marisha turned away as I followed her line of vision.

It was Sage Rothschild, Declan's wife. I had just seen her husband beat and rape a dead woman. Averting my gaze, she filled the space between us with her white caftan flying behind her.

"Demi! Where the hell have you been?" Sage tilted my head up.

"I'm so sorry, Mrs. Rothschild… I was assigned to help out."

"You sneaky little bitch. You did it!" Sage let out a laugh before crossing her arms. "You got to the bottom floor where the men go and play, didn't you?" She was truly beautiful. Her face was glowing and her shiny blonde hair sat in perfect waves.

"Why did you and Declan decide to come here?" I looked around nervously. There were more couples checking in.

"Demi, is everything okay? Is Declan okay?" Sage tilted her head and looked at me with immense concern.

"Mrs. Rothschild…" I began as my heart pounded against my chest. This woman had a family with the man I saw down there. I saw a normal, everyday kind of guy turn into a monster.

"Demi." A cold hand snaked around my back. Turning around, my lips parted as I looked into his eyes. Bradley.

"How…" My voice cracked as tears filled my eyes. "I knew it was…" I began, but he cleared his throat.

He plastered that signature faux smile across his

face. "Have you seen the wonderful film, Titanic, Mrs. Rothschild?"

His nails dug into my flesh as Mrs. Rothschild looked between us and made note of his hand.

"Yes, I have. It's one of my favorite movies." Her jaw tightened as she saw the way my spine straightened and my shoulders tensed with Bradley's touch.

"Do you think there was enough room for Jack?" Bradley glanced over at me before smiling back at Mrs. Rothschild.

"No. There was never room for Jack. Truthfully, I'd have let him drown. He was nothing more than a one-night stand on the ship."

I looked up at Bradley. I needed to talk to him. He was the only one who knew everything and more. He knew what I'd been through, and I knew him—or most of him.

"I think there was room, but Rose was scared. She'd spent her whole life drowning and finally needed to prioritize putting herself first," I said.

Something shifted inside him. I could see the way the hatred and rage softened into the deep emotional connection Bradley and I had from the moment I'd walked into the Ivory estate.

"Okay then, this is weird and not what I expected a six-figure resort to get me, but I'm ready to have help in getting dressed for tonight's masquerade ball," Mrs. Rothschild said.

Bradley and I stared at each other for a moment longer before I pulled his hand off mine.

"Mrs. Rothschild, shall I help you get ready for the masquerade ball?" I waved her over in the direction of the guest suites.

"Yes, and please stop calling me that. It's Sage." She looped her arm into mine. I turned and peeped over my shoulder and saw Bradley standing there. Closing my eyes, he looked the same as the first time I ever saw him. Perfectly coiffed blonde hair, stark green eyes, hollow cheekbones, and pale skin.

"What the hell was that?" Sage nudged me as I swiped my card to access the guest suites. I stayed silent until we walked into her room and the door shut behind us.

"You should request to leave with Declan now." I looked around her room and frantically opened her closet.

"Demi! What are you doing?" She shouted at me as I paced around the suite.

"I'm looking for the cameras!" I was out of control but didn't care.

"Demi." Sage grabbed me and shoved me against the wall. "What is wrong with you? Of course, they'd pair me with a psycho on my one vacation in years!"

Tears formed in her eyes as I panted from racing around her room.

"Sage, I'm sorry, but this place isn't safe for you. You don't understand where Declan is."

Sage slammed her hand against my mouth. "I don't want to hear it! I'm here to enjoy massages and drink pink cocktails while lying poolside. They told me that we'd be assigned a quiet little bird to help us with anything and everything. After all that I've been through!" Sage stepped back and took a deep breath as I realized I was making a grave mistake. If she reported me, I'd be killed. I had to keep my mouth shut. Sage, a rich housewife, didn't need my help. The nightingales and the doves—who were all just innocent girls being bought and killed after torturing them—needed my help.

"I'm so sorry, ma'am." I changed my entire demeanor immediately.

"Help me get ready for the masquerade ball. I need something to look forward to before tomorrow's visitation day!"

"Visitation day?" I questioned as I looked at the gown she was holding.

"For my baby, of course." Sage smiled and turned away.

My lips parted as I looked out the oceanfront balcony doors.

Baby?

"I have a secret, Demi..."

Chills splattered across my arms as Sage smiled and grew closer to me.

"I had two beautiful children from my first husband. They were taken from me when the world claimed I was not fit to be their mother. Now they are with some perfect family and have forgotten that I even exist. I was wasting away when I was admitted and found a new path. But then my uterus was stolen from me and in order to keep Declan happy, I need a baby." She kissed my cheek, then spun and walked away.

CHAPTER
SEVENTEEN

WE WERE MOSTLY silent the rest of the time. I helped curl Sage's blonde hair as she did her makeup. She decided to reject the offer to have Kandi come in and do it for her, preferring it just be the two of us. I had to bite back the looming questions about Sage going shopping for a baby. Had I heard her wrong? Why did she lie to me about having children that lived with her already, and what did she mean that her uterus was stolen from her? She seemed like a genuine woman. But then again, when had I ever found someone who was truly the person they portrayed themselves to be?

"Declan and I may see each other tonight," Sage said excitedly. "They said some of the husbands may not be there to keep things exciting. Plus, these masks are just darling!" She lifted her exquisite bedazzled white mask that matched her stunning ivory gown.

"I think this whole all-white concept is quite soothing." Sage smiled at me through the mirror as she applied the signature nude lipstick all the female guests received in their welcome bags.

"Mm-hmm…" I nodded as I zipped the back of her gown and took a step back.

"I'm sorry." Sage turned slowly and leaned her backside against the vanity.

"About?" I asked cautiously.

"I shouldn't have been such a nosy bitch and had you hunt down and spy on the men. Whatever you saw was probably just men, well…being men." She shrugged.

"Sage, I need to know how you both found out about La Gabbia and why you chose to come here." I was nervous. She was already agitated with me, and she could easily snap and report me.

Sighing, she walked past me and went to the sitting area of her suite. It overlooked the ocean but had the glass between the cream boucle chairs. I knew she didn't want to go out and mess up her hair.

"Sit with me, Demi. For once, I'm an hour early." She patted the empty spot beside her.

"I was the daughter of a criminal. I never knew what

wealth and love were like. My mom died from a drug overdose when I was young, and everything was a blur after that. I craved this life…one where you're not fighting for your next meal. I was married and had a sex addiction that ultimately tore my family to shreds in many ways. I had always been attracted to men that pretended to love me but just hurt me instead. When I met Declan, I knew everything would change. But he wanted a baby more than anything. He chose me and knew I didn't have a uterus. It was part of…recovery for me."

Sage turned to me as the sun shone brightly in the clear, blue skies.

"I can't give him a child of his own, and Declan was upset but he chose to marry me because he thought I was the most beautiful woman he'd ever seen. Declan was worried because he wants our child to be perfect. He wants him to have blue eyes, blonde hair, and light skin, of course."

I looked over at her. "So, your surrogate is here?"

Sage patted my hand. "You really are the new girl around this resort, aren't you? They ought to improve your training, but perhaps that's why they keep every department of the resort separated."

We both looked back at the crystal-clear water. It was strange being so secluded on a private island where there weren't laws or regulations. I thought I was in the Bahamas, but it turns out Ivory Island, surrounded by deep ocean waters, is its own piece on earth where there is quite literally no escape. La Gabbia had its own in-house hospital, security, and everything a human could need. Alister even had his own food and drink supplier, so he never had to go through a single person. He was the king of it all.

"I believe it's time for you to take me down to the masquerade ball." Sage tapped me.

I stood and nodded. "Yes, it is. I'm sorry I don't know much about anything around here. I promise to research and know exactly how to best serve you tomorrow when you go to…"

"See my baby!" She clapped excitedly as I shuddered.

I couldn't get the image of her husband raping a dead woman out of my head, or how he strangled me before almost doing the same to me. That man was going to be the father of an innocent child?

But I pushed through and forced myself to do what I always did when surrounded by the chaos the Ivory family created, and that was to pretend I was okay with it all.

———

The ballroom was all white with fairy lights and fresh peonies decorating the entire room. Every single woman was wearing a white ballgown that resembled a wedding gown, and suddenly, I realized this was staged to look like a wedding day.

It wasn't a masquerade ball, it was...a vow renewal celebration?

"Ladies, please take your seats as soon as possible." I looked at the stage and saw Jamie, one of the doves I'd met earlier.

"Come sit with me, Demi." Sage waved over.

I shook my head because I watched the other girls line up on the side of the ballroom with their hands folded in front of them. "I will check on you soon, Mrs. Rothschild." I moved out of the way for the other wives to sit down.

The lights dimmed as I took my place between Marcie and another girl. "I'm Lacey." She smiled and wiggled her fingers at me.

"Shh..." Marcie shook her head at us as the room went completely dark and there were hushed whispers all around.

"Ladies, we truly hope you're all enjoying Ivory Island and La Gabbia resort. When my uncle created this resort on his private island, he had one thing in mind and that was family. Making sure families stayed together, and those who wanted to become a family with children could do so privately."

Everything became pitch-black, but I'd always recognize his voice. It was Bradley speaking.

"Why is everything dark? They even turned the small lights off." I hated this feeling of terror while everyone else was blissful.

"Shh…" Marcie elbowed me.

"You see, here at La Gabbia, we believe that the bond between a husband and wife remains sacred and holy at home; but while here, we can explore and experience things that may be causing rifts. When your husbands were invited to attend our Euphoria program, we didn't force them to bring you, their doting wives—they chose to."

There was joyful chatter in the darkness as the women must have been so thrilled that their husbands wanted them to join them.

I rolled my eyes as I pressed my back against the wall. "I know many of you are here hoping you can go to our Life Center and meet your newest family member. Others are here to remember why you're worthy of love.

"But ultimately, we are here to celebrate it all, and tonight, before we begin our ball to celebrate each of you, we have our very own special vow renewal between one of our couples that leaves in the morning after they have completed our sacred program.

"Of course, none of this is possible without the dedication of our team members, who we lovingly call our nightingales and our doves." My eyes slammed shut as lights flashed above our heads.

The women all clapped for us, and Marcie whispered, "Curtsy!"

The lights cut off and a screen flashed behind Bradley, who I could now see clearly. He was wearing a fitted, three-piece cream tuxedo, and he smiled straight at me, although I knew there was no way he could see me.

"Now for our nightingales." There were black-and-white images flashing behind him on the projector of young women wearing black tulle dresses, their long legs dipped into black heels. Their faces were void of any emotion and their hair was neatly pinned back.

"These ladies have been serving your husbands and are fully trained in working through the stresses a man can endure."

There was light chatter amongst the wives, but nothing rage filled.

"You were told to sign an NDA to protect this safe haven we have established, and in exchange, you go home with a husband who is happy to be yours. Some of you will go home with a new family member, while others will join the waitlist. I hope each of you has been enjoying the full pampering and service you deserve."

There was a spotlight on stage and the screen shifted to an image of a young couple. "This is Kim and Todd. They were married for eight years before Todd began showing signs of interest in his secretary. An emotional affair is far more daunting than a physical one, as many of you know." Bradley paused and brushed his hand across his clean-shaven face.

"They've always wanted a child together, but Kim didn't want to sacrifice her beautiful body, especially after Todd's indiscretion. On the verge of divorce, Todd was informed about La Gabbia and had selected to attend our Euphoria program with a special invite to visit the Life Center with his wife. Today, they've completed their stay with us, and I'm so thrilled to help them renew their vows before they go to the Life Center." Bradley took a step back as more lights flicked on.

A man and woman made their way to the stage wearing wedding attire. Kim was clutching a bouquet made of peonies, causing an innate response of anxiety to course through my body. But that wasn't what had my heart pounding. It was Todd. His eyes were desolate as he walked across the stage to meet his wife in the middle. Kim was clearly giddy with excitement as she saw her husband and looked into his eyes while opening her free hand to him.

He looked down at it before glancing at Bradley. His eyes were tinged red, and I could see a bruise across his neck. Bradley's jaw ticked as he shook his head slightly at Todd, who immediately straightened his shoulders and dropped his hand to Kim's. I knew he had done something, just as Declan did and was doing. I knew he probably raped a corpse or innocent young woman. He probably made her do all the sick things he dreamt about doing to his wife.

"Dearly beloved, we are gathered here today in the vision of God to join this man and this woman in holy matrimony. Marriage had been protected through the ages for the stability, trust, and holiness it brings to an individual, a family, and our world as one community. Once we join them in marriage, they are becoming a new family, and raising a life after is of utmost importance. We know we cannot simply gain a life without sacrifice, right, Todd?" Bradley paused and smiled at the tense groom.

Nodding too many times, Todd immediately looked at his wife's hand—though he hadn't once looked into her eyes.

I didn't listen to the rest of the absolute trash Bradley was spewing. "You may kiss your bride."

Bradley was beaming as Kim leaned in, but Todd stood there, staring at her hand.

"They made me chop it off," he whispered, but they were wearing microphones for all of us to hear their vows.

Kim squinted and leaned forward. "What did you say, honey?" She glanced at Bradley.

"They made me chop her hand off. She bled out slowly, Kim. So slowly and painfully. Then they said she'd be used for men who preferred an imperfect body. The room... They make you..." He started to weep, and Bradley immediately snapped his fingers. Two men dressed in all white suits raced up the stage to drag him away.

"Wait! Where are you taking him?" Kim shouted as she chased after her husband. There were gasps and gossip coursing through the other women, but every single one of us doves stayed quiet, as if we all knew what was coming. But just like the crowd, all of us were left in nothing more than the dark.

CHAPTER
EIGHTEEN

"LET'S GO, DEMILION," Bradley mocked as he aggressively tugged me down an elevator. He wrapped a blindfold over my eyes as he clutched my hand.

"Bradley, please just stop." The air around me was frigid, as if we'd gone even lower into the ground.

We were wearing the assigned white platform shoes now, where no sound echoed in what I was certain were stark hallways.

"Please, Bradley!"

He shoved me against the wall, causing me to cry out in pain from the brick wall against my back.

"Demi, shut up!" he hissed before he slowly pushed up my blindfold. I was staring straight into his green eyes. His facial expression immediately softened as soon as he looked at me.

"Hi." I offered a trivial, dejected smile at my first

love. The first and only man I had ever truly trusted in my life. The only man who made me believe someone cared about me. The man I thought I had poisoned and killed in the middle of an ocean when he betrayed my trust.

"Hi," he replied and brushed his index finger against my face. "You tried to kill me." My eyes widened as he said the words with no resentment, but complete despondency laced into each one.

"I trusted you, Bradley…even after everything your family put me through. You never mentioned you were Ian Ivory's son." I choked back the tears that stung my eyes.

He cupped my hands and pressed his forehead against mine. "I know, I know…but this is all I ever wanted for us. I dreamed of us getting to Ivory Island and eventually taking over La Gabbia. We could make it ours; we could end all of this and turn it into something you want." His minty breath brushed against my face as a single tear rolled down my cheek.

Grabbing his hand, I looked into his eyes. "You want to end all of this?"

. . .

"Demi…" He took a deep breath in. "I missed the way you smell. I missed these brown eyes. I'm so glad I put the tracker on our boat for Uncle Alister to track. I couldn't have lived with myself if I knew you were dead. Granted, I would have saved your dead body the same way…" He paused and pressed his lips against mine.

I turned my head and pushed him off my body. "Bradley."

He had known all along that we were going to end up here, and that us being saved was never a coincidence or an accident. "You knew I'd see the photo album of you as a child with Ian and Conrad?"

What kind of sick game had he played with me?

"I wanted you to know the truth, Demi. Ian, my father, wouldn't let me tell you. He told me he'd kill you after…after having his way with you."

My head was spinning. Everything was starting to make more sense. "I loved you then, Demi. I love you now, and I'll love you forever." He brushed away the tears from my face.

"You are my soul's mirror." His dimple deepened as I broke my gaze and looked down the dark hallway. The walls were all black brick, and only one light behind us flickered.

. . .

"Bradley…" I blew air out before looking back to him. "What is this?" I shuddered.

"Tonight went terribly, Demi. Our resort has been compromised because of the incident with Todd and Kim. Alister wants to see us both to discuss some changes. I know we have much to catch up on, and I know we will, but tonight we have to go see what he needs. Demi, you married my brother; you are an Ivory. One day, I'll finally get to make you mine as you were intended to be. This is our family business, and we must save it. I know you tried to kill me because you were scared, but the truth is, this was our only place to go."

I was an Ivory. Granted, I had murdered my husband after we consummated our marriage, but I was still part of this sick family.

"Bradley, I'm scared." As much as I had every reason and more to hate Bradley and not trust him, ultimately, he was the only person I was familiar with and knew. I also knew he was in love with me. Having someone love you held more power than any form of violence ever could. I controlled him in a way he didn't even know, especially now that he knew I wouldn't hesitate to kill him if I had to.

"I know, my sweet Demi…but just play the game. We must." I nodded at him as he laced his fingers through mine, and together, we walked down the cold, dark hallway. I let my hand brush against the black brick walls as we made our way down. There were divots that were no longer brick, but rather a cold steel to blend in.

"Bradley..." I whispered and stopped. "What is this?" I felt as if my eyes were closed because I couldn't see anything. Tracing my fingers against it, I knew without a doubt it was a door. I turned and walked a few steps further and felt another.

"Before we have beautiful nightingales, we must have the caged girls." His arm wrapped around my waist as he tugged me away. "You have to stay quiet."

"They are kept in total darkness?" I was shaking as memories of Ian Ivory's caged girls came flooding back. The stark, sterile bright white rooms, where the girls were deprived of senses and turned into obedient wives for the rich.

But this...this was the opposite. These girls were kept in total silence and darkness. This was far more terrifying because they didn't know what evil was lurking.

"It's different, Demi. Darkness helps us heal. It's therapeutic to cleanse your soul and learn how to please and give, rather than to take."

"We have to help them..." I knew I shouldn't have

said that—they were words Bradley would never agree with.

"We will. We will, my love." He tugged me down the hallway until we reached the end. "Lift your palm and press it against the door. You'll feel it." We both did so, and suddenly, the door opened slowly. It was still too dark, but I could hear the door slide shut behind us.

"Do it again." We both pressed our hands against the door I couldn't see, and it slid open, revealing an enormous space with a gold chandelier hanging over an expansive conference table.

I knew they had the first door so no light would emit into the hallway for the caged girls to see.

Alister Ivory was sitting in a suit at the head of the table, with half the table filled with men in all white suits and the other in all black.

Two seats were empty.

"There's my right-hand man and right-hand woman..." Alister chuckled as he stood. His eyes immediately dropped to where Bradley's hand was holding my shaking one. "Why are you touching her, Bradley?"

"Uncle Alister, she was tripping in the darkness." He

released his hold and took a nervous step away from me. "A dove isn't accustomed to the…"

Alister's jaw clenched as he made his way around the table and shoved Bradley out of his way. My lips parted as I watched him look at me with sorrow. He knew something I didn't, of course.

Alister smiled down at me and waved to the empty seat next to his.

"Come sit, Demi…" I was freezing. Everything about this area of the resort was icy, cold, and dark.

Alister pulled the chair out for me, and I slid in, tugging my dress down. All the men around the table were staring at the binders in front of them.

"Demi and Bradley…" He flinched as he said our names together and sat in the oversized velvet chair. "I hate saying your name with anyone else's." Alister winked at me before tapping his fingers against the binder. "We are looking at page three."

I stared at the binder in front of me. This felt familiar, but I knew it was all a new twisted game I'd have to fight to live through.

Except, one thing I couldn't fight was the feeling deep inside that made me think I may not survive this one.

Flipping the binder to page three, I gasped. It

looked like a yearbook. Images of women wearing the same black, off-the shoulder blouse. Each girl was staring blankly, wearing identical necklaces—a small bird pendant.

"My darling, Demi, this is our current class of nightingales. You see, we've been at a bit of a standstill to obtain more inventory, so I'm very unhappy right now. But we will prevail. We always do. Don't we, gentlemen?" I looked up and each man nodded quietly.

"But if you'll flip to the next page, we are examining our other portion of this resort, which is the Life Center." Alister licked his finger and flipped the page for me.

It was divided by eye color, skin color, and hair color.

"The eight of you have been my most trustworthy team, and it's been extremely important for us to keep you all healthy and fit. We've never had a dissatisfied customer from the Life Center."

"What is this?" I looked at Alister before glancing at the men at the table. They were all staring at me, and I fell back into my chair when I saw their eyes. All green. Half of them had shiny black hair, while the others had stark blonde.

"Demi, our clients are wealthy men who have worked incredibly hard to leave a legacy behind. And they expect their legacy to be perfect. Sometimes breeding between a husband and wife isn't the best option. Say your wife has medical issues, or she's unable to carry a child, or perhaps you're not fond of the way you both appear... At the Life Center, we allow couples to come in and design their—"

"Uncle Alister, I'm so sorry for the interruption." Bradley's cheeks were red as he stood. "But there was a huge mishap at the vow renewal today."

"No, wait...Alister. What..." I was trembling. I needed to know what he was telling me. What were these couples designing? Why didn't Bradley want me to know?

"What mishap?" Alister slammed the binder shut.

"Todd, our latest graduate of the program, broke down and almost revealed everything to his wife. We had to go the nervous breakdown route and medicate him. His wife believes us and is more concerned about making it to the Life Center. But the other wives were shaken up. The doves have been told to go full force on making sure everyone is taken care of and forgets this mess with the masquerade gala with endless drinks laced with our special pill." Bradley didn't want me to hear what Alister was saying, so instead he was distracting both Alister and me.

"What a fucking mess! How did we not recognize a weak, pathetic link?"

"I'm sorry, Uncle Alister. We've admitted him to the psych ward."

I erupted into laughter as all the men stared at me. Alister froze and looked at me. "Demi!" He lifted his hand and slapped me hard, his thick gold rings slamming into my cheek. My ears rang as I cried out.

"Demi!" Bradley sprinted over, but before he could reach me, Alister shoved him violently.

"Alister!" I shouted.

"Take him away!" Alister snapped at the man sitting closet to him, who immediately grabbed and dragged Bradley out.

"Shut your fucking mouth, Demi." Alister's eyes were filled with something I'd never seen before, not even in the eyes of his monstrous brother.

Staring up at him while clutching my cheek, I knew what I had to do and how irresponsible I had been. "I'm sorry, Mr. Ivory." I pulled myself up by holding on to the chair and for a moment, Alister watched me struggle as my shoe had fallen off.

Sighing, he reached his hand out and drew me upright. Was Bradley going to be alright? I knew better than to ask.

Alister's face shifted. Something about my presence always made him soften even after a violent outburst.

"We are done here." Alister spoke to the men surrounding the conference table. I didn't want to be done here, but my throbbing cheek was a reminder that I didn't have a choice. I wanted them to go through the binder and listen to everything else they were planning. I wanted to know the ins and outs of this sick resort.

The room lights turned off as the others silently left. "Demi, come with me." Alister held my hand and led me to the back wall, where he pressed his hand against the brick, and it slid open. There was another dark hallway with small lanterns flickering. He waited for the door behind us to shut before stepping forward.

"This is where I keep them…my own precious little birds. My beautiful nightingales." I could see the white of his teeth flash in front of me as my stomach flipped.

"I thought the other hallways had them?" I whispered as we slowly walked.

"No, no, those are a mix of nightingales and breeders," he said with pride.

"Alister, what are the breeders?" My voice shook as I trembled in the freezing air.

He slid his suit jacket off and wrapped it around me. "They help us keep the Life Center stocked. Don't worry, once they test positive, they get to move out of the breeding area to a more comfortable Life Center bed."

I pressed my hand against one of the doors. "The Life Center?"

"Where couples can become families," he answered as I looked over my shoulder and tugged his jacket on.

"They are surrogates?"

"You could say that..." He pulled me away from the door.

"And what are the roles the nightingales have to do?"

I knew none of this was as simple. He was keeping pregnant woman hostage? How were they becoming pregnant?

"Nightingales are the ones who serve and create Euphoria. They create the escape for the men to become better husbands and even better fathers. If a man has a place to release his rage, then he won't release it elsewhere."

"Declan Rothschild..." I started. "He was choking me; he almost killed me and then you forced him to have sex with a corpse. Who was that woman?" I choked back my tears as I pressed my hands against my neck and looked at Alister, who was illuminated from behind by the lantern.

"A nightingale who had served her time, and served her time well. Once you're a nightingale, you serve La Gabbia for eternity."

He smiled down at me as he wrapped his arm around me. "I love that you're curious. I love that you're an Ivory woman. It's been years since I've been in the presence of one, Demi. Mrs. Demi Ivory."

I was Conrad Ivory's widow. *I was an Ivory for eternity.*

"I need you to stay away from Bradley..." He slid his palm over one last door.

My lips parted in shock. We had walked straight into an elevator with only one letter. "P" for penthouse. His home led straight to these wicked hallways.

"What if I don't?" I was playing with fire, but I had a plan.

"Then I will cut small slits into his body and let him drain out. I'll serve his beautiful blood to our guests in their daily wellness smoothies, then force a nightingale to have sexual relations with his rotting body."

"You are sick." The elevator doors slid open as we walked into his penthouse.

"Demi, for all that you have been through in a lifetime, I'd have assumed you were more immune to nature's laws."

Shaking my head, I peeled Alister's coat off my

body and threw it to the ground. His eyebrow lifted and he smirked with amusement.

"Nature's laws?"

"Go take a bath and get into bed. We must work tomorrow. I need you more than ever, Mrs. Ivory."

He may hit me and play with me as his puppet, but I knew Alister Ivory had a soft spot for me. Was it because his brother's son trusted me enough to marry me? Or was it the fact that Bradley was also in love with me? Whatever it was, I knew my life was safe.

For now.

CHAPTER
NINETEEN

ALISTER WAS asleep next to me. I missed my room with Marcie. There was no discussion of me moving into his home, but suddenly, my small bag of belongings was neatly lined on the bathroom counter. A custom robe hung in the closet with my name on it, and even the slippers by the bed—which were my size —sat neatly on the floor.

I wondered where Bradley was and if he was okay? I needed to go back down to the lair that held the girls. I needed to understand how to help them.

My heart was racing as I laid next to Alister and waited to be sure he was asleep.

Sliding out of the bed, I tiptoed out of his bedroom and walked into the living room. The balcony doors were open, so I made my way and looked outside. I welcomed the warm breeze as I hugged myself tightly. The sound of the ocean crashing made me realize I had never gone down to the coast. After being saved from the ocean, I never thought to go back to it—not that I'd been allowed to leave these walls in the time I've been here.

I could have spent hours outside, soaking up the salty air and the silence that was only laced with the waves of the ocean.

But instead, I turned back into the penthouse and looked around cautiously before grabbing one of the cards from a bowl I'd seen. Alister had a stack of black metal cards I had seen him swipe to enter where he was keeping the girls.

I was wearing a lace, black nightie, but I knew it was too risky to look for anything more. I didn't have much time.

Sliding into the elevator, I held my breath and was thankful for everything in this pit of hell being as silent as possible. Swiping the card, I hit the bottom floor button and watched as the penthouse disappeared behind the door.

Not even a minute later, it opened to the dark hallway. I could smell death in the air and feel the pain behind the doors. Slamming my hands against my ears, I sucked in a breath of air.

"I'm sorry, I'm sorry!" I whimpered, seeing my

sister's bloodied face and then the girls I'd left behind at the Ivory estate when I fled and saved myself.

Taking deep breaths, I wiped away the tears streaming down my face.

Looking down at the card in my hand, my fingers shook as I took a few steps down and waved the card against the scanner.

The small red light turned green, and the door slid open.

A small rattle echoed against the floor.

Taking a few steps in, the door slid shut behind me. I could tell this wasn't the main entrance to the floor. Flinging around, I panicked but then...

"Please...I miss my mom."

Her voice was so meek, but I couldn't see anything —it was completely dark. Putting my hand out against the wall, I kept walking forward.

"Ow!" she cried out as I jerked back and dropped down. Blinking repeatedly, I looked forward and then, she smiled.

I flew back and gasped as her teeth stood out against the otherwise pitch-black space.

"You're not Marisha," she rasped. I remembered Marisha—the woman with the long, dark hair in the black gown.

"No...no, I'm not."

She wouldn't stop smiling. I pushed back a bit and

suddenly, she began crawling toward me. I could see the outline of her body move through the room.

"Who are you?" I closed my eyes as the fear felt like too much to handle.

"Please stop." I felt a cold hand brushing against my face as I held my breath.

She traced my face with her bony fingers. "Name?" she asked, her voice regressing to almost a child-like one.

"Demi," I replied. I could feel her breath on my face as she traced my face with her fingers.

"You're so beautiful, Demi," she whispered.

"How long have you been in here?" I shook as I felt the floor around me. It was warm and wet.

"Sorry, I couldn't hold it." She pulled her hands away and moved from me.

She peed. Squinting, I wiped my hands on my nightie, cringing as the pungent urine stung my nose and soaked my feet.

"What's your name?" I stood and placed my hand against the wall.

"Caged girl number three," she answered, and I could hear her moving around.

It was too dark and cold.

"Do they ever turn a light on?" I asked as I took a few steps backward, beginning to feel claustrophobic and anxious.

"I haven't seen lights in months. I can't wait to be a nightingale. I've heard there's light when you serve the gentlemen."

"I'm going to help you get out. Just tell me what your name is?" I asked again as my heart began to race. I needed to get out.

"Caged girl number three." She laughed quietly. "Demi, I don't want to get out. I want to stay here and serve. For the first time ever, I'm feeling peace. I used to jam needles into my arm, Demi...Demi...Demi." Fear started to pool in my stomach as I pressed the keycard against the wall, but it wouldn't open. Her footsteps grew closer as I panicked.

"Heroin?" I asked as I turned and ran my fingers against the wall in a panic.

"Mmm...yes." She sighed and her cold fingers wrapped around my shoulders.

"I'll be back."

"Don't leave me, Demi...Demi..." She pretended that her voice was echoing as she changed the tone. She began smelling my hair, inhaling loudly.

"Please stop." I slammed my palms against the door until finally, the door slid open.

Stumbling out, I fell to the ground as the door quickly shut behind me. The small lantern that was lit was completely out, and I couldn't see anything.

I pushed myself off the ground and leaned against

the wall and began walking. Alister had brainwashed these girls the same way Ian had.

But the difference was, in some sick and twisted way, Ian Ivory created submissive brides. Alister Ivory was creating submissive sex workers, who were ultimately killed.

I think that was what scared me the most, knowing what I could see on the surface was so little compared to all the layers underneath.

CHAPTER
TWENTY

I COULDN'T TELL which way I was going when the only lantern had blown out, so I hoped for the best as I made my way down the narrow, cold hallway. Patting my hands against the wall, I wondered where the damn elevator had gone. Once I felt the end of the hall, I waved my card wildly and a door slid open.

"Help me," I whispered. It was another room. I wasn't prepared to interact with another destroyed woman who was convinced she was living a wonderful life.

I stepped into the empty space as the door shut behind me and then a second door opened. A small amount of light poured in as I covered my eyes. Suddenly, it was too bright, even though the light was mostly dim. Slowly opening my eye, I saw it. A giant golden cage. It was life-sized, and a bed was in the middle.

"Oh my God." I breathed out as I could see a man's bare back. Looking up behind the cage, I froze, my eyes wide. There were women hanging upside down, blood draining from their bodies as their hair straggled, and their eyes were taped closed. I couldn't see it on the black floor, but the dripping echoed as the life drained out of them. There were moans that shook me out of my trance, and I looked back at the bed. She sat up with her arms wrapped around the pale back, and her deep brown eyes met mine.

I gasped before slapping a hand over my mouth and stumbling back.

It was my sister.

It was Layla.

Her eyes grew large as she pushed the man off her. He turned and looked at me.

Bradley.

Bradley and my sister were in bed together. In a cage.

"Demi?" Bradley jumped out of the bed and grabbed his pants, but just as he came closer and I stared at the girl I thought I'd let die, everything went black and my body crashed to the cold, hard, marble floor.

———

"Demi..." His voice was gentle. "Demi, please open your eyes." I didn't want to open them. How could you want to live so badly, but at the same time, want to end it all?

"Demi..."

I took a deep breath as my head throbbed and the light beeping in the background taunted me. "Bradley..." My voice cracked.

"Demi." He sighed as he brushed the hair out of my face, but I slapped his hand off me.

"My sister is alive. My sister is alive!" I screamed. Bradley looked alarmed as he glanced around the room. I didn't even think to check where I was, and truthfully, didn't even think I cared.

It was a stark white space that resembled a hospital room.

"Demi, you are dehydrated, you are sleep deprived, and under extreme distress." Bradley lifted a cup filled with something steaming. "Drink it, Demi."

I pushed it away and forced myself to use any bit of strength in my body to sit upright.

"No. You don't get to gaslight me and make me

think I'm crazy. She was there. You were fucking my sister, and there were women hung upside down, bleeding out." I licked my dry, cracked lips as snot dribbled out of my nose.

Bradley tilted his head and watched as tears poured out of my eyes. They weren't tears of sadness; they were ones of anger and exhaustion.

"Demi, think about what you just said. Please. Your sister, Layla, died in an apartment after you stabbed her to death to put her out of her misery. You think there were dead women hanging upside down as blood drained from them?"

Closing my eyes, I was shaking, feeling the IV needles deep in my flesh and I began doubting myself.

"Demi, Alister flew to Miami for the day to handle business. You are lucky he thought you'd gotten up to work. Mrs. Rothschild has been asking about you and needs you to be back serving her. She refuses any other dove." Bradley placed the mug down and rested his elbows against his knees before running his hands through his hair.

"Demi, this is an all-inclusive resort for wealthy couples to come and heal their marriage and expand their families. There is nothing to it. No one is here against their will. You poke and prod until someone gets hurt, or worse, someone or many people die." He looked back at me.

"Once you're in this family and have seen what you have, there's two options: one, you accept this as your new normal, or two, you kill yourself or be killed. That's it. You'll never escape this family. They will never let you go, and most of all, you're forgetting that you are an Ivory."

"I've decided you will no longer be exposed to the Euphoria program. Being a nightingale is intended for the women who were on death's door...the women we saved."

"Saved them?" My forehead creased as I shook my head. "Those innocent girls are rotting in sheer darkness, deprived of sight and all their senses. They are expected to feel grateful to serve and be used, raped and tortured by rich men who want to feel what? Appreciated? Powerful? And then...you let them die so they can serve men as corpses." My heart raced with fury.

"Demi?" Bradley and I both looked at the door. Nothing made any noise here; everything was quiet, and I knew we were always being watched or heard.

"Mrs. Rothschild is looking for you. She's very upset and even asked for her husband to be returned so they could depart early, unless you came back to serve her." Marcie paused and crossed her arms. Her shiny blonde hair was perfectly placed in a low bun.

"Demi needs more rest," Bradley replied. Every time I closed my eyes, I saw the image of Bradley sleeping with my sister and the bodies hanging in the background.

I could hear their moans and my shriek. I could hear my heart pounding against my chest as the world crashed in around me. Layla and I looked almost the same, except for the small birthmark she had on her cheek that was never noticeable since she covered it with makeup. Most of our lives people had assumed we were twins.

"Demi has rested plenty," Marcie said sternly as she reached over and yanked the needles out of my arm. Bradley tried to block her, but she pushed him away as I cried out in agony.

"Get up, Demi. We cannot lose one of our richest clients over your little dehydrated-induced hallucinations." Marcie tugged me into the hallway and my head spun from the sudden crass movement.

"Easy, Marcie. Easy, now." Kandi, the makeup and hair stylist, was waiting in the hallway with her white makeup box.

"I think our Demi needs to stay in heaven and far away from hell." Kandi winked at me as I held on to the doorframe. Everything was sterile and all white.

There were nurses walking up and down the hallways with blonde hair, green eyes, and the old-fashioned nurse outfits and hats.

"Demi, this is inside of La Gabbia. When you live on a private island and in a resort, then you have no reason to leave. We have our own little airport right outside for the private planes to land, and beyond that it is our haven, right, Marcie?"

Marcie wasn't smiling or showing any emotion beyond watching Bradley over my shoulder. "Get her ready and drop her off to Mrs. Rothschild, Kandi. I need to have a word with my…"

Bradley's jaw tensed. "I'm not your employee, Marcie. Alister would never give you that control."

Marcie smirked, and for the first time, I saw something inside her I'd never seen before.

Evil.

"I'm going to warn you once, Demi. If you don't start behaving and doing your job, you'll be one of those girls hanging upside down and drying out to be used…"

"Marcie!" Bradley put his hands up as I looked between them.

I wasn't crazy. I saw what I saw. And now, I knew my sister was alive.

CHAPTER
TWENTY-ONE

"MRS. ROTHSCHILD." I folded my hands neatly.

She slid her sunglasses down the bridge of her nose as the white caftan she was donning flew gently in the breeze. She was lounging by the balcony that quite literally hung over the ocean. It was stunning. The gorgeous, bright blue water and the warmth of the sun felt unreal.

"Finally, you're back. My God, they paired me with some dumb ass who gave me Stepford wives vibes. I needed you back, Demi, or else I was about to jet on my private jet." She waited for me to laugh, but I think I had secondhand embarrassment for her.

Waving her sunglasses at me, she laughed. "See, this is why I needed you back. You're not a kiss ass."

I forced a smile, although my mind was spinning as I thought about my sister and the women in that room.

"And remember to just call me Sage, please." She pointed at the empty seat next to her. "I request Zen time with a view. Really, I was hoping for a sexy, young pool boy to admire while here, but no, even in paradise, it's all just beautiful women serving us." She beamed at me.

"Can I get you anything else?" I asked politely, the shake in my voice apparent, no matter how hard I tried to conceal it.

"Sit with me. I'm lonely." She laid back on the lounge chair and slid her sunglasses back on. I hesitated for a moment, but ultimately, remembered that the role of a dove at La Gabbia was to entertain, serve, and worship the rich, bored housewives of the men who were funneling funds into this sick resort.

"It's beautiful out there." I was wearing a white suit-style romper with gold buttons. Crossing my legs, I squinted as I shielded my eyes with my hand.

"What is my husband doing down there?" Sage turned to me and took a long sip of champagne. I could see peony petals floating in the glass. "I know you got down there, and that's why you've been missing."

. . .

I shook my head and kept my eyes on the ocean. There was not a single person lying in the sand—it wasn't allowed. The rules of the resort included not leaving the premise unless you were signed up for beach-side yoga or soul cleaning, which I had no idea what that even meant.

I looked at her. "He's watching football, drinking beer, and bitching about you to the other guys."

Nodding slowly, she processed what I had said. She peeled her sunglasses off her face and revealed her beautiful eyes that were mostly blue, but tinged with green.

"You're a terrible liar. Did you know Declan and his ex-wife divorced because he would beat her black and blue? They'd be having sex, and he'd suddenly just want to choke the life out of her as foreplay." Sage looked back toward the ocean.

"Why did you marry him, then?" This made complete sense to me, considering Declan tried to suffocate me and then enjoyed beating up a corpse before raping her.

"He chose me, and I'm such a pick-me girl." Sage tilted her head up toward the sun.

"Does he ever hit you?" I instantly regretted the question as soon as it left my lips.

"Yeah, when he's had a terrible day at work. He's in finance and does all that stock trading stuff. I don't know…I guess losing massive amounts of money can mean you just want to beat your wife after a work party." Sage shrugged as I listened to the grief in her words.

"Better to be beat by a finance guy with millions than a drunk in a trailer, am I right?" She let out a dry laugh that I recognized as one of reassurance. Layla would do it when we were trapped inside a small dark closet for hours on end in our trafficker's small apartment. She'd make dark humorous jokes, ending with that same laugh to make me feel safer and think she wasn't worried.

"No, I don't think you deserve that at all. I think, as women, we've just gotten so used to feeling powerless."

Sage sat up. "Demi, the most dominant woman is the one who can have a powerful and wealthy man fall in love with her. Once you have him on a short leash, you can rule the world."

I flung my feet back over and slid my padded white shoes back on. "What about a woman just becoming powerful on her own?"

Sage clicked her tongue and shook her head. "In this day and age? No, darling Demi, you must have a man on your team. You can destroy the rest that way. No one touches a powerful woman with a powerful man."

I didn't necessarily agree, but then again, I didn't exactly disagree. I'd witnessed first-hand just how deep these wealthy people could dig. How much they could bury without even so much as a red flag waving.

They could get away with anything.

"Can you get me one of those smoothies? It's some berry-floral one?"

"Of course." Sage waved me away as I stood, and I brushed my hands through my hair. I missed my thick black hair that was always coated in coconut oil before Layla and I got sold by our own parents.

Our parents... It had been a very long time since I thought about them. My heart ached as I made my way through the gorgeous resort. I was thankful to be out of the lower level. Maybe Bradley and Marcie were right; I'd need to learn how to just accept this as my forever normal and be obedient. Why did I think I could be some sort of Nancy Drew and single-handedly go against wealth and power?

I walked through the hallways and stopped only to look at the photographs. It was the same sort of sorority house photos. Every single photo was of a woman with blonde hair and the eerie smile that sent chills up my spine.

———

I knew I couldn't waste time and anger Sage. This was an easy job for me, and after last night, I needed to stay under the radar. Alister would return, and I needed a track record of me caring for Mrs. Rothschild. I walked into the kitchen where I had forgotten about the unique outfits, or lack thereof, for the staff.

But then my stomach flipped as I remembered the screen.

It was what the men were getting to watch. That's why the girls were wearing heels and nothing but an apron and tiny lace shorts to cook in. It was part of the entertainment for the men.

"Could I please get the berry-floral smoothie?" I asked one of the girls who was washing a wineglass.

"Are you talking about our wellness smoothie, Pretty in Pink?"

"I think so…"

"Yeah, just go over to Taylor. She's making them." I nodded and slid against the wall toward the back, hoping to not be a part of this sick production.

"Taylor!" I waved at her as she was chopping fruits and vegetables on a cutting board.

She wiped her brow with her forearm and smiled at me. "Hi, need something?"

"One Pretty in Pink, please." This felt like a normal

job. It was kind of a relief to just be…normal for a moment.

Taylor blew out a breath. "You should learn how to make it, too. That's our most popular smoothie."

"Yes, I'd love to." I washed my hands at the sink next to her and dried them quickly.

"Strawberry, ice, banana, spinach, raspberries…" She paused as I finished adding the ingredients into the blender.

"That powder right there…" She flinched as I reached for a container labeled, osso blend.

"What is this?" I opened it and grabbed the measuring spoon.

"Bone blend."

My lips parted as I looked at her. "When the caged girls…"

"You mean, the nightingales?"

"They're the same. The nightingales are the caged girls. Once they are finished and used, they get well… It's just their bones."

Taylor looked around. Luckily, we were tucked away into the side of the kitchen that couldn't be seen well. She slid a small container of something in a deep shade of red, almost black. "Alister swears this is some youth smoothie because it contains the bones and blood of beautiful, submissive women."

. . .

"I'm not putting this in there," I whimpered as my fingers shook.

"You must, Demi. Don't stray." She grabbed it from me and put in two heaping spoons of it. Then, she handed me a bowl of peony petals.

I gagged as I put the top on and began to blend everything. I knew where peony flowers grew at Ian Ivory's home, and I wondered where the graveyard was here on the island.

"If this one was hard to make, then you really don't want to know what's in the pineapple smoothie."

"What?" My eyebrows knitted together as I shuddered.

"Semen."

CHAPTER
TWENTY-TWO

"THAT TOOK YOU LONG ENOUGH." Sage smiled as she took the smoothie off the white marble platter.

"You don't have to drink it. It may not taste great since I took so long to bring it back to you," I rambled as she looked at me with confusion.

"This is La Gabbia's most talked about smoothie. People swear you drink it for the entirety of your stay, and you leave with a face as smooth as a baby's butt." My stomach churned as Sage took a sip.

"How much longer are you and Declan here for?" I took the seat next to her as she looked forward.

"Another week or so. I believe Declan extended it." She stirred the icy smoothie around.

"Hello, ladies." I abruptly jumped out of the lounger and stood. It was another wife and Jamie, both dressed in white dresses. They both had blonde hair with piercing green eyes. I sucked in a breath as the other wife made her way closer.

"It's such a beautiful day. Sage, you've been hiding from all of us, now, haven't you?" She snapped her fingers at Jamie and pointed at the lounger I had just moved from.

"Wipe this clean. Sage, I don't know why your... dove was sitting in our seats." She clicked her tongue with disappointment and disgust.

Jamie tugged a wipe from her pocket and began cleaning the chair. "Ms. Sabrina, please take a seat. May I bring you anything else?"

Sabrina looked at me, her head tilted. "You look familiar." She brushed her fingers through her blonde hair as she studied me carefully.

I glanced between Sage, Sarah, and Jamie before following Jamie's lead and taking a step back.

"I know you from somewhere." Sabrina took out a tube of nude lipstick and painted her lips.

Jamie cleared her throat and nudged me slightly. "I'm sorry, Mrs. Sabrina... I don't know you."

She nodded, her lips pinched to the side. "Of course not."

Sabrina and Sage began to make conversation as the sun beat down on Jamie and me. My palms and neck grew sweaty, but it wasn't because of the heat...it was because I did recognize her. I recognized her instantly and didn't know what would happen because this was feeling all too familiar, too terrifying, and much like a reoccurring nightmare I was trying to escape but knew there was no way out.

"Have you seen Daniel since check in?" Sage asked Sabrina.

"No. Have you seen Declan? I mean, in the contract it was made quite clear that we had to follow the rules to not be charged that ridiculous resort fee, but it also made it seem like there were far worse repercussions if we bent the rules." Sabrina shrugged her shoulders.

"I know. It was the NDA that was included that really made me think we'd have to play nice here. Besides, it's great not having the husbands hovering around. I think this is the most freedom I've received since well...forever." Sage finished her smoothie and nodded at me to take the empty glass.

"I mean, even prior to marriage, you and I both were enrolled in..." Sabrina glanced back at us and sighed.

"Anyway, I'm loving this. It's all such a nice break," Sage quickly interjected.

Sabrina laid back into her chair. "It truly is."

"Girls, you may be dismissed. I'd like some one-on-one time with my old friend." Sage waved Jamie and me away.

"Let's go, Demi. We must head over to our assessment, anyway. Have a wonderful day, ladies. Please page us if you need anything," Jamie said as I paused an extra moment, taking Sarah in.

Jamie let out a small cough, breaking me out of my trance, and we spun around on our white padded shoes and made our way out.

"We need to go down for our assessments." Jamie looked at me. Her eyes were a shade of pale green and her blonde hair was matted to her scalp, trailing into a tight, neatly plaited braid.

"Assessments?" I lifted a brow and followed her.

Jamie didn't answer. I followed her through the narrow white hallways that were set up like a maze. Looking down at my feet, I hated the same white padded shoes we were forced to wear at my previous residence. There was no noise, but it didn't make sense. Why would everything need to be all white, sterile, and clean on these parts of the resort? Down below is where they were caging the girls.

I picked up my pace to catch up to her. "Hey, Jamie, do you know a girl named Layla?"

Jamie started to walk faster, and her skin flushed when I grabbed her arm. "Jamie, please."

"Demi, your sister died here. What you saw wasn't her, I promise." She peeled my fingers from her arm before sighing. "Please, we can't be late. The doctors, especially, get very upset."

"I saw her, Jamie." My voice trembled as I closed my eyes and could clearly see my sister in that room with Bradley.

Jamie grabbed me by the neck and pushed me against the wall. "Do you know what these images are, you stupid girl?"

Gasping, I peeled her hand off me. Turning, I looked at the colored sorority or graduation-like images. Each individual frame held a photo of a young woman. "No." I shook my head.

"Have you ever wondered why these images aren't a group photo or in one of those frames that can hold countless photos?"

Nodding, I brushed my fingers against my neck.

"It's so every single time one of the girls is killed, they get moved to the black-and-white hallway. The goal for us girls here is to stay in this hallway as long as we possibly can. Demi, you may think you're the favorite, but you're not. You are just one of us." Jamie tugged my hand and led me down the hallway.

"Here." I squinted at the photo. It was me. I thought these would be used for an ID badge, not for this.

"Wait…" I took a step back and froze. There were hundreds of missing spots in between frames.

"I just thought they put the photos in some sort of way..."

Jamie began walking away, so I followed her. "If one of us doves cause any kind of trouble, we risk being put in a cage and going through treatment."

"Treatment?" I questioned as the pit in my stomach grew larger.

"Total darkness to deprive our senses before we become a subservient nightingale. That's actually a blessing, considering some of the defiant girls...well, they went straight to the fridge."

I didn't know what any of this meant beyond the cages and darkness I had witnessed first-hand. "The fridge?"

"You don't want to know, Demi. Promise me you'll just stop. You're going to get yourself killed, and one of us will get dragged down with you, too. Alister Ivory is si—"

"Alister Ivory is what?" A voice behind us was low and husky, but it seemed to shake the floor beneath our feet.

Turning slowly, Jamie and I both took a step backward.

"Alister Ivory is what?" There he was in his black

suit, his eyes darkening as he folded his hands behind his back and took a step forward.

"On your knees," Alister boomed as Jamie's body began to shake. She dropped to her knees, and then he cut his eyes to me.

His jaw ticked as I stood there, my body growing cold. "On your knees."

Jamie dropped her head down and stammered, "I'm so sorry, Mr. Ivory. I'm so sorry, sir."

"Demi!" he hissed at me, only raising his voice slightly but making more of an impact as if someone had yelled at me.

I dropped to my knees. We were off in the employee-only side of the resort, unfortunately. Had we been on the side closer to our guests, there is no way he'd have risked anyone seeing this.

"Now, my precious little obedient dove, tell me what you were going to say…" Alister lifted his hand, revealing a small shiny knife with a carved handle.

"Sir, I was…" Jamie was sobbing as she choked on her own spit. "Sick. Alister Ivory is sick," she said quietly.

Alister tossed his head back and laughed. My chest was rising and falling rapidly as I looked at Jamie, who kept her head down.

• • •

Alister tipped her head up with the knife and looked at her. "You were always supposed to be a nightingale, you know that?" He smiled. With his other hand, he reached into his pocket and took out a small clear bag. "Demi, my beautiful raven, open this for me."

My fingers shook as I took the bag from him and opened it.

Leaning in, Alister brushed his index finger and thumb together, then whispered, "Close your eyes, little dove." He tucked the knife away and pulled out a small pair of tweezers.

Jamie's bottom lip quivered as tears rolled down her face rapidly. "Please don't do it."

"Mr. Ivory," I interjected. Alister didn't look at me; instead, he began plucking her eyelashes out.

Jamie screeched from the pain. "Demi, darling, please shut her up or I will."

"Jamie, please..." I gasped as he took the eyelashes and put them inside the small bag I was holding. Grabbing her hand in mine, she squeezed it so hard, the immediate ache in my bones hurt.

The jar. The jar in his room. I had seen it full of eyelashes.

"Mr. Ivory, I'm begging you. Please stop. You can

take mine," I rambled as Jamie's face grew pale and her sobs became unbearable.

Alister stopped after he took the eyelashes from one of her eyes completely.

He moved over to be in front of me and looked at me with a satisfied grin. Brushing his finger against my lashes, he smiled. "Why would I ever make you less beautiful, my raven? Besides, I already took some of them. Now, if I ever hear any one of you speak my name or disrespect me again, you will be dissolved."

"Get to your assessments now. Demi, I want your IUD taken out." Alister opened his palms to me. Placing my hands in his, I stood on shaky legs. Jamie was still on the floor, sobbing in pain.

No. I didn't want to know what was coming for me. I didn't want to know what the next event would be.

I just knew I wasn't powerful enough. I never was, and I never would be.

I couldn't save myself, let alone hundreds of women.

I needed to escape.

I had to save myself.

CHAPTER
TWENTY-THREE

"TODAY WE ARE BEGINNING our assessments for the doves first, then the nightingales, and then lastly, the breeders. Since all three groups of employees have gone through very different training, we want everything to be kept separate." Bradley paced the stage wearing a white tuxedo.

"If you've been here for some time, then you know that you'll go to your physical check-up with Dr. Davenport, the dear friend of Dr. Noah Wimberly, who was a highly respected surgeon in our community. Then you'll spend an hour of reflection in your original training quarters, where you'll have a dietary evaluation, be weighed, and then cleansed with our peony tea. If you're a new employee, you'll need to take an updated photo," he said.

I looked at the girls around me, some I recognized,

THE CAGED GIRL 173

while others I had never seen before. I noticed some girls were missing from the crowd, and I turned to the girl next to me. "Hey, have you seen Jamie?"

She didn't turn, ignoring my whisper. I turned to the other girl beside me. We were sitting in clear, acrylic chairs in an all-white room with too much bright light that had my head hurting.

"Have you seen Jamie? She's worked here for quite some time."

The girl smiled at me. "Sure, what does she look like?"

"Blonde hair, light green eyes." I paused as I glanced around the room filled with women in matching white uniforms, with matching green eyes and perfectly done platinum blonde hair.

She smiled at me. "That's going to be hard to narrow down. There are so many people in here, and I'm sure your friend is somewhere."

I looked up at Bradley, whose eyes were fixed onto me, and murmured, "Yeah...maybe."

Alister had asked me to go ahead to the assessments while he had a word with Jamie. I knew there was nothing I could do to change his mind. I heard her crying and sobbing as soon as I walked away, and I knew he was plucking the eyelashes from her other eye.

But I didn't think he'd do anything else. All she did

was make a silly comment about him and use his first name.

The girls began to stand in perfect lines, and then were directed to separate sections.

I lagged and waited until I could turn and walk up the stage to Bradley. "Demi...did he touch you?" He didn't make eye contact with me and pretended to be reading the stack of papers from the oddly dirty podium. "I want to hold you, but I know...I know they may be watching." His voice was filled with heartbreak as his eyes flicked around the now empty ballroom. "You have to tell me... Did he hurt you? Did he—"

"No. He never does anything. He just...wants me there." I placed my hand on Bradley's, knowing the risk. "Bradley, tell me I'm not crazy. Tell me that what I saw between you and my sister... She's alive, and you...you and her were..." My heart hurt just saying the words.

Bradley took a deep breath and moved his hand away from me. "Demi, this place makes you lose your mind. It makes you see things that aren't there; it makes you hear words that aren't spoken, and most of all, it makes you question things that can have you killed. If your sister was alive, I'd have risked my life to let you know that. Please, Demi, go to your assessment."

I turned away and was about to leave the stage when he grabbed my wrist from behind. "Demi…one day, you and I will escape once and for all. I promise, no more Ivory's. Just us. You'll wear a beautiful white lace dress and your big white hat, and I'll have your Nike Jordans waiting for you so we can run."

Tears built in my eyes. The Nikes were the shoes Bradley snuck to me at the Ivory estate. I had told him when I was a little girl, I'd draw a check mark symbol on a cheap pair because I'd always wanted them after seeing a picture of a celebrity wearing them in a magazine.

"One day." I moved his hand off me and walked away.

"Miss Demi, so good of you to actually join us." Taylor smiled at me and pointed toward a hallway. "To the left. You'll be up next for your physical with Dr. Davenport." She checked my name off her tablet.

"Demi Ivory," a deep voice called out from behind a white screen. I could see his shadow as he stood.

The girl behind me widened her eyes when she heard my last name—a last name I hadn't accepted as my own.

Walking around, I paused. He was a handsome man with light hair that I could tell had been dyed. He wore green contacts, and even his face looked like it had some makeup on it to lighten his tone.

"Mrs. Ivory, I'm Dr. Davenport. Mr. Ivory has asked me to remove your IUD that was inserted upon your arrival, as per La Gabbia's employee protocol."

"I'm not his wife," I said as he handed me a white hospital gown.

"I am aware of that; however, we do ask you put this on before we commence your check-up and remove it."

"I don't want it removed," I said, taking the gown and unzipping my dress in front of him. He averted his eyes and spun around.

"You're about to be elbow deep in my vagina; I'm pretty sure I'm not going to act coy and hide my panties and dress from you."

He cleared his throat but remained turned around as I piled my clothing onto the exam table.

There were no emotions or modesty left in my body —it was stripped away from me the moment I entered the Ivory estate in Charlotte.

I slid onto the table. "I'm ready, but I do not want the IUD removed."

"Mrs. Ivory, I do what I'm told by Mr. Ivory, as he is the one who signs my checks." Dr. Davenport flashed an arrogant smile. "Now, if you do not oblige, we can do this the hard way, which involves an injection and being tied down." He pulled the latex gloves over his hand and let it snap against his wrist mid-air.

Closing my eyes, the angry tears brewed but I fought them back. I flinched as he took my IUD out.

"Very good, Mrs. Ivory. I just need to do a quick exam, and then you will be on your way to the next station. Nurse?" he shouted out, and a moment later, a woman in an old-fashioned nurse's outfit came in.

"The vaccine please." He nodded as I looked between both.

"What vaccine?" I sat up and saw her holding the injection needle.

"Gardasil, dear." The nurse smiled at me before patting my arm and whispering, "Just lay back and make a fist for me."

"What is Gardasil?"

"Prevents HPV, Mrs. Ivory. It's in your best interest to have it." Dr. Davenport smiled as I hesitated for a moment before letting the nurse inject me.

I knew I couldn't fight whatever Alister had ordered,

not with how Jamie went missing after simply saying his first name out loud.

"Ouch," I muttered as she jabbed me with the needle.

"There you go, dear. I'll leave you and Dr. Davenport to it." She winked at the doctor before leaving.

"While the medicine is kicking in, I'll do a breast exam, Demi."

"Kicking in?" I tried to sit up, but my arms felt weak. "Wait, it's a vaccine… Why would…" I trailed as my eyes grew hazy.

He ran his hands all over my breasts as I mumbled words that didn't make any sense.

"Wow you were impacted a lot faster than some of the other pretty little doves, weren't you?" He grinned before removing his gloves.

Trailing his cold, bare fingers down my abdomen, he pushed my legs apart before slamming four of his fingers inside of me.

"Ah!" I cried out, trying to move my limbs, but they wouldn't. "No." It was all I could muster out.

He began rubbing my clit, and then as I blinked over and over again, fighting the tears and haziness, I watched him lick his fingers. "Mmm…delicious."

My heart shattered, remembering those very words

were said to me by Dr. Ian Ivory late at night in my bedroom back at the Ivory estate.

"Who…are…you?" I cried as he continued to assault me.

He rolled back on his stool. "Dr. Davenport. You may not remember me, darling Demi, but do I remember you. I purchased a product from your former boss… my beautiful wife. But then she became defected, so I brought her here, hoping Alister Ivory could repair what his brother had wronged me with.

"Apparently, my beautiful wife, Daisy, is back to training and learning how to please. I thought I wanted an obedient virgin wife, but now I'm realizing I may need a bit more of a whore."

He stood and continued to lick his fingers. "Alister assured me that if they couldn't fix her, I'd be able to have a replacement with anyone I want." Crossing his arms, he smiled at me. "The Ivory lifelong guarantee carries between families, too. Aren't they just the best, Mrs. Ivory?" Winking at me, he turned and left. Dr. Davenport's wicked laughter echoed as I laid on the cold steel exam table, half-dead.

. . .

"Now it's time to perform our surgical procedure. It's lovingly referred to as the husband's stitch, in which we add an extra stitch post childbirth to tighten the vagina. Especially with your upcoming nuptials, we need to make sure you're perfectly tight." Dr Davenport snickered.

I wanted to scream for help, but whatever they injected me with was causing my entire body to grow weaker by the minute.

"I haven't…had a child."

"Oh, I know, sweetheart. But you're a dirty whore who has had sex before, and we need to make you a virgin again."

I wanted to die.

Perhaps, I was already dead, and this was my afterlife.

CHAPTER
TWENTY-FOUR

"DEMI, you need a shower and have Kandi do your makeup and hair. You look terrible," Marcie said as she brushed her long blonde hair and I laid in my bed.

"Marcie, do you know where Jamie is?" I was staring at the ceiling, trying to not replay what Dr. Davenport had done to me a mere few hours ago. I was in agonizing pain, even though they injected me with a cocktail of pain medications and slathered numbing cream all over my vagina.

"I don't know. I think she left the resort and went back home."

"Yeah, because that's a likely explanation." I rolled my eyes, knowing Marcie was just lying to me so I would let it go. "Marcie, can I ask you how you really ended up here?"

• • •

Marcie stopped brushing her hair and put the gold vintage hair brushes down neatly on her vanity.

"I found myself like most of the girls here, Demi. No one loved me, no one cared where I was, and now here, someone must know where I always am. I have a home. I have a job and a place that is my own."

"I miss my sister." I wiped the tear rolling down my face. "All this time I thought I had killed her, but she was here. How... Did you know her?" I pushed myself upward in bed and looked at Marcie. She was sitting in nothing but a white lace bra and matching lace shorts.

Marcie spun around in her chair. "Isn't she the reason you were led to the Ivory estate in Charlotte? Didn't she betray you?" Standing, she pulled a white dress over her body. "Demi, stop being pathetic and just live your life."

"You need to go back to Mrs. Rothschild today; she's been asking too many questions about her husband. She gets to go to the store today, and that will help distract her from the massive mishap we've had with her dumbass husband. The store and Life Center are on the tenth floor. Make sure to use your badge and have Mrs. Rothschild bring her documents."

I nodded but was barely listening to the rest of what Marcie was talking about. "What happened to him? What happened to her husband?" I brushed my hand across my neck, remembering our interaction.

"Didn't he almost choke you to death and try to rape you?" Marcie flicked her eyes over at me.

Nodding, I slid out of bed and sat at my own small vanity. I did look like a wreck.

"Do you think Alister Ivory liked that?" she asked me.

I shrugged. "He made him have sex with a dead woman."

"He has still yet to pay the price of touching what is Alister's."

"What is his?"

Marcie flicked her hair over her shoulder. "You."

My breathing hitched. I knew he took a special interest in me.

"Demi, Mr. Ivory wants you to meet him in the peony garden tonight at eight."

Chills ran up my arms as I looked at her. "There's a peony garden?"

Marcie nodded. "Of course. Where else would the good ones get to rest?"

"Marcie..." But before I could even ask what she meant, she left the room.

What did Alister want from me? I brushed my hair into a tight ponytail and quickly wiped the smudged eye makeup off completely. I wanted to kill Dr. Davenport, and I would, but I knew I couldn't do anything I wanted to without someone else. Someone far more powerful.

I needed to go tend to Mrs. Rothschild and find Bradley. I wasn't crazy; I know I saw my sister. I needed to find her, and I needed to find Jamie, now. I had to figure out where these girls were disappearing to.

Exhaling, I looked into the mirror. "You cannot be good anymore, Demi. Good has only hurt you." Swiping the nude lipstick across my lips, I smacked them together and smiled, even though I cried with every step I took. I had to ignore the burning pain between my legs.

Why be a victim when you can just get ahead and be the villain?

———

"Demi, today I get to visit the store and then, I get to see Declan. I'm getting quite homesick now and triggered here, if I'm honest."

Sage Rothschild was wearing a fitted white jumpsuit, small pearls, and clutched her designer bag to her chest. She was looking around with paranoia seeping out of her.

"Okay, that's fine. We can go to the store, and then

I'll ask the front desk about Declan and when you both are reuniting," I reassured her. I had no idea what the "store" was, considering I'd never been, and Mrs. Rothschild was my very first actual guest I'd been trusted and paired with.

"Thanks, Demi." She patted an embroidered hand-kerchief against her forehead.

We walked side-by-side until we made our way to one of the narrow hallways that led to the elevators.

While Sage kept her eyes forward, I was looking at all the colored images of women plastered on the walls.

"Oh my god," I breathed out. Pausing in front of a missing spot, I glanced around. The photos were hung in alphabetical order.

"Jamie…" The photo was missing completely. "No…no." Guilt hit me as it was my fault for pushing her to talk about Alister and the sick things happening behind the façade of a beautiful resort.

"Mrs. Rothschild, will you give me a moment? I'm so sorry."

She looked at me and then back to the images. "What is it?" She placed her hand over her heart and followed me as I sped up and walked to the other hall-way. The hallway that held black-and-white images of girls.

Racing to the letter 'J', I slapped my hands across my mouth. "Jamie," I whimpered when I saw her black-and-white image framed next to others.

It was my fault. She was so scared and followed the rules. I just had to push her to speak up and talk to me.

Sage dug her nails into my arm and tugged. "Demi, I really would like to go to the store."

I looked at her and noticed she was wearing light green contacts, which sat slightly off her pupil. They weren't her natural eyes.

"Sage…" I began, but quickly stopped myself. I'd done enough damage.

Swiping my badge against the white elevator doors, they opened silently. She stepped in first and then I entered.

Pressing floor number ten, I closed my eyes. "I'm sorry," I whispered.

"About?" Sage asked with agitation.

"Nothing. Sorry."

The doors opened, and we walked out into a strikingly bright and beautiful space. It was completely white with minimalistic furniture.

A woman with a neat blonde bun, green eyes, and nude lips greeted us. "Demi and Mrs. Rothschild, so nice of you to visit our stores. It's shopping day!" She clapped her hands excitedly.

. . .

"Here's a catalogue for you, and Demi, if you'd like one as well, to help provide your expert insight on Mrs. Rothschild's purchase."

I took the catalogue and walked over to the small bistro-style seating with Sage. There were sparkling pink drinks waiting on the table and peonies neatly displayed in a vase.

Sage was happily looking through the catalogue and circling items. I couldn't see what was in it since she had it propped upward. Sitting down slowly, I winced in pain.

"Are you alright?" Mrs. Rothschild asked with genuine concern.

Pursing my lips, I gritted my teeth together. "Yes." But I wasn't. I slammed my knees together and wanted to cry from the brutal pain from the stitches Dr. Davenport put inside me.

"Definitely light only. I don't want brown." She smacked her lips together.

I brushed my hand against the white cover with small gold letters. "Bambino in Gabbia," I whispered.

Opening the first page, I skimmed the words.

It's an honor at La Gabbia to provide couples

control and opportunities to grow their families. Alister Ivory, founder and owner of La Gabbia, knew that an all-inclusive resort meant just that. All-inclusive to provide both husband and wife with the worldly things that fulfill our hearts and feed our souls. Desire and pleasure fuel men to be better husbands and fathers; rest and rejuvenation fuel women to be the best wives and mothers. Mr. Ivory grew up in an unsettling environment and knew the value a healthy set of parents could provide a child. Therefore, we welcome you to the Life Center and hope you find the prized possession you're looking for. If you've put a deposit down on a specific model, please let guest services know.

What is this? Baby furniture? I thought to myself.

"No, I just told Declan we should have put a deposit down on that light-skinned one I loved. These aren't the right ones. I mean, a made-to-order brown one wouldn't be so bad. I suppose the genetic component is even better than some of these light ones. Especially since the mother is in-house, and we know more." Sage tapped her nails against the marble table.

"I don't understand." Flipping the page, I sank back into my chair. "Oh no."

The items listed in the catalogue were babies.

CHAPTER
TWENTY-FIVE

"WHAT DO YOU THINK, DEMI?" I was flipping through, page after page. The ages of the child were next to them. Two weeks old, four months old, six months old, and then I flipped towards the end...

"Discounted items." I gasped and saw babies around a year old with a red number next to it.

Customizable options were available, but a special request must be placed two years in advance.

"Demi?"

My head was spinning as I looked through each page, and finally, there it was. A page that made the stomach acid crawl up my throat.

"Breeders," I mumbled and looked at images of women. They were the nightingales and doves, all divided up. Their stats were displayed next to their photos: weight, height, eye color, skin color, genetic, and medical history.

"Honestly, I might just tell Declan I want to place a special order with the mother known as Raven. She's got the best medical history, and I think with a white male's sperm and her beauty, we might just have ourselves a brilliant, beautiful little one. Hopefully, the skin will be lighter, but that's a risk we might just have to take."

"That's my sister." I saw the image of Raven on the page that Sage was fawning over. "That's Layla."

Sage's forehead crinkled as she looked at the image, and then back to me. "Oh, my goodness, what wonderful news. I knew she looked familiar... Apparently, she's able to be bred the fastest."

Closing my eyes, I could see it all over again—Bradley in bed with Layla. Is this why? Were they...

"I think you...we...should request a special visit with her to make sure she's the woman you'd want to carry your child, Sage," I said as my heart pounded rapidly.

. . .

Sage paused for a moment and then looked back at me. "This is why I wanted you to come with me; I just knew it'd be useful to have some extra help. But I do like the sound of that. Besides, for two million dollars, we should have a bit more say." Sage snapped her fingers in the air until the girl from the front desk came over.

They chatted as I stared down at the image of my sister. It was like looking at a reflection of myself. She hadn't changed much, beyond her once beautiful brown eyes growing more and more lifeless.

"I think it's really nice that you and your sister have taken to working at the same establishment."

My eyes filled with tears as I looked through the photos. Where were these babies coming from.

"Demi?"

"Yes, thank you." I nodded quickly.

"I'm going to go put the deposit down for a custom baby. I'll be right back, then I want to go shop for the gorgeous hair extensions here. They only do it with real human hair." Sage stood and walked back to the front desk.

I went back to the beginning of the white leather-bound book. There was an entire page designated to eye colors, hair color, and skin tone. How would they even guarantee all of this, and who even agreed to have these babies?

The nightingales weren't pregnant; they were down there, caged up to be used as sex dolls.

"Guess what? We get to meet her now." Sage was jumping up and down excitedly.

I stood quickly. "Wait, now?" I brushed my hands nervously against my dress as I followed Sage and the girl from the front desk.

"Yes, yes! She's in her fertile window," Sage shrieked, but was quickly silenced by the lady in a white turtleneck and pencil skirt.

"Ma'am, please, we must keep our voices down. You, of all people, should know why."

Sage's face flushed as she straightened her shoulders and clasped her fingers together. "Yes. Of course. My mistake."

"We will need to change clothes to visit the breeder's floor. There's also a contract to be signed, and you may not speak to her, simply type what you'd like for her to read. She's not permitted to have communications. Words and language can often cause us to have too many...thoughts."

"Of course. I know." Sage closed her eyes for a moment, as if she was replaying something in her head.

"Shall we, Demi?"

"Yes." I followed behind them into a small dressing room.

She opened a closet and there was a row of black dresses—all identical sheath dresses with small labels with sizes.

"These would have looked amazing with my Chanel pearls." Sage grabbed a size two, and turned away to a dressing room to change.

"Demi?" I looked at the pale woman in front of me with piercing green eyes.

"What is all this?"

She tilted her head and brushed her index finger against my cheek. Leaning in, I could feel her cold, minty breath on my skin. "Hell." Pulling away, she smiled before handing me a dress. "Let's all get ready quickly. Raven only has a few minutes before she needs to be fertilized."

I wanted to just die.

"She's not a plant. She's a human being." I looked at the woman's name tag. "Kori, how could you...go along with all this?"

"Along with what?"

"She's being raped, isn't she?"

"Please do not talk about our precious breeders that way. You know, Demi, I'm not sure you should be joining us, anyway. I've been told you have a meeting with Alister Ivory tonight."

"No, Mrs. Rothschild has specifically asked me to go with her. Please, don't do this, Kori."

She smiled at me with her eyes lowered. "One chance. Open your mouth, and you will have the same thing happen to your tongue that happened to Jamie's."

"You know what happened to Jamie? Please, please tell me!" I slammed my lips shut as Kori's eyes widened.

"Demi, let's go quickly change. Kandi just left us a whole new stash of wigs and hair extensions, too! They got a fresh batch of hair in to make them." Kori shot me a look before pointing at the other side of the closet.

Each wig had a small name tag, and I knew exactly what that meant. Walking toward the wigs, I selected one. "Karina," I whispered. I had met her in my brief stint on the Euphoria floor.

Shaking my head, I pushed past Sage and Kori.

"These are gorgeous! I always wondered what I'd look like as black-head. No, wait, that doesn't sound right? Brunette? No, this is dark black hair... Hmm... it's fine."

I quickly changed out of my all white ensemble and tugged the tight-fitted black body-con on myself.

"You have to wear your hair down. Just quickly

grab a wig, too. There's too much gel in your hair." Kori shook her head at me and aggressively handed me one before rushing away.

Placing the wig on my head, I brushed it with my fingers, but there was a tangle. Looking at the long, black hair, I squinted.

I tugged the object out. It was…flesh?

"Kori?" I called out.

She came in immediately, already fully dressed. "What is it now?" she snapped at me.

"What is this?" I lifted it to her.

"Oh, silly goose, it's just a piece of what's her name? I think you are wearing the Karina. Karina's scalp." She opened her mouth and started to chew it.

"Kori…" I gagged.

"Yes, it's definitely fresher than some." She licked her lips and winked at me before turning back to the hallway. "Let's go, ladies," Kori chirped.

I followed them to the elevator. "Demi, you'll have to use your badge, too."

We all scanned it before Sage lifted her wristband

and scanned it, too. It looked like a normal wristband one would get at any all-inclusive resort.

The elevator dropped down and suddenly, we were on the floor I knew was where the caged girls were. The girls who, if they were lucky enough, became the nightingales and were freed.

I scoffed at the silliness of it all. Freed? To be abused, raped, and then...ultimately killed?

I began to turn toward the side of the hall where I'd already been. The side that led to the room I had seen Bradley in with my sister. I knew I wasn't crazy.

I just hadn't had a moment to absorb the fact that the guilt I had carried all this time wasn't even based on reality. I didn't kill my sister; I didn't take her life. But she did betray me. She sent me to Charlotte. She was a part of why my life had now become a constant game of cat and mouse.

I was wrecked and ruined.

"No, Demi. This way," Kori whispered.

"It's so dark." Sage covered her eyes and started to panic.

"Sage, deep breaths."

"It's all black... Why is it so dark? Where is the clean white and bright..." She was breathing heavily as we made our way down and finally entered a room.

"Mrs. Rothschild, enough. You must compose your-self. I know, trust me, do I know. This is hell for me to come down here, but you cannot speak out, you cannot be this way." Kori waved her hand over Sage's body.

"Hello, there," a soft voice called out in a hushed whisper.

The room was enormous. We turned and there it was.

A giant bird-like cage that had a swing inside.

And on that swing sat a woman wearing a long, flowing black gown, and her long black hair was draped over her shoulders. The only sound echoing and slicing through the silence was the slight creak in the golden metal as she swung.

"I'm Raven." She looked through the darkness at us. Alister referred to me by the same nickname.

But she didn't look directly at us; she looked behind us.

The small candle flickered and illuminated her, but we were in the dark completely.

"I wasn't expecting the three of you." She smiled slightly.

"Raven, we have a special VIP guest. She's interested in becoming a mother to well...a made-to-order child. She doesn't want any from our shop, but rather one she can be a part of the journey with."

"That's lovely," Raven said. But it wasn't Raven, it was Layla. My Layla. I was frozen in place.

Sage leaned in and whispered, "She looks just like you, and you her, Demi."

Kori glanced between us. "Absolutely no word of relation or this is all off."

"Of course, I'm sorry." Sage immediately walked away from me.

"You are breathtakingly beautiful. Do you stay in this?" Sage brushed her hand against the cold metal.

"This is my home. I'm to be kept safe here." Layla continued to slowly swing as her gown dragged.

She was a vision.

This was so sick and twisted that she was here in an actual cage. How could Bradley allow this? How could…

"I wanted to know if you'd choose Declan and I to receive the next life as ours? We have a mansion in Rhode Island. We have four cars. I was…well, put through etiquette lessons when I was younger and lost. This life would be cared for and loved…"

"This is sick, and so are all of you," I whispered to Kori.

Kori looked at me with anger. "Keep quiet."

"That voice…" Layla said softly. "I know it."

My heart stopped. I took a step forward as tears fell down my face and everything started to blur.

"Lay—"

"It's time for you to lay down." A cold, strong arm tugged me backward.

"Bradley…" Layla said, her face lighting up.

"Hello, my beautiful Raven." I turned to him as he looked at me with agony painted on his face.

Slapping my mouth with my own hands, I cried into them and stumbled back toward the door.

"Well, you're just in luck, Mrs. Rothschild. The male fertilizer is here." Kori clenched her jaw as I hunched over in the corner crying.

Sage drifted away from the cage and toward Bradley.

"This is truly the greatest all-inclusive resort, isn't it? This is where dreams come true." She wiped away a tear from her face.

"I'm Sage Rothschild. It's a pleasure to meet you. You're just as beautiful as she is. We'd like the full medical records of both, if that'd be alright. I know my husband Declan would really like those. He's a perfectionist." She smiled at Bradley and brushed her hand across his face.

"My beloved," Layla called out as Bradley walked to her.

"Mrs. Rothschild, we will have all that and more in the detailed files once Mr. Rothschild and you confirm payment. Mr. Ivory will want to meet with VIP clients

—he's particular about who gets Bradley and Layla's precious baby birds." Kori smiled.

"Of course. Of course. And just look at them! They are so in love. We wanted a loving environment. It's proven, you know..." Sage looked at Bradley and Layla. He brushed her hair away and kissed her neck before he pushed her on the swing.

"Kori, I need to go..." I swallowed the vomit in my mouth. "Please." I clawed at the door, then lifted my badge and scanned it against the keypad.

It opened. I fell into the darkness and ran toward the elevator, gasping for air as I felt someone's hands wrap around my throat.

Falling to the floor of the elevator, I scanned my badge and pressed the floor of my room.

But the elevator kept going upward. It opened on the very top floor, where Alister Ivory's penthouse was.

I clenched my fists as I stormed out and looked down at the black-and-white-checkered foyer. It was new. It used to be all black marble.

"Greetings, Miss Rao." A faint voice startled me. I hadn't been called by my maiden name in years. It was Marisha, the beautiful woman with long, dark hair and golden skin that matched my own.

"Mr. Ivory has requested you bathe and dress for your special dinner tonight with him. I will be assisting you." She reached her hand out to me and smiled.

"The floors..." I stared down at the black and white.

"Yes. Aren't they beautiful? You inspired them. Mr. Ivory is mostly a fan of all black, but he said that the purity you emit made him want to tie in the doves and nightingales with his design." Marisha wiggled her fingers at me. I placed my hand in hers and together, we walked to Alister's stunning all-black bathroom. There was no light beyond a few candlesticks flickering in gold candelabras.

I was numb. I stripped out of the tight dress and watched as Marisha filled the dark tub with water.

Sliding into it, I was surrounded by steam.

Marisha ripped peony flowers and sprinkled them into the tub. "Peonies have so many health benefits, did you know that, Miss Rao?" Marisha placed the remaining peonies into a vase, and then moved the candelabra closer. Sitting on the velvet stool, she poured a milky white substance from a glass bottle into the water.

"What is that?"

Marisha dipped her hand into the water before brushing it against my face.

"Peonies can aid in inflammation reduction, increase fertility, assist with mood disorders..."

Taking a small loofah, she began washing my body, pouring more of the liquid onto it.

"Tonight is going to change everything, Demi. I hope you know how lucky you are." Marisha began scrubbing my hair and massaging my scalp.

"He wants your hair to be worn black again." It had been a very long time since my hair had been worn without an itchy wig or being bleached blonde. The bright, blonde had become my new identity in some sick way. It was comforting, especially after seeing what darkness represented at La Gabbia.

"Okay." I closed my eyes and let her take over. Because tonight was the night... I was going to kill Alister Ivory and end it all.

CHAPTER
TWENTY-SIX

I STOOD in front of the golden arch mirror, staring at myself. My hair was shiny black and long—Marisha had put in extensions and had clipped in black feathers on the sides of my hair. My eyes were lined in thick black eyeliner, with my lips painted a deep red.

"You look gorgeous. I can see why he chose you to be..." She sighed and clasped her hands together.

"Chose me to be, what?" I brushed my hands against the black tulle dress. It reminded me of a ballerina's outfit.

It felt strange wearing anything but the all-white I had been trained to survive in.

"The favorite girl, of course. Tonight is the ceremony."

My heart dropped as I flung around and grabbed

Marisha's arms. "No, what do you mean, Alister chose me to be the favorite girl? What does that mean here?"

Marisha looped her arms into mine. "It's your wedding day, silly." She shuddered as I fell back into the mirror.

"No...I can't marry him. I..." I gasped for air as panic rose inside me.

"I must confess, Demi. I always thought he'd have chosen me. We've worked closely together for so long." Marisha handed me a cup full of pills. "Here."

"How is it feeling?" She looked down at my crotch.

Heat flooded my cheeks as I looked at her. "If I'm getting married in a few minutes, then doesn't that mean tonight is my...wedding night?" I grimaced at the thought of having sex with Alister Ivory, especially considering my body was still in pain.

"Yes." Marisha turned away. "The pills are painkillers. Just take them, and it'll be okay."

"He likes...well, you'll see soon enough." She paused. "I'll need to go get dressed now, too. The ceremony is starting soon."

I looked at myself in the mirror. This was such a peculiar outfit to wear for what was apparently my wedding day.

If I married him, I'd become his wife and have full access to everything. Maybe this is exactly what I needed. Sometimes I regretted how I acted out in a panic and wave of emotion after being forced to marry Conrad. Had I played the part of the obedient wife, then perhaps I would have exposed the Ivory family back in Charlotte. Perhaps I would have saved them... the caged girls. I didn't even take the time to memorize their faces. They were all bald, green eyes, and thin. That was the extent of seeing them.

"It's time, Demi."

I looked at Marisha and brushed my hands against the tulle skirt. "Here." I followed behind her and she handed me a bouquet of red roses, ivory peonies, and one single sunflower. I couldn't help but smile at the flower. It was such a happy, beautiful color.

"It's a tradition Mr. Ivory has always dreamed of starting. A single sunflower. The flower that closes for its fear when darkness pours in." She shrugged as we made our way to the elevator.

Gripping the bouquet between my hands, I closed my eyes and prayed to a god I didn't know existed.

I begged her to give me the strength to save the rest of the girls here and free me of the pain I'd been carrying my entire life. I pleaded with her to help me get back to my sister and find out that she didn't betray me. I prayed to be set free from this gilded cage once and for all.

"What are you praying for?" Marisha whispered.

I opened my eyes and looked at her, feigning a smile. "I prayed that she would bless my marriage to Alister."

Marisha tilted her head and slanted her eyes at me. "She?"

"If there is a god who will help me...well, it must be a woman. No man would answer these prayers." I turned back and waited until the doors opened.

They opened directly into a peony garden.

"Shall we?" Marisha opened her hand to me. I looked at it, but shook my head and took a step forward.

It was breathtakingly beautiful. There was a light echo of music floating through the warm, salty sea air. A piano and perhaps a harp? I looked at all the gorgeous fairy lights that twinkled against the otherwise dark sky.

The scent of peonies was overwhelming but refreshing from the otherwise sterile, often bleach-scented environment of La Gabbia. There must have been some special way they were having peonies bloom in this makeshift garden on a private island.

"Stand here." Marisha pointed. "You'll know when to walk down the aisle when the music shifts. And look, perfect timing! The rest of your bridesmaids are here." Marisha smiled.

I looked behind me, and my lips parted in shock. It was Mrs. Rothschild and a few of the other guests I had seen with the other girls. All of them had their blonde hair neatly pinned back, white ankle-length dresses, and small bouquets of peonies gripped between their palms.

"Why would they be my bridesmaids?" I whispered to Marisha. The women all had green eyes. How do the guests of La Gabbia all look like that?

"We treat our VIP guests extra well, Demi. Well, looks like it's my turn. See you at the altar." She winked at me.

The music shifted into the song Alister once recited lyrics to me from.

"All of Me" by John Legend.

I took a step forward until I curved around the tall palm trees and saw him. Alister Ivory was standing under a stunning canopy of peonies and lights, his skin permanently sun-kissed. His shiny black hair was combed neatly, and his dark eyes widened as he saw me.

There were guests seated and just a few bridesmaids lined on one side, and then one groomsman stood with Alister.

Bradley.

My jaw ticked and my eyes filled with tears as I pictured him kissing my sister. He knew she was alive this entire time; he watched me live every day in agonizing pain and carrying the guilt of her death. He made me fall in love with him, even though he was in love with her.

Was he impregnating her so they could sell their babies? Was this their first time, or had she done this before? Sage and Declan Rothschild would take the baby of my sister and the man I thought I loved.

Bradley's eyes stayed on mine as I walked down the aisle, but I looked away and back at Alister, who was staring at me in awe.

Once I got to the altar, I handed my bouquet to Sage and placed my hands into Alister's without a second thought. My hands shook in his and I kept my eyes lowered as I whispered, "This is quite a surprise." I lifted my gaze to his. "I didn't know we were getting married."

Something was different in Alister. The way his face had softened when he saw me. The way his lips were slightly parted as he watched me carefully.

"Alister?" I said quietly, my heart racing. Jamie was punished for saying his first name and here I was, announcing it in front of others.

Alister blinked and looked at the older man who appeared in religious garb and an all-white cloak. "Father John, welcome."

"Dearly beloved, we are gathered here today to join Mr. Alister Ivory and Demi in holy matrimony. Marriage is a sacred bond between not only two humans, but two souls. Demi, you may repeat the vows after me, and Mr. Ivory, you will do the same after your bride." Father John nodded to me.

"I, Demi, take you, Alister Ivory, to be my husband to have and to hold from this day forward, for better, for worse, for richer...and richer." I paused, and Father John nodded as I repeated what he had said. I knew for sure Alister had edited the original vows.

"In sickness and in health, until death bring us even closer." Marisha nudged me and handed me a black wedding band. My fingers shook as I looked up at Alister. His jaw clenched as he held his hand out for me. Sliding the wedding band on, I realized I wasn't okay. I wasn't as strong as I thought I'd be. This was the second time I was getting married against my will into this sick family. But this time, I knew I had to keep myself composed. The most powerful person aside from an Ivory man had to be an Ivory woman.

"I, Alister Ivory, take you, Demi, to be my wife, to have and to hold from this day forward, for better, for worse, for richer and richer, in sickness and in health, with death never parting us. Even in your after life, you will serve me, worship me, and pleasure me." Alister's words poured out smoothly as he slid a massive, radiant-cut diamond ring onto my finger, followed by a thin band.

I glanced at the guests and squinted. I'd been so nervous on my walk in that I didn't focus on them. I took a step away from Alister, but he quickly gripped me.

"Are they…" I felt faint. There were a few rows of women that alternated between white and black dresses and hair.

But they weren't alive…they were corpses, somehow sitting upright. I recognized one. Jamie.

Gasping, I turned back to Alister. "Alister, you killed her…"

"You may now kiss your bride!" Father John called out as Alister cupped my face and dipped me downward. His lips locked onto mine as my eyes stayed open in shock. Lifting me upright, I looked at Bradley, whose eyes glistened.

"They are dead. What… Why did you kill Jamie?"

"It's to show you, my beloved, that even when you're no longer here earthside, I'll never let you go. And this is what happens if you dare disrespect me." He smiled and lifted our hands into the air as the bridesmaids cheered and clapped. We walked down the black-and-white-checkered aisle.

Alister leaned in and kissed my neck. "You are mine forever, even in death."

CHAPTER
TWENTY-SEVEN

I STOOD in front of the mirror wearing the black lingerie Alister had selected for me. I missed the white. I suddenly missed the Ivory estate. Had my life really become this way that I was missing one hell over another.

"Demi, my beautiful raven, I'm ready for you..." Alister called out. I walked out of the room wearing the four-inch Christian Louboutin stilettos he'd left for me to wear as well.

"I could have worn white..." I mustered up the courage to say as Alister looked up and down my body.

He was shirtless and sliding his pants off.

A small smile curved on his face. "No, my sweet Demi, I prefer you to wear black for me tonight. White is pure and clean and doesn't depict the darkness I know is scorched into your soul from what they put you through. I know you don't want to hear this, but… I think you are quite the favorite girl around here. It doesn't seem like it now, but that's far better than being the caged girl. Now come sit on my lap and let me adore you." He guided me into his bedroom. The fragrance from the fresh flowers scattered everywhere and the candles flickering set a romantic stage if this was a normal newlywed dynamic. But here I was, Mrs. Alister Ivory. I knew I'd hold more power if I succumbed to him. This was my final chance of survival. I'd escape this hell eventually, I just had to be patient.

Pulling the blanket back, I screamed.

There was a dead woman wearing a white lingerie set.

"What is it, my beautiful precious raven?" Alister came racing around toward me and looked at her.

"Alister…" My body shook violently as I stumbled backward and clutched my chest.

"My bride, what is it? What is it?" Alister grabbed me and tugged me back toward the bed.

He began kissing my body and taking the lingerie off. "No, please…" I whimpered as my skin grew cold.

"Lay next to her," he whispered in my ear as he pushed me onto the bed.

I felt nauseous.

"No, Alister, please…don't do this."

He slid his briefs off and exposed himself.

I slowly turned my head and looked at her. She had short blonde hair straggling around her decomposing face.

"Alister," I cried, "I'm begging you…"

"I saw the video footage of Dr. Davenport assaulting you before your procedure."

I was hyperventilating as he adjusted the dead woman next to me.

"This is his beloved wife, Jenna. You see, his first wife, Daisy, who had a familial connection to the Ivory family, was returned by force and he received this lovely girl he called Daisy, too. He loved her so much that he pleaded with us to fix her, and in exchange, he'd work here as a doctor until we found someone else more permanent. When I saw the footage of him assaulting my soon-to-be bride, after he knew who you were to me… Well, I had to make sure he paid." Alister handed me a gold box. "Here, my love."

Sliding away from the corpse next me, I began hyperventilating.

"Open it, my beautiful raven."

Sliding the top off, I cried out before flinging it across the room. Alister laughed as the bloodied fingers flew all over his room.

"I chopped each finger off that touched you, before

cutting his wife with thousands of slits and letting her bleed out in front of him. We let some of the girls drain upside down in a special room. Then, I slit his throat and brought a special bottle of wine for us to share this evening." He nodded toward the glass bottle sitting on the bedside table and two glasses.

"The blood of your enemies will always be auspicious to drink, my love." Alister poured the thick liquid into the goblets before looking at me.

"Please have her removed," I whimpered as I turned my head away. The floral scent of the room no longer lingered—I could smell decomposition.

"Oh no, not yet, my bride. You see, I know you're still sore after your surgery to...well, make you my virgin bride. I want you to see me as a caring, loving husband. But it is very important as a man of higher power to consummate our marriage on our wedding night, one way or another."

Brushing his hand through Jenna's hair, he smiled. "She's not as beautiful as you, but her pussy will have to do."

Towering over her, he wrapped his hands around her neck. "I already had them cut it a bit, but I wanted the privilege of doing this." Twisting her neck in one swift motion, he tore Jenna's entire head off.

Slamming my eyes closed, I covered my ears. I could hear her screams even though they didn't exist. I could hear her pleading for her life and not paying this price for her husband's sins. As usual, that is what women had to do since the beginning of time…pay for the sins of a man.

I heard a loud thud, and then Alister was lifting me toward the body. "No, no…Alister…" I cried.

He tilted my body in a way where my head was resting where hers was just moments ago.

"Open your eyes and make the sounds of pleasure for me. I promise, my virgin bride, you'll feel me deep inside you soon enough."

I kept quiet as he pushed himself inside the dead woman. Clenching my teeth, I swallowed the stomach acid that rose into my mouth.

"Demi," he shouted and slammed his hands around my neck. I gagged as he smiled and thrusted inside her.

"Yes, baby…it feels so good, doesn't it. You feel so good…" He moaned as his hands left my throat and grabbed my breasts.

"Alister…" I sobbed.

"I love when you say my name, my beautiful raven." The scent of death had me in a nightmare haze.

My new husband was having sex with a dead woman's body.

He exhaled in a euphoric trance before pressing his

lips to mine. "You are perfection, my love," he said into my ear as I cried hysterically.

"It's okay, it's okay…Demi." His voice shifted from the sick monster I just saw moments ago to concern.

"How can you be like this, Alister?" I pushed his body away from mine and scrambled off the bed.

"Get dressed, Demi," he boomed as a loud knock echoed on the door. I quickly grabbed my robe and tugged it over my body, then hid in the bathroom. Locking the door behind me, I could hear him snap his fingers and then voices speaking to him. My back slid down the door as I panicked.

"Clean her up, then take her into the bath."

He was going to bathe her? Then what? Have her stuffed and displayed for me?

"It was a fucking disaster, Bradley. She didn't take to the ceremony. I don't know if I should have her tonight and do the blood ceremony. But we must at least do that."

"She's not a virgin. Conrad married her." Bradley's voice cracked as he spoke. He was, after all, the man who took my virginity because I begged him to let me have one choice in my life.

"Don't fucking say his name and my wife's name in the same sentence. I need her to compose herself. Ian was powerful because Daphne was by his side, and I need Demi to do the same. No other woman understands us the way she does. If she wanted to run, she wouldn't have gotten on that boat with you."

"If we don't do the blood ceremony, then the marriage isn't sealed. We didn't…" I heard more footsteps and wondered if others were there to clean up.

"She knows about her."

"Shut your mouth, Bradley! She doesn't know anything. That isn't the woman she thinks it is."

"I need a female front to recruit more nightingales since we are killing them too quickly. Then the breeders…well, you already know we've faced countless miscarriages and issues. The only way to keep inventory up is having a face like Demi's out there."

"Uncle Alister, have you ever thought that there is an end to all this?" Bradley's voice shattered me, and the pause had my heart stopping.

"Do you know what the greatest gift in the world is, Bradley?"

I wiped away the tears streaming down my cheeks.

"Power," Alister filled in. "Without power, you are nothing. This legacy the Ivory men have created is nothing without power. Lucrative businesses, all inter-connected, fuels men to want to be more than average. Average men do not make the world flourish, powerful men do. I have single-handedly given the gift of life and family to couples who should have that. The poverty-stricken classes reproduce rampantly. If wealthy couples don't have legacies, then what will become of this world?"

"Where is she?" Bradley asked.

I assumed Alister pointed to the bathroom because the footsteps grew closer and louder.

"My wife is upset with me, isn't she?" Alister said mockingly as he harmoniously knocked on the door.

Each thud had my stomach flip as I pressed my back against the door harder in hopes he wouldn't open it.

"What do you want, my love?" he crooned.

I cleared my throat. "I want to talk to my sister."

The door unlocked. Slamming my eyes shut and clutching my knees to my chest, I was terrified as he pushed it open.

"Your wish is my command, my queen."

CHAPTER TWENTY-EIGHT

"IF YOU OBEY ME, you can know anything you'd like. You are now a proud co-owner of La Gabbia." Alister and I were now sitting on the balcony overlooking the stunning ocean. The white sand glistened as the sun rose and gave it life.

He dragged me out by my arm, sliding me against the marble flooring into the bed that no longer had the dead woman lying in it. Bradley flinched as agony was clearly painted across my face.

He forced me to drink a cup of tea, and before I knew it, I was unconscious and woken up to breakfast in bed.

"You have the most beautiful eyelashes I've ever seen." He reached over and brushed his fingers against them.

I moved his hand away from my face. "Is that why you collect them? Just because they are beautiful?"

He looked back at the ocean and sipped on his cappuccino. "Papa hated my eyelashes; he said they looked like the lashes of a girl. He and Ian would mock me about them. Papa and Ian were blonde, with light eyes and pale skin. My mother...she was beautiful like you, Demi. Skin that had this golden glow and big dark eyes." He paused and leaned his head back before cracking his neck side-to-side.

"Then one day, he saw me playing with a doll— Mother had purchased it at a market in the islands on a vacation. He took the doll and tore her dress off and waved it in my face. He told me to look at her gorgeous naked body. He told me that women are here to pleasure men and nothing more. He called me some obscene names, and then he leaned forward, reeking of bourbon, and ripped my eyelashes out. When I cried and fought back, he summoned Ian, the brother who should have been protecting me, and had him pin me down as he plucked each eyelash out. Then he had Ian make a wish, and my brother did. He wished that I be exiled from the family." Alister laughed and opened his arms to the ocean-front view. "Now look at me... alive on Earth's most beautiful land, as the world's most powerful man, and my brother… You killed him, my love. You are truly the love of my life."

There it was, the making of a monster. I looked at the man sitting next to me. The one who created an all-inclusive resort, housing women who were being brutally raped and then murdered by powerful men. Women, so delusional with their wealth and prestige, that they thought adopting a baby was nothing more than an exciting shopping trip.

"Then why would you do all this?" I waved my hands around us. "You know how painful toxic masculinity is… Why the cages full of women? What would your mother have said?"

He paused and nodded slowly, as if he were processing it all. But then, like a light switch went off inside him, he looked at me and smiled. "You stupid little bitch, I'm saving the world by creating happier couples and flourishing families." He tossed his head back and laughed hysterically.

Fear ran through my body as I watched the man who was now my husband have no emotion beyond inflicting pain.

"You're not doing any of that. You are a monster. You are wrecking lives." I didn't have even a second to process anything else before his hand covered in the thick gold rings rang across my face, creating a crack echoing from my jawline.

"Ah!" I cried out, immediately dropping my face between my knees. But he didn't stop.

"Please," I choked out as the iron from the blood seeping into my mouth triggered a gag reflex inside me.

"Please…" I begged. His black dress shoe slammed into my face, causing my vision to blur.

"Alister…" The world was spinning as I lifted my hands and tried to protect my face. He had me pinned down and with my legs spread.

I screamed so loudly that my ears rang. The surgical procedure Dr. Davenport had recently performed wasn't healed yet. The stitches were ripping, and my body was on fire.

"Please…" my voice trailed as I grew faint.

He kept going while my breathing hitched and life around me began to dissipate.

Was this finally the end? I had tried to understand this family and take them down. I had tried to finally make my life worthy and meaningful, but perhaps everyone wasn't meant to have that.

Perhaps some of us were meant to simply be irrelevant to the world.

My eyes were closed as everything in my body ached.

"Open your eyes, wife," he boomed. Slapping me, the sting of his rings crashed into the open wounds on my flesh.

I forced myself to look at him. He looked different; he looked like a wild animal.

Taking a knife, he slit his arm and his blood gushed out over my face. Grabbing my arm, he did the same motion before dropping the knife and slamming our exposed arms together.

"We are one, and there is no escape, Demi Ivory. You don't understand. That woman's corpse in our wedding bed is nothing compared to what I will do to you if you die. I will have you preserved, serving me until my final days, and even after I will find you in our next life and make you mine."

"Uncle Alister?" a familiar voice called out. I blinked away the blood in my eyes that no longer had lashes protecting them.

"The blood ceremony is complete, nephew. It's complete." He smiled proudly as I watched Bradley race to me. I thought he'd lift me into his arms and take me to a safe haven, but instead, he wrapped his arms around Alister and patted him on the back.

"Congratulations, uncle."

CHAPTER
TWENTY-NINE

I SLOWLY OPENED my eyes but kept blinking since the darkness still surrounded me.

My body ached as I lifted my head. I wasn't on a bed; I wasn't in my bedroom or Alister's.

"Hello," I rasped as the taste of blood still lingered on my tongue. Brushing my hands against the cold floor, I pushed up. "Ah!" I cried out as my ribs ached.

They had to be broken. Spitting out the thick saliva and blood from my mouth, I hunched over and patted around. There wasn't an ounce of light. Wiping my eyes, I looked around.

Nothing but darkness and silence.

A small sound echoed as I jerked back.

"Hello?" I whispered again.

"Shh…" Her voice had my eyes widen and I fell back into the rough brick wall.

I was in the cage.

"There's been a mistake," I panted as I bumped backward into the corner of the small space.

"Shh…" she whispered again.

"Who are you?" I cried as fear and panic rose inside me. "Please help me!"

"Shh…they'll come for you and hurt us both," the girl whimpered.

Cradling my ribs, I slid back down the brick and held my knees to my face. I was scared. I was terrified. How foolish had I been to test an Ivory man? I made the same mistake again.

"Who are you?" I asked again.

"The caged girl," she replied and my heart shattered. Did this mean I was going to be one of the nightingales? Every caged girl was deprived of their senses through this dark and silent space, so they'd feel grateful upon release and serve the male clients however they desired.

"And now, so are you." She let out a sigh as I sobbed into my knees.

It was freezing cold; I couldn't see anything, and all I knew was another person was in a small cage with me. A cage that I knew resembled one dogs were kept in at shelters.

My head was pounding as I shuddered in a thin, wet gown.

"I'm so thirsty," I said quietly.

"Please stop talking; they'll hurt us," she pleaded.

"Someone help!" I cried again, feeling claustrophobic and suffocated. I began crawling around the small space until I felt her.

She was cold and thin.

"We can get out. When do they bring us food? When do they open the cage?" I asked with panic.

"They won't bring us anything now because we are talking."

I patted my hands against her face. Her cheeks were sunken in, and I could feel a tear trail down her cheek.

I stayed silent, knowing yet again, it was my fault someone else was hurting. Everything I thought I was doing was to free all these girls. No one helped my sister or me when we were children being sold by our parents. No one came looking for us, and now these girls… The unloved, unwanted girls were being abused by power and wealth.

"I'll save you, I promise." I kissed the top of her head as she trembled.

The air reeked of feces and urine, and I forced myself to close my eyes. There was no escaping the darkness.

———

Time didn't exist here. There was no end and no beginning without light. We shared one small bowl of what I assumed was oatmeal. No words were exchanged, I couldn't see the person who came down. We were both given a small cup of water, and the other girl with me refused to speak.

If I spoke, we didn't get food. If I cried, we didn't get water. I learned very quickly to stay silent.

If not for me, but for her. I lifted my finger and pressed it against her mouth before lifting her hand and pressing it against my chest.

I had learned that when she could feel my heart beating, she smiled. I could tell by the way her cheeks lifted and her lips curved upward.

I wanted to speak to her. I craved the comfort of another's voice.

But it would be selfish.

So, I just stayed quiet and stared into the darkness,

knowing we'd eventually get some form of food. I'd let her have more since she was far too thin.

Brushing my fingers through her long hair, I began to braid it. I pressed my finger against her mouth once again to make sure she approved.

She did.

Another smile.

Every night I'd whimper in pain as my rib protruded out. I knew it was broken so I tore off a part of my gown and wrapped it around my chest in hopes it would alleviate the pain. But this wasn't physical pain, this was emotional turmoil.

Part of my mind began playing tricks on me. I'd hear her voice and mine, even though our mouths were closed. I thought I'd see a flicker of light, but realized it was my imagination dancing wildly through an empty abyss.

"You must be his perfect wife. It's the only way you'll survive. Just save yourself. That's why I did what I did. It will be a waste if you don't survive and live. Please, Demilion," she whispered so quietly into my ear that I pinched myself to make sure I was awake and alive.

A door opened. They'd make sure when opening the first door that it closed all the way before sliding the screen in front of the bars.

They didn't want us to see even a sliver of light

because that would give us some form of hope. All this time I had feared bright lights and white, but now I realized this truly was a hell greater than all.

No wonder the nightingales were subservient. They'd rather please these sick men than be thrown back here.

A warm arm grabbed me and dragged me to my feet. "No, wait," I called out as her hand released mine. "Who are you?" What did she mean it's why she did what she did?

"Goodbye, my sister."

My entire world shattered as the cage slammed shut. The second door opened and shut behind us.

Light. A small flicker from the lantern hanging in the narrow hallway made of all black bricks. I slammed my eyes shut before slowly opening them.

Falling to my knees, I realized it'd been so long since I even stood. My body didn't have the strength.

"Demi, please, let's go." Opening my eyes slowly and shielding them from the light, I looked at him.

"Bradley, my sister..." He lifted me and carried me in his arms. His lips were in a tight line as we walked to the elevators. This entire time I was with my sister. I was with Layla.

"Save her, Bradley. Put me back. Kill me. Just let her out. You congratulated him, Bradley," I cried and choked on my own saliva.

Bradley didn't speak as his eyes flicked to the red light in the corner of the elevator.

They were watching us.

"Alister wants you to receive medical care and rest today. Tomorrow is your orientation as the co-president of La Gabbia." He glanced down at me and instantly shut his eyes, as if he were in physical pain looking at me.

I couldn't stop crying. My sister and I had spent time together in a dark closet when we were trafficked in Nashville. And now this...

What did Layla do? What did she mean I had to be the perfect wife to survive?

"The next time, he'll kill you and her."

"Was my sister with Alister?"

Bradley carried me out of the elevator and looked over his shoulder before walking forward and then making a quick halt before turning around.

He was getting us on camera that we were heading to the right place. Scanning his badge against a door, it slid open, and we walked in. I kept my eyes closed. Everything was bright and all white.

Feeling something on my face, I opened my eyes. Bradley had put sunglasses on me.

Laying me down on the bed, he immediately

walked to the wall-to-wall window and drew the curtains closed.

"Demi..." He sighed before lifting me back up and carrying me to the bathroom. Turning on the faucet with one hand, he checked the water and slid me into the oversized tub, then quickly lifted my gown off my body.

"Ah!" I cried out as the warmth burned my skin. The clear water instantly turned shades of brown, red, and black.

Sprinkling in Epsom salt and soap, he dropped to his knees and turned my head toward him.

"I don't understand anything, Bradley. I'm so tired, I'm so scared. You must go back down there and get my sister. You...you love her." I rested my head on the curve of the tub as the water covered my aching body.

"I don't love her, Demi. You know that. It's always been you..." His eyes filled with tears as he took a washcloth and began cleaning my face.

"The cage, the way you were kissing her... You're sleeping with her. Of course, you love her, Bradley. You have to save her. Why is she there? I thought..."

"Alister is making you see what he will do if you don't obey him, Demi. This is how he makes everything work. He finds the weakest link in you. How do you think he gets all these wealthy couples to never leak what he does here? He has videos of their wives and the men. He could incriminate them all."

"Why can't we just call the police? There has to be someone," I whimpered as he scrubbed my arms and body.

"Demi, the most successful people in life know two things: everyone has a price tag, and everyone has something or someone to lose. When you know the answer to those things, then you hold the power to destroy them. Alister Ivory knows that and more. He has the police trembling in their boots if they get on his bad side. He owns this island, so who would come? Some of the guests here are federal agents and police officers."

"So, what am I supposed to do, Bradley? How can I save these girls and my sister?" I sank deeper into the water until it brimmed my chin.

"You know what you're supposed to do. You're supposed to realize Layla sacrificed her life for yours. You're supposed to realize that this is it, Demi...for all of us. There's no saving the nightingales, the doves, the caged girls, the favorite girls; there's no saving me or you. This is our reality. The sooner you accept it and stop acting like some one-woman army, then you will live your life and let all of us live, too. Because if you don't, Demi...he will slaughter her and me and air us to dry out the way he does to the rest of them." Bradley began draining the tub and turned the water back on.

"Some people have to learn to accept that there will be no light in their life and that they simply need to adapt to living in the dark. That's us." Lifting the attachment, he washed me off.

"I don't understand what Layla did for me. She led me to the Ivory estate in Charlotte. She ruined my life..." I removed the sunglasses and blinked repeatedly.

"Do you remember Trent?" Bradley filled the tub with clean water and continued to rinse me off.

My chest tightened at the mention of his name. "Of course, I remember the monster who turned Layla and me into caged girls before we ever met an Ivory." Trent was the man my parents trafficked us to. He kept us in a closet in an apartment in Nashville, where the music from the bar below radiated so loudly, no one could hear us screaming. He'd rape, beat, and attack my sister. He'd withhold food and force Layla to do unspeakable things to save me.

"Trent is an Ivory—was an Ivory. He's Alister's cousin's son."

My lips parted as I felt sick to my stomach.

"Demi, you just don't understand how much this

family is interconnected; they're everywhere. You can run, but you will never be able to hide. Look at what happened to us in the ocean. You tried to kill me, and then we were found by Ivory employees. Every boat, car, plane, train, everything that an Ivory touches is tracked. There is no way out."

"But what does this have to do with Layla?"

"There's two positions that an Ivory cannot fill and must be filled by women the men will marry or reproduce with." He paused as I covered my breasts with my arms. Now that I could think somewhat clearly, I felt embarrassed to be on display in front of the man who took my virginity—and who I'd just seen have sex with my sister.

"What are the two positions?"

"The favorite girl and the caged girl." He brushed his hand through his hair. "The favorite girl marries the son—in your case, it was Conrad. You were supposed to be the perfect wife and take over the family business. The caged girl is sent here to Alister's private island, where they reproduce as back up inventory for wealthy couples. The caged girl is also the girl who sets an example for the nightingales, the doves, and any other woman who steps foot within these walls of what happens if you don't obey." Bradley took a deep breath.

"Trent told Layla that being selected as the main caged girl was basically being dead while living. It's hell, Demi. You don't understand how much Layla's gone through. She was in sensory deprivation, both light and dark. Then she's had…"

"She had what?" I asked while tears streamed down my cheeks.

"Demi, you're healthier and genetically better than her, according to the medical records we have on you both. Trent told Layla that you were going to be sent here, but she refused. So, she set everything up for you to get away. She wanted you to kill her, so she'd never have to be the caged girl, but Trent found her in time. He saved her to send her here and make his money."

"She wants you to be the favorite girl because that means you get to rule beside him. You get to live a life of luxury."

I looked at the soapsuds in the bath. This wasn't survivors' guilt, this was just…living guilt. Guilt that I was alive, and Layla had done all this in order for me to, what? Get the better position in the Ivory family?

I turned and looked at Bradley. "Why us?"

"Conrad, Alister, and Ian saw you both from the binder of girls that have been trafficked. Everyone blurred together. Many became the prisoners or caged girls that you saw, and others are here in the morgue for…other purposes. But you and Layla had something the Ivory's craved. You both spoke to them from the pages. You reminded them of their mother, who was loving but also the most loyal woman in the Ivory family."

I let out a dry laugh. "We are living the American dream, aren't we?" I wiped away the tears from my face. "What do I do now? How can I help my sister the way she helped me?"

"Just be Alister Ivory's favorite girl and an amazing wife, Demi."

"Why should I do that?" I shook my head.

"Because Layla is pregnant."

My eyes met his in shock. Sadness washed over his face. "There's a client…Mrs. Rothschild. That's why she came in to see us. She wants a mixed child with excellent genetic makeup. Nearly perfect."

"But I just saw you together in bed. How is she already pregnant?" I sniffled.

"Demi, we've been together for a while now. We are nothing more than breeders for Alister, but we are also married. The only way Alister will let us both live somewhat peacefully is if you keep him happy." Bradley held my hand in his.

"We've been through a lifetime together, and yet, we never got our chance. I want you to know everything I did was to keep you safe, to keep us safe. When we got here, Alister forced me to marry Layla. He wanted you to see me with her and know there was no chance for us. Alister is obsessed with power, wealth, proving himself worthy, and most of all, well...you." Bradley pressed his lips against my hand.

"I'm begging you to force yourself to fall in love with him, Demi. It's the only way we can all survive."

CHAPTER
THIRTY

I SAT in the sand and looked at the crashing waves. Now I understood why people run away to the ocean. My problems felt much smaller as the powerful ocean danced in front of me.

My sister was still alive, and Bradley was married to her. Layla was being used like a dog, breeding babies for wealthy couples who were coming here to have their darkest desires, fantasies, and wishes come true.

All while Alister Ivory made millions of dollars and was one of the most influential men on earth. He was dominant because, with a snap of his fingers, he could inflict damage on anyone who'd been in his presence.

He dangled the idea of escape in front of their faces, and they ran away from their realities to live out what they thought would be their dreams.

Layla let me have the better path—being the good wife and living in luxury—while her body was beaten, neglected, abused, and babies were ripped from her.

I was too tired. I wasn't mighty, let alone capable of saving anyone. Dragging my fingers through the soft, white sand as my hair picked up in the salty air, I knew this was it. I wanted to live. I didn't want to die, and I didn't want my sister or Bradley to die. I knew I had to accept Alister Ivory as my husband. Looking over my shoulder at the stunning black and white resort, I smiled.

This was all mine. Perhaps I was having some kind of psychotic breakdown or maybe a different Demi was coming out to protect me. I just knew I had to do whatever it took to survive and keep the ones I loved alive.

Our fate had been sealed, and sometimes, no matter how hard you try, destiny will overtake any ounce of effort put into trying to alter it.

The only way to keep my sister alive in better living conditions was if I obeyed Alister Ivory. He made it clear that if I ever defied him, he'd put us both in a cage.

What good was coming for any of us by fighting him? He almost killed me. I could become someone else…a woman I never wanted to be. *I could be the evil yet obedient wife he wanted me to be.*

"Demi." His voice wove into the breeze.

He sat next to me in the sand. Turning my head, I looked at Alister Ivory. My husband.

"Alister." I forced a small smile.

"Here." He lifted a necklace with an evil eye pendant. Putting it around my neck, he whispered into my ear, "This will protect you from all the evil in the world, my precious little bird."

I looked into his eyes and brushed my hand against the necklace. "Will it protect me from you?" I spoke softly.

Alister stared into my eyes for a brief moment before looking back into the ocean. "Nothing can protect you from me, my raven."

Nodding, I cradled my knees and winced as my ribs ached—a painful reminder that I wasn't invincible. He wrapped his arm around me and tugged me into him. "I love you, Demi."

I bit back the laugh that tickled my mouth.

"Why do you love me?" I drew a little design into the sand.

"My family didn't love me, either. My father's prodigal son was Ian. I had to become this, Demi. I needed this. It's given me purpose and value. This is what you need, too."

He paused as I closed my eyes.

Sometimes we have to become evil because we were never given a chance to be good.

"I'm sorry for tearing your eyelashes off." He caressed my eyelids. The sand stung my eyes without them. He tugged out a packet of false lashes and stuck them onto my eyelids carefully. I was frozen in fear and not going to protest as he patted them down.

"You are damaged like me, but you're also just as resilient. These couples come here with money to escape reality, Demi. What is so bad about helping them do just that? I'm giving these babies homes and families who have always wanted them. You and I both know more than anything what it's like to be unloved."

Something inside me shifted. I didn't know what I felt but something changed.

Alister Ivory was right.

We were both misfits.

He never lied to me the way Bradley and Conrad had. He always told me exactly what he was and how he was.

I looked at him. "Where are all these babies coming from?"

"Demi, La Gabbia is a full-service resort. We

provide everything one could dream of. We are gifted with one life...one precious life that is fleeting. Every day we grow closer to death, and since I was small boy, I fantasized about an escape. And that's what I have created. Look at this, Demi." I studied him carefully as he waved his hands around. He was wearing an all-white linen outfit. I hadn't seen him in white before. His preference of black clothing and darkness molded into who he was.

"People are shunned and made to feel embarrassed by their darkest desires, but if they don't expel that rage and lust somewhere, then how will they be adequate fathers, mothers, wives, and husbands?"

I wanted to scream and tell Alister that this wasn't the way. But the passion in his eyes about this empire he had created made it clear that there was no way I would ever get through to him.

"I understand now." I opened my hand to him. And in some sick way, he did make sense.

"I need you to promise me something, Alister." My chest tightened as I was about to make the biggest trade-off.

He laced his fingers with mine. "What is it?"

"You have to let Layla and Bradley go. I'll be every-thing you could ever want in a wife and partner. I'll make this business my entire world. I just need you to let them go."

Alister smiled at me. "Demi, the moment you realize I don't have to negotiate is the moment you will learn to be happy. Bradley and Layla have impeccable genetic makeup. The made-to-order products will be perfection. The price these couples are willing to pay for their custom-made—"

"It's not a product, Alister; it's a *baby*. It's a child. It's my sister's baby." I took a deep breath in.

"Demi!" He put his hand up and silenced me. I flinched back in fear he'd hit me.

"They will not be let go of. You will be the best wife, partner, and eventually, the mother to my children, and in return, I will not peel Layla's nails off. I will not slit her throat and allow her to bleed out. I will not chop Bradley up and blend him into our wellness smoothies. I will not skin her face and sew it onto another nightingale."

I closed my eyes.

"Do we have an understanding?"

I nodded. There was no negotiation.

"Wonderful. Now, if you'll stand up and come with me, I'd like to take you to the live cinema tonight as my date. You are to be introduced to the business and be more involved. As my wife, I'd like you to be by my side. Truthfully, I'll need you to occasionally come with me to check inventory on all fronts. It's becoming a challenge to have no one to lean on the way I know I can lean on you, my Demi."

He stood and brushed the sand from his pants before lowering his hand to lift me up.

Wincing again, I shook my long, white cotton gown off.

Glancing once more at the ocean, I thought about drowning.

"And if you ever think about killing yourself, the torture that Layla and Bradley will endure, along with any child they bring into this world, will shake the earth to its core with their screams."

"I understand." I clutched Alister's hand and together, we made our way back to La Gabbia.

CHAPTER
THIRTY-ONE

"I FEEL like we haven't seen you in forever!" Taylor and Kandi were standing behind me, brushing my hair out. I no longer wore the blonde wig. I wasn't used to my black hair anymore, and part of me missed the blonde. It fit more with the woman I had become versus the girl I was.

"I heard you were in the cages," Kandi whispered as Taylor shot her a look of disdain.

I looked at them through the mirror. "I'm not sure if you both know, but I am Alister Ivory's wife, and I expect that you limit your useless conversations and uphold respect for me." I gritted my teeth as Kandi stared at me in shock.

Taylor cleared her throat. "Of course, Mrs. Ivory." Everything would be different now.

Kandi smiled at me quickly. "Mrs. Ivory, is there any specific hair or makeup style you'd like today?"

I didn't smile; I didn't gossip. I simply nodded. "Leave my hair down in loose waves, and I'd like dark eye makeup but the classic Ivory nude lipstick. And Kandi, your lips have too much of a hint of pink in them. I shouldn't see that again. You need to follow protocol."

Kandi nodded and grabbed a tissue before quickly wiping her lips. "I apologize, ma'am."

Closing my eyes, I let them work on my hair and makeup. For the first time in my life, I felt...*power*.

And my God, didn't it feel nice?

———

I didn't recognize myself as I stood in front of the oversized mirror, brushing my hands against the black beaded gown.

"Mrs. Ivory, it's time." A young woman named Anu, who I remembered meeting earlier, came over and handed me a gold ticket. She was the one who hid me under the cart to see Euphoria for the first time.

I took it from her and slid it into my bag. "Thank you."

She led me down the hall and down to the bottom floor of the resort. "Mr. Ivory is waiting for you."

. . .

"Excellent." I stared forward and waited for the doors to open so I could exit.

Leaving the elevator, I walked toward the ballroom that had "Cinema" blazed in gold above it.

Two men dressed in all white opened the doors with their heads bowed. Waltzing in, my lips parted. It was mostly dark beyond a screen and stage. Every single row was filled with men wearing black suits and clutching popcorn in their hands.

I walked down the red carpet until I saw him. Alister stood immediately, his eyes trailing my entire body before his gaze locked onto mine.

"Perfection," he mouthed before quickly putting his hand out for me.

Taking it, I looked around. All the men had stood.

Were they standing for me?

I took a seat and so did they. "Demi, you are breathtakingly beautiful," Alister whispered in my ear with our hands still laced together. "I think you'll love tonight's film production. It's a mix between an action, romance, and horror film."

My throat felt dry as a man came in a red-and-white-pinstriped outfit and brought popcorn to Alister and me.

Taking it from his hands, I sat back, and the lights went completely dark.

A black-and-white film started to play, but I instantly recognized the location. It was La Gabbia.

My heart began to race as Declan Rothschild filled the screen. Was this what I thought it was?

This was the man who would take Bradley and Layla's baby away. This was the man who would raise their child.

He was having sex with the dead woman that replaced me after he had choked me to nearly dying.

Her body flung around as he aggressively defiled her. His moans of pleasure sent chills up my spine.

I glanced over at Alister, who was smiling. This is what our wedding night had been. What was this obsession with…

The scene changed from Declan to one I stopped breathing for.

It was my sister. Layla was sitting in the life-size cage, swinging while another woman was being raped by a man I didn't recognize.

She was grinning as his hands wrapped around the woman's throat and he assaulted her. As soon as he finished, he let the corpse fall to the ground before he moved to kiss my sister.

"Just in case you thought Layla was unhappy here, my love..." Alister said before pressing my hand against his lips.

I couldn't stop watching. The crunching of popcorn echoed around me as I felt my skin crawl.

Another woman came in. Jamie. But it wasn't really her. Jamie's face had been peeled off and put on another woman, the stitching on the other girl's face grotesque.

Bile rose in my throat as tears stung my eyes.

My sister and the man continued kissing and groping the other girl wearing Jamie's face. She was clearly panicked and pleading for them to stop. I gasped as I watched the flesh loosen around her jawline.

I could see the fear in her eyes and looked around. The men in the audience were smiling with delight. A few seats over from me, I saw one of the men rub his crotch.

"Please help her," I said to Alister under my breath, and he squeezed my hand tightly. Layla tugged out a knife and the man held Jamie down. Layla began cutting into her flesh, but not with long gashes or sudden jabs. She placed intricate cuts on the girls' flesh as she screamed and sobbed. The scene changed again.

I let go of Alister's hand and covered my mouth. Everyone around me was completely unbothered.

The woman was naked and hung upside down from the cage, bleeding out alongside other women who were all wearing another girl's face. The stitches were spaced out so the flesh curled and fell forward.

"Alister," I gasped and looked at him.

"Let me…" His eyes shifted and he looked at me as if he would kill me in that moment. Pools of blood flooded the floor of the cage.

My head felt fuzzy as the film continued, cutting to new scenes.

It was an all-white morgue. But then it went black.

The Caged Girl was written in bright red letters at the end.

CHAPTER
THIRTY-TWO

"WE ARE a society of men who have been hand-selected to keep the legacy of what real men should be like alive," Alister boasted as he stood on stage with one hand snaked around my waist.

Each man in the audience had a glass of champagne.

"Declan Rothschild has always wanted to be a father. Understand, I don't simply grant wishes, especially when it comes to a customizable child—I must be selective. Declan wanted to have a child born to a woman of strength. My precious little nightingales make for the perfect breeders; however, not all have the strength you just saw. Raven is special. She has immaculate genetic makeup, she is obedient, and she is beautiful. She gives and doesn't take as a woman should. Jamie was a dove, who was naughty and disrespectful, so now we must cleanse her body and make her useful elsewhere. We took her face and put it on another woman who was obedient in hopes that Jamie's soul could learn that skill. As you know, La Gabbia doesn't believe in wastefulness. We reduce, we reuse, and we recycle." A sinister grin grew on Alister's face as he looked down at me.

"As you all know, I recently married my own beautiful bird. You see, when I met Demi, I didn't know where to place her. She's obedient like my precious doves, but she's got a very dark side, like my nightingales." He brushed his hand across his mouth.

"I just know she'll do whatever it takes to continue this legacy. Many do not understand our kind—they say we are a dying breed of men. If you've been to the therapist here for your one-on-one session, you know we aren't sick or tainted. We are masculine men who crave full control in all forms."

I didn't understand what Alister was talking about. Society? I licked my lips as the men lifted their glasses in the air.

"To never healing. The only healing that needs to be done is for those who are broken, and we, gentlemen, are not broken. We will create a legacy the same way my father did for my brother and me. We will release our inner rage and become better fathers and husbands. We will know that La Gabbia is our source of solitude, and our families can have the other version of us. We can mask who we are, knowing we have a place where we can be seen."

"Cheers!" Alister lifted his glass and drank. Saving just a bit, he handed it over to me. "Drink it, my love. It's infused with the peonies we grow on fertile soil. It's time we prepare your womb for my seed."

Stomach acid tickled my throat.

Drinking the remainder of the champagne, I looked at the crowd. These men were wealthy celebrities, bankers, doctors, singers, financiers. These men had trust funds and bank accounts larger than anyone could ever imagine.

But these men were all sick.

———

"I need to understand what this society is exactly?" I sat at my new, hand-carved vanity Alister had gifted me as Kandi and Taylor helped me get ready for bed. It was Alister's rule that I always looked presentable and had them help me with every outfit change, including bedtime.

"Mrs. Ivory, we don't know anything about your husband's society. We are here to simply work and serve you both and the rest of our beloved guests." Taylor cleared her throat and continued to brush my hair as Kandi removed my makeup and began doing my skincare.

"I'm sorry for how I spoke to you both earlier." I looked at them through the mirror. Truthfully, they were the ones who'd worked here the longest.

"Nothing to apologize for, ma'am." Kandi rubbed some fancy serum into my skin.

I had to tread lightly. "He was talking about some society, and that's why La Gabbia was created."

Kandi looked at Taylor before sighing. "Mrs. Ivory, La Gabbia was created as a piece of heaven in a world that is otherwise mostly hell."

"Heaven? For whom, exactly?" Taylor coughed out.

I put my hand up and asked them to stop. "I know they are abusing women here. But where are these women coming from, and how come none of the wives are questioning anything? They are here just enjoying the amenities without a care?"

"Some come here in hopes that their husbands will heal and change. That they won't bring home their fantasies. They believe Mr. Ivory will make their husband's fantasies come true here so they can act normally in their real life." Kandi squeezed some cream out of a tube.

I looked at the tube, seeing no label on it. "What is that?"

"Alister— I mean, Mr. Ivory asked for me to start using this skin-tightening cream on your face."

Looking at the tube, I saw it had a small list of ingredients, and written in small gold font, "La Gabbia Skin-Tightening Serum."

Squinting, I looked at the list.

Ivory seminal fluid. Organic peony. Rose water.

"Seminal fluid?" I looked up at Kandi, whose cheeks flushed red.

"It's Mr. Ivory's…"

"His semen? He wants me to put this on my face?" I threw the tube at the vanity. "He's making others use this?"

Kandi nodded and looked down at her feet.

I wanted to tell them we had to put an end to La Gabbia—it was the last known Ivory business. But then I remembered, I couldn't. That vigilante part of me had gotten me nowhere. I looked around at the gold-encrusted, but otherwise, all-black room and remembered how incredible it felt to be up on stage as everyone respected my husband and me.

Did I want to go back to the cage? Did I want to become my sister?

My sister. My heart ached at the evil I saw oozing out of her.

"That's fine. Please apply it." I closed my eyes and let Kandi rub the 'serum' all over my face.

After the ladies helped me prepare for bed, I slid into the tight black lingerie Alister had selected for me.

My body ached in every sense possible, but tonight I knew he'd want us to consummate our marriage.

I knew I had to succumb to him and every desire, no matter what or who he brought to our bed.

This was my life.

I was Mrs. Alister Ivory. It was my entire identity and the only identity I could uphold that would protect me from becoming one of the other girls here. The ones that could be recycled and reused.

Kandi and Taylor left, and I tugged the thin robe open, letting the lingerie be on full display.

"Alister." I brushed my freshly painted black nails down my cleavage.

He turned away from the ocean-front balcony and looked at me.

His jaw clenched as I let the robe slide down my body.

"Demi," he breathed out as the sea air blew the curtains. I stared into his dark eyes as I began unbuttoning his dress shirt.

"You did incredibly well with your speech, and the film was one of the best I'd ever seen." I licked my lips as I peeled his clothing off.

His head tilted as he watched me unzip his pants. "You enjoyed the film? Even though..."

I looked at him as he stepped out of his pants and gripped my arms.

"Even though, what?"

"Your sister..." he asked curiously.

"I don't have a sister. Raven, as you call her—which I do not approve of you calling her that since you call me the same name—is nothing more than an employee. Our employee. Am I right, my husband?" I asked as I leaned in closer with my lips brushing against his.

"What would you prefer I call you? You are my most precious bird, after all..."

"I'm not your bird, Alister. I'm your wife, and as such, you will treat me that way. I have ideas and dreams for us and our future children. Tonight, when you discussed our...legacy, I realized I wanted to make sure that they reap the benefits of all the hard work their father...and now, their mother, has invested. I want them to have an even bigger empire. I am Demi, your wife. I will not be one of your—"

His hands wrapped around my throat, and he tightened them. "Demi," he rasped as he dragged me off my feet.

Gagging, I fought back the fear I felt in my lungs as my breath grew erratic.

Throwing me onto the bed aggressively, he pushed my legs apart and pushed inside me.

"Ah!" I cried out. I never quite healed from the surgery the demented doctor had done to me.

Clenching my eyes together, he continued as my nails dug into his skin.

"Please, st—" I cut myself off as he tugged a knife out and began carving it into the flesh right under my collarbone.

I began bleeding. He leaned in and began licking up the blood seeping out of my skin.

"Your blood will keep me alive longer," he groaned as he dug into my skin even deeper.

"Alister," I cried. The pain was too much, but I forced myself to moan.

"We will rule the world together, my queen." He began choking me until I lost my breath.

CHAPTER
THIRTY-THREE

"AS MY WIFE, you are free to roam the grounds of La Gabbia." I sat in the lace robe and sipped the piping hot cappuccino. The skin around my neck was raw and light bruises were already appearing.

I stared at the ocean in front of us. "Does everyone get an ocean-front balcony?" I asked, realizing that I was choked to near death as I consummated my marriage, and now, I was wondering about the varied views from the balconies of the resort.

Alister looked at me. "Every room has an ocean-front or ocean view; however, some come and request our..." he paused and smiled, "VIP floor." I kept my eyes on the waves. "You should drink some peony tea today."

. . .

"What is that?" I looked over and saw a woman with a small white steaming cup that I had seen before.

"This is Sarah; she will be your right-hand woman from this day forward. She's here to help you navigate anything and everything you need." Sarah was blonde with green eyes; she was wearing a short white dress with nude lipstick. Her icy, emotionless stare sent chills up my spine.

"Here you are, Mrs. Ivory." Sarah handed me the cup of tea as I looked at Alister.

"It aids with fertility." He smiled, and his eyes dropped to my abdomen as I took the tea.

"Are fresh peonies used to make the tea?" I asked calmly.

Alister nodded. "From our own garden here with top-quality soil. Sarah can take you there whenever you'd like. I find it very tranquil, and sometimes you can hear...well, the cries."

"The cries?" I took a sip of the tea, closing my eyes, knowing the soil these peonies grew on came from pain and grew from death.

"Demi, I have business to handle today, so please feel free to enjoy a massage, pampering, and more. If you find yourself lonely, Sarah is here to fill in your day. I don't want you to have to work right now, my love, but soon, I'll need you to come with me to...help restock inventory."

. . .

"Restock inventory?" I questioned as Alister stood and Sarah immediately bowed her head and dropped to her knees.

"It's easier when a beautiful woman is there. They are more trusting." He winked before leaning down and kissing my forehead. "Bye, darling, I'll see you tonight."

He turned away and I stared at Sarah, who remained on her knees. "You can stand up..." I whispered as soon as I saw him leave.

She nodded and slowly stood. "Would you like me to reserve your private session for the spa, Mrs. Ivory?"

I put the tea down and stood. "Actually, I'd like you to go back to your room and stay there. I'm going to lay down and nap a bit. I'll call when I want to do something." I forced a smile and yawn while stretching my arms over my head.

Sarah looked nervous but quickly picked up my teacup. "Mrs. Ivory, I just thought I could create the perfect day for you, and Mr. Ivory was very intent on me staying with you for the entirety of the day." She backed away as I pushed past her and walked to the bedroom. My palms began to sweat when I saw the bed we shared last night and how I went unconscious after Alister choked me. He knew exactly how much pressure could leave me unconscious versus how much would kill me.

"Sarah, I am tired and do not want to be watched while I sleep. As you can imagine, last night was very…busy with my new husband, and I'd prefer to be rejuvenated when he sees me. Do you think he'd appreciate a grumpy wife just because you pushed me to go out?" I peeled my robe off and pulled the blankets back as Sarah quickly raced around and fluffed my pillow.

She began tucking me into the bed and stood back without any emotion. "I understand, ma'am. Please page me when you're awake." She tapped her nails against the small pager before turning away.

Closing my eyes, I pretended to fall asleep and waited for her to leave. I laid there, thinking of everything La Gabbia encompassed and what Alister had said. Was he right in saying that this was essentially a place where people could safely live out their fantasies and then go on to be normal, productive humans? Why was I convincing myself in his favor?

I got out of bed and made my way to the closet. Walking inside, the lights turned on immediately.

I sucked in a breath as I stopped in the middle. Every single outfit was all white. The platform shoes that made no sound were all lined up neatly in one section. Dresses, slacks, blouses, and then as I made my way forward, I stared down at the oversized island in the middle. All-white dog collars, in different styles, were displayed neatly. "Oh no," I breathed out as I lifted one and read the engraved tag.

Demi Ivory. Placing it down, I knew I didn't have much time before the day would end back into a night with Alister. Who knew how much time I had here or alive, given who these people were.

I turned the corner and the lights turned on again. Looking down, I noticed the floor had gone from white marble to black marble. The clothes and everything were identical, except now, they were all black.

I glanced at the oversized mirror and quickly peeled off my clothing before turning back and selecting a white dress. White felt safe to me.

Grabbing white lace gloves, I tugged them over my hands before brushing my hair and pinning it into a neat low bun. Quickly making my way to the elevator, I stumbled back as soon as the doors opened.

"Bradley." I gasped at his bruised eye and swollen lip.

"Mrs. Ivory." He glanced up in the corner of the ceiling. "I was asked by Uncle Alister to come and bring you with me today. He said there is an urgent need for an inventory restock and we need to take care of it today for our buyer."

"I don't understand." I shook my head as he nodded for me to go into the elevator with him.

"You will soon enough." We were silent the quick rest of the way up. I knew there was a high chance the elevator, and everywhere we went, had cameras.

The doors opened, but I didn't recognize the floor we were on considering Alister resided in the pent-house. Opening a second door, I squinted as soon as the bright sunlight hit my eyes.

We were on the roof of La Gabbia. My lips parted as the wind blew my hair and I immediately held my dress down. The one-hundred-eighty-degree views of the clear ocean was surreal. But I couldn't take it all in with the loud echo. Turning, I saw Bradley near a heli-copter. "We have to go, Mrs. Ivory!" he shouted over the blades of the helicopter chopping through the warm air.

"Bradley," I said, but knew he couldn't hear me. "Let's run away."

He held his arm out and helped me get on as I looked at him with confusion. Handing me head-phones, he slid his on before waving me to a small seat.

The pilot was wearing all white and didn't look back at us.

I buckled my seatbelt. "Demi, listen to me, what we are about to do is something you have to promise not to stray from. If we don't successfully do this, then Alister will kill Layla, me, and many of the other girls."

I adjusted my headphones and looked at him pleadingly. "What are we doing, Bradley? Let's—"

"There's no running from this life, Dem." He shook his head sadly. A single tear rolled down my cheek as soon as he said the words I already knew. "I'm sorry," he added as I looked forward so I wouldn't sob.

"Sorry for what?" I rolled my shoulders back and sniffled, feigning confidence.

Bradley put his hand over mine. "I'm sorry that most girls get to live out their dreams and you will only get to live out your nightmares." I closed my eyes as his words pierced through my heart.

"How is she?" I asked as I wiped tears from my face.

"Nauseated, but unbothered for the most part. She's good at dissociating and listening."

"If Layla and I had any emotion about all this, then

we'd never stay alive." Bradley and Layla were literally like dogs being forced to breed babies and give them up. I looked out the window and at the ocean below. If I ran away once off this helicopter, I could start over. I could be someone else.

"He will find you. An Ivory never loses its property." I looked at Bradley and touched the small mouthpiece.

"I'm not property." I clenched my jaw and closed my eyes, letting my head fall against the headrest.

People condone lying. But sometimes the greatest survival skill is to lie just enough where you believe it and the lie becomes your truth. I knew I belonged to the Ivory family, and in order to keep Bradley, Layla, and the rest of the innocent girls alive, I had to stay. I was just another piece in Alister Ivory's game.

CHAPTER
THIRTY-FOUR

"WELCOME TO MIAMI, DEM." Bradley slid his headphones off and then took mine from me. We exited the helicopter carefully. It was scorching hot, and the palm trees towered all around us.

Bradley took my hand, and a door opened on the rooftop we had landed on. A man and a woman appeared.

"Hello, Mrs. Ivory." An older woman with bright white, slicked-back hair eyed me carefully. The man was wearing a neatly pressed white butler-styled suit and pursed his lips at Bradley's hand that was clutching mine. He immediately released it.

"We decided to get the baby birds as requested by Mr. Ivory to prevent you having to go out into the field to find them."

Baby birds? I swallowed as my throat grew dry.

"Come this way." The woman directed us through a door and down a narrow set of metal stairs. We were all wearing the same platform shoes that emitted no noise against the otherwise cool steel.

I gripped the banister tightly as we paused in front of a second door. "Usually, we use Alister's dark therapy, but because he wants you to analyze each bird before selecting them, we've chosen to go with the white therapy route for this batch." The man with piercing green eyes winked at me.

"A word with Mrs. Ivory in private please? We will be right behind you." Bradley nodded the older couple off, and they stopped and turned away to exit the room. The door silently slid shut as I walked to the wall and pressed my back against it.

"Bradley…" I scratched my neck.

"Demi, listen to me. You cannot crack. We have to select the inventory, and they'll be shipped back to Ivory Island. If you do anything that is even slightly alarming, then Ian and Daphne will report you."

"Did you just say Ian and Daphne?" Fear slammed throughout my body as I looked at him with terror.

"Demi, every older couple that works for the Ivory family are now called Ian and Daphne in memory of…"

Cringing, I rubbed my arms. "This is all…insanity," I whispered.

"I need you to choose four birds based on this." He handed me a form, composed of four lists.

The first one read: Male, brunette, prefer blue over other colored eyes. Will accept hazel. No scars, visual birthmarks. No obesity permitted. Please make sure he is extremely good-looking. Check teeth. No health concerns. $550,000 paid in full.

"Bradley, what is this?" My heart was beating violently against my chest as I scanned the rest, including requests for two females.

"Alister Ivory runs an all-inclusive resort for the one-percenters, Demi. Your husband owns the first and only resort that quite literally provides anything and everything their heart desires, which would otherwise take too much time or would be shunned. Fantasies and families...that is what he specializes in." Bradley typed a code on the keypad.

"The sooner we do this, the sooner we can get back home and move on with our lives."

I bit back a laugh. *Home? Life?* We walked through the door, and I immediately shielded my eyes. The light was far too bright and bounced off the stark white walls and floor.

The massive space was cut into small, opaque, cage-like boxes. "I think this one will fit the bill for the small female bird requested by Mr. Ivory." The woman called Daphne pointed and scanned a badge against the door. I brushed my dress and as soon as the door slid open, my eyes widened.

"Oh my..." Bradley pinched me. I winced and immediately composed myself. A little child was sleeping on a small white cot, wearing a white gown. Their head was shaved, leaving a short layer to be able to identify their hair color.

Deep down, I hoped this was some child found on a street and needing a home.

"We were able to find her. She needs a new home. One with love and safety." Daphne said calmly. "She'll need some time in either the dark or light therapy program if they want a more obedient child. She did bite when we first got her..."

"Found her?" I looked at the little girl who was staring at a small bowl of white rice and plain yogurt. The two meal items I asked for when I was found in the ocean, knowing it was the only way they'd believe I would also obey and that I could be brainwashed. I knew as soon as I saw the two people in the ocean with their blonde hair and green eyes that they worked for the Ivory family.

"Well, the baby bird's mother was too busy drinking and left her unattended. Honestly, we saved her. These parents don't understand that children are meant to be protected from monsters." Daphne smiled as I moved forward and looked at the small tag attached to the child's gown.

"She's going to miss her family," I whispered as I read the date of birth, weight, and height. "Isn't her mother looking for her?" I looked at Bradley, who immediately shook his head.

"Of course, she is. But the child will be far happier with the couple Mr. Ivory has chosen. Why not place these children with wealthy families who can provide organic meals and private schools?"

I thought my sister was being forced to give birth to provide babies for a few wealthy resort visitors. Why take these children?

"We will take her. I think she fits what the Matthews were seeking." Bradley walked away to the next, and as soon as the door opened, a shriek echoed.

"Mama!" a little voice screamed. I ran over and pushed Bradley out of the way.

It was a little boy.

He was wearing an oversized white T-shirt and was sobbing while screaming, "Mama!" He tried to run out, but Ian, the older man, took a taser and jammed it into his small frame.

"No!" I shouted and dropped to the floor next to him.

"Great. Now he's damaged," Daphne hissed as she looked at his body that slammed into the hard floor.

"No, we need him and the little girl." Composing myself, I quickly stood, even though I wanted to lift the child into my arms and hold him. "My husband asked me for four new restocks, and I will not leave until we do so." I exhaled slowly before brushing my hands against my dress and shooting Bradley a look. He was stunned.

"Yes, ma'am. We will have them ready and shipped to La Gabbia tonight. The little boy is unfortunately the son of some big-time social media influencer who is posting about him daily. Be wary when altering his eye and hair color once it grows back." Daphne bowed.

That was perfect. I knew exactly what I needed to do. "And don't you dare ever use a taser or anything on them for the remaining hours they are here. I need to resell and not have to mark products down because you couldn't care for our products properly." I straightened my shoulders, and we continued to look at the next two children.

I could save them. I would save them. I just had to figure out a way to kill Alister Ivory.

CHAPTER
THIRTY-FIVE

"YOU DID WELL, Demi. It was a good performance." Bradley spoke into the headset as we flew back to Ivory Island.

"Performance?" I scoffed and looked at my nails. "I'm simply trying to contribute to my husband's lucrative business." I ignored Bradley for the rest of our journey back to the resort. He was unsettled, but truthfully, I didn't know how much of what I said to him was a lie or what I was starting to become.

No one is truly born evil. We absorb bits and pieces of it until eventually, we become it.

After exiting the helicopter, Sarah and Taylor were standing with a tropical drink and a hot towel for me.

"Mrs. Ivory." They both bowed their heads as we made our way back inside. I was mentally exhausted. I wondered when the children would arrive to La

Gabbia. I made my way back to the penthouse and took a few deep breaths.

"My love, you're home." His voice startled me as I flung around with my hand on my heart.

"Daphne and Ian informed me of your selections, and I've notified the buyers. They are thrilled and are sending payment shortly. I raised the prices to a million each, and the Rothschilds will be shelling out almost three million for the custom product. You did so well, my love."

"Of course. I wanted to show you that I could fit into your world, Alister." I brushed my hand against his facial hair and smiled at him.

He leaned in and kissed me. "I have to run to handle a situation but take the rest of the day off. Enjoy yourself at the world's biggest escape." He left me in the living room.

"Alister, why all the black in some places, but white in others?" I called out as I spun around in the all-black living room.

He paused and turned to look at me. "My father and Ian believed white represented cleanliness, structure, and purity. I believe that the dark is truly where we find ourselves the most. The dark is where your mind is forced to become stronger and resilient, Demi. But my doves thrive better and are, in fact, more obedient after completing white therapy. My nightingales are more subservient after completing dark therapy. They don't want to go back to being alone with their minds. It's brilliant combining both. Just like a game of chess wouldn't be possible without black and white."

Nodding, I licked my lips. "Thank you for taking the time to explain, darling," I whispered before turning away and heading to the bedroom.

"Why don't you go see a movie on the Euphoria floor tonight? I hear they've put together an excellent film."

My stomach tumbled. "Okay, I'll do that."

"Please wear black. The nightingales aren't accustomed to anything else, and we like to keep the aesthetic perfectly matched," Alister said calmly. I looked at the man in front of me before he turned away to leave. How was this the same man who had sex with a corpse on our wedding night? The same man who choked me to near-death?

I suppose that was the thing about predators: they have the power to mask and shift into anyone they need to be in order to hunt their next prey.

I made my way to the closet and tugged out a pair of black slacks and a black blouse. Standing in front of the mirror, I looked at myself. I didn't think I could go on much longer. Thoughts of killing myself seemed far more soothing than ambitious thoughts of raging war with someone far more powerful than anyone or anything.

But if I died, Alister would kill Layla, Bradley, and the children. The sounds of the small boy screaming for his mother would haunt me. I closed my eyes and thought about the moment my parents sold Layla and me to traffickers. A white-haired woman tricked us to come with her, and now…

I was that woman.

Brushing my hair, I put in the small diamond earrings from the jewelry box on the island before swiping on the nude lipstick. It was easier to be Mrs. Ivory than it was to fight her.

Alister recommended I go watch the movie at the cinema tonight, and I needed to show my face there before I went exploring.

Grabbing a black fur coat, I slid my arms into it. I wanted to see Layla; I wanted to talk to her and understand what she had been through. I wanted to find any way to free her from the cage she'd been in for years.

It was supposed to be me. I was the favorite girl, but she took my place. Being used to produce babies for others against her will and being forced to stay in the dark for most of her life…

The elevator doors opened, and I entered the cold,

dark space. The black brick walls taunted me and rico-cheted the sensual music that was playing.

"Welcome to Euphoria, Mrs. Ivory," a woman greeted me. "Would you like a drink, ma'am?" She lifted a champagne glass filled with red bubbling liquid.

"No." I lifted my hand that was covered in lace gloves and moved away. "I'm here checking on things for my husband." I waved her off. There was a caged girl on stage, dancing, as rows of men were seated and staring at her. I took a seat in the back and watched.

She wore nothing but a black lace lingerie set while twirling on the pole in the center of the enormous cage.

Her face was desolate from any emotion as she kept her eyes down. It was mostly dark in the space beyond the few lanterns flickering. Glancing over to the side, I watched as the nightingales began lining up with trays and bringing them down the aisles.

Squinting, I saw there was a small bottle of lotion and Kleenex tissue boxes on the trays. I watched as the men took them from the girls and began unzipping their pants.

My heart raced as I watched many of them pull their penises out and stroke them. "Gentlemen, today's lucky winner is Max Teller. Max is an investment banker, hailing from New York City. He will do the honor today. Mr. Teller, thank you so much for your donation to the La Gabbia Life Center." It was Marcie, my former roommate and, at one point, my only friend.

The man she had called walked on stage with a large grin painted across his face. Slowly undressing, he took off his belt and kept it clutched in his hands. The music shifted and then, Mr. Teller lifted his belt and began swinging it aggressively. He slammed it into the girl's tender flesh, and her face drained of blood at the first hit. I gasped as I gripped the handles of my seat.

I clenched my eyes shut until I heard the crackling of the leather belt melting into her skin repeatedly. Her cries pierced through my soul. There were men all around me, masturbating to the violent scene in front of us. Mr. Teller rubbed his penis before dragging the girl by her hair to the ground. "What is this?" I said out loud, though no one was listening.

He shoved her mouth on him and forced her to perform oral sex.

She began gagging with tears racing down her face. Shoving her off him, she fell back, and he whispered something to her. I saw when the fear took over her thin body, and she turned over quickly and, on all fours, crawled away from him. Trembling, she pulled herself up with her bony hands gripping the cold steel.

My heart stopped as I slid forward in my seat.

"Oh, my beautiful raven, you've found yourself the live-action film..." Alister came around and sat beside me with a box of M&M candies.

I kept my eyes on the girl in the cage as she clutched the bars and pressed her body into it as if she could melt away into them. "Alister..." I breathed out.

He wrapped his hand around mine and shoved an M&M candy into my mouth. "The best part is coming. This is our Russian roulette night," he murmured into my ear. Mr. Teller stood behind the girl and lifted a knife.

I bit my tongue as I sat there in a room full of men pleasuring themselves to the pain of an innocent woman.

He began cutting into her skin. Small, swift, and quick slits in her flesh as blood began pouring out of her.

She screamed as she flung around, trying to fight him off. "Alister, please." I was about to stand, but he dug his nails into the back of my hand.

"Remember, Mrs. Ivory, if you show me you can't handle this position, you'll be just another one of those girls to me." A sinister smile grew on his face.

"And if you disobey and intervene, then not only will people die, but I think I may just want you to be the caged girl, so you see just how lucky you are…" He nodded toward the gilded cage as I watched the girl bleed out. Most of the men surrounding us were drinking champagne or eating snacks while watching her fight for her life.

I watched her become lifeless as she bled out and the entire floor was muddled with her blood. Mr. Teller smiled down at her before crouching over her body, spreading her legs and then feeling her pulse.

His smile grew larger as he pushed himself inside her.

"She's still nice and warm," he moaned out, to which the audience cheered. He tossed his head back as he continued defiling her and blood spewed out across the floor.

Alister brushed his face against the side of my neck and smelled my hair. "Demi, I wish you could understand what death feels like. The way a woman feels after she's dead is unmatched. That's why I love you so much…" He turned my face to him.

"When I look into those big, brown eyes, I see that you're dead inside. We've all chipped away at parts of your soul, and now, nothing is left. That's such a beautiful way to be." He pressed his lips against mine and I tasted my own tears I didn't realize were seeping from my eyes.

"Just don't make me really kill you. Not that I wouldn't enjoy fucking your corpse just as much."

THIRTY-SIX

"HOW HAS NEWLYWED LIFE BEEN, Mrs. Ivory?" Taylor and Kandi were back and brushing my hair. I ignored the question.

"I'll just use the wig collection today." I knew those wigs came from the innocent lives that were ripped away from them. The hair extensions and wigs were also made-to-order for the visiting wives, who were thrilled they came from humans.

"You'll be visiting the wives today at the pool for a luncheon, and Mrs. Rothschild wanted to say goodbye to you before they leave." I looked at them through the mirror.

"Is her husband leaving? Declan?" I questioned.

"Yes. Of course, he is," Kandi said.

"Declan and Sage Rothschild paid one million

dollars for their all-inclusive stay here," Taylor added while filling my lips in with a nude shade.

"And for their custom baby…" Kandi shot Taylor a look of disdain.

"They are now paying three million dollars." Taylor continued to gossip as if we were simply a group of friends having coffee.

"Mr. Ivory asked that we remind you to let the ladies know about their retail and souvenir options. The window for purchasing a live child is now closed until their next visit, but they can still buy custom wigs, skincare items exclusively made at La Gabbia, and a few other items."

Kandi fastened a short blonde wig on my head. Brushing the sides down with my fingers, I fluffed the bangs. "I love it," I said without hesitation. I actually did. It felt more like me. Like the girl I had to become at the Ivory estate in Charlotte when all this changed my life.

I left Kandi and Taylor to head to the pool. My white gown was draped over my shoulders as I glided down the hallway with the platform shoes.

Pausing for a moment, I looked at the images. More were missing. I knew that the girls had been moved to the other hall into black-and-white photos. That meant they were slaughtered. Intently looking through the photos of beautiful young women, I froze and dragged my finger against one.

It was the girl from the cage. The girl that… She was smiling proudly in the image.

"Excuse me, Mrs. Ivory." Sarah startled me and took the frame down.

"There was a removal request. Jane has to be moved to the other wall…the wall of the angels." Sarah smiled at me. "She truly served La Gabbia well," she added before prying the image of the young girl from the frame.

My heart didn't ache. I didn't feel sad. I didn't feel…

"I don't feel," I said with my hand against my chest.

Sarah looked at me curiously. "You're a lucky one, then." She smiled before leaving with the photo of Jane.

———

"Welcome to the farewell ladies brunch!" a man wearing an all-white uniform, stark blonde hair, and piercing green eyes said.

All the doves were donning the same short, white dresses, slicked-back buns, and eye makeup that made the green of their eyes stand out in harmony.

It was all so beautiful. Hundreds of fresh white and pale pink peonies decorated the long tables that were set across a clear acrylic floor to cover the pool.

"Mrs. Ivory!" he called out with a large smile on his face. All eyes darted over at me as the ladies stood and clapped.

The doves and man instantly bowed as I made my way to the head of the table.

I clasped my hands together to stop them from shaking. I wasn't prepared for this kind of positive attention nor respect.

"Welcome to La Gabbia's farewell brunch. My husband and I are so very honored you chose to spend your vacation with us. We cannot wait for you all to come back soon. I know many of you had shopping on your mind, and if you were unable to finish it, please notify your assigned dove and she will make sure you are able to place any orders. I know our skincare is the best in the world, along with the custom lipstick." I brushed my fingers across the fresh peonies, knowing the skincare had Alister's semen blended into it. The lipstick was blended with blood and whatever else Alister desired. I shuddered thinking of his wall art composed of lips.

"Alister and I truly appreciate your presence. We know the real world is challenging. It's hard to carve out time for your marriage or yourselves, and that is why La Gabbia exists. La Gabbia is where your dreams and fantasies can come true. It's the sliver of the world where the word 'no' does not exist. Now, please enjoy your meals and then we will finish any last-minute shopping before we say our farewells." I sank into my chair and stared down at the salad in front of me. Lifting the drink, I swirled the blush-pink liquid before taking a sip.

The clamoring and clattering of all the wives chatting happily as they noshed on the delicacies constantly being served after spending however much time their vacation was booked for was fascinating to me. Did they know while they were sunbathing that their husbands were slicing young women up and raping their corpses? Did they know they were playing out their fantasies with bondage and toys before putting their suits back on? Did they know the children they were adding to their families were crying for their mothers?

Did they care? Maybe. Did they feel? Absolutely not. I took a bite of the chocolate cake in front of me before sitting back and sliding on the pair of sunglasses that were in my purse.

The blazing island sun was beating down on my shoulders and the ocean in front of us looked stunning.

It was truly stunning. I pinched my forearm as I felt darkness and evil grow inside me. I was enjoying this life in some way. I was better than everyone around me. And for once in my life, I was untouchable.

"Mrs. Ivory, when you're all finished, I just wanted you to know that Mrs. Rothschild would like a private word with you, if possible." A girl that had to be Sage's assigned dove tapped me gently.

"Don't touch me." I brushed at my shoulder before standing.

Who was I becoming? What was I becoming?

I made my way into the private pool-view rooms above the kitchen, where the girls were still cooking in nothing but aprons and being filmed as part of the cinema selection for the Euphoria floor.

"Mrs. Ivory, you've done well for yourself in such a small amount of time, my friend." Sage Rothschild stood by the window and smiled at me. She had sunglasses on, a scarf wrapped around her neck, and was sipping a glass of Ivory champagne.

"I suppose so, Sage." The clear action of using her first name was an easy display of my shift in power.

"I ordered a custom product." She slid her glasses off and looked out to the pool. "Declan and I thought we'd select something from the inventory, but they were all too...dated?" She waved her hands.

She was going to become the mother to my sister

and Bradley's child, and here she was, calling that child, my niece or nephew, a custom product. But more than her being the mother of that child, the fact that Declan, the disgusting vile man who nearly killed me, would be their father? The man who choked me and didn't understand the word 'no' pleading from my mouth? The man Alister let live solely because he was concerned how it would look if a prominent, wealthy white man went missing at his resort?

I knew I didn't have much say in any of this. I had too much to lose if I tried anything.

But suddenly, I thought about something that may be my own little project here.

"Sage…may I ask you a personal question?"

She looked at me with interest as I waved her over to a table. "Do you love your husband?" She paused. "Actually, let me ask you this… How did you meet?"

Her presence shifted almost immediately.

She grew closer to me and brushed her finger against my face. "Mrs. Ivory, you really don't remember me, do you?"

"Sage…" I tried to back away, but she grabbed my wrist.

"Close your eyes and think, Demi," she rasped. "You were just their little housekeeper. You came into Dr. Ivory's office to clean and pulled the curtain back. I'm sure you thought you'd see trees or something pretty, didn't you?"

Her voice grew deeper and raspier. "I was one of the caged girls you left behind to die—just like you did to your own flesh and blood. And look at the poor girl, she's giving life while you steal it."

My breathing grew rapid as I looked into her eyes. "You were there? You were her?" I choked out as I peeled her hands off me.

"Declan bought me out of the catalogue. I won." She chuckled.

"Sage, I didn't know... I... Wait." Goosebumps scattered across my arms as I stood and pressed my hands against the glass window.

Suddenly, everyone outside, all the wives, stopped.

They looked at me through the window and smiled. Most wiggled their fingers in small waves, while some even blew me kisses.

Blonde hair, green eyes, perfectly pale skin, white dresses, and...submissive personalities. They stayed with the doves on the all-white floor. Their meals were all white.

Rice, yogurt, peeled radishes, vanilla cake, and milk...

I flung around, and Sage was standing there, grin-ning. "We're all just precious little birds, finally set free."

It felt like the entire world was closing in on me. I'd never escape this sick, all-white world. These women were so happy to be here because it was better than the cages they all came from. There wasn't just one caged girl; there were hundreds, if not thousands walking this earth. These women were the custom-made brides from Ian Ivory.

"Sage, listen to me. I have an idea..." My voice trembled as I walked toward her. It was all intercon-nected. The Ivory family was everywhere. They made sure to have businesses that poured into one another. Wealthy men needed obedient and submissive wives, so they sought out Ian Ivory. Then, once they were married and bored, they needed an escape and their wives wanted children...

So, they came to La Gabbia. "Why do so many of you choose to take children from here?" I questioned.

Sage rubbed her hands against her abdomen. "When we get purchased by rich men, we are expected to be submissive and use our training from the white therapy. Some of us try to fight back when they... torture us. There is a one strike rule. They say we are being hysterical, so they force us to get hysterec-tomies." She switched her entire personality. "But now,

Declan and I need a legacy. We need children to fill our home. My children were stolen from me when I let sex and booze consume me. The Ivory family saved me."

"Oh my God," I breathed out in shock. "Sage, do you love your husband?"

Something changed in the way she looked at me. "Of course." She anxiously looked to the corner of the room.

I glanced up but didn't see any cameras. "Sage, no, I need you to tell me. I won't say anything. I'm not…"

"Says the woman who abandoned us all."

I shook my head. "And look where we all ended up. Together. I didn't escape hell."

It was as if a mask fell from her face and Sage blurted out, "I hate him. I hate the way he hurts me. I have heard La Gabbia helps tame their male rage. But I hate the way he…controls me. I hate the way he locks me up in the all-white dog cage at home and laughs while pleasuring himself."

"I have an idea about Declan. I want to keep him here," I said quickly, knowing it was only a matter of time before Alister would wonder what I was doing.

"You could inherit all his money. You could raise your child. You could break all of this. You could have the means and chance to live on your own terms and give that to the baby."

A single tear rolled down her cheek. "He's too powerful. Everyone would question where he went."

"It'll be a boating accident; I can set it all up. Somewhere farther away from Ivory Island. We can't afford to have our resort or island in any headline."

Color flushed in Sage's cheeks. "What would you do to him?"

I shook my head. "You don't need to know; all you need to know is this is your chance at freedom. I just have one request." Rolling my shoulders back, I said, "You must promise to update me about the child and raise them in a life of sheer happiness. If I find out you are hurting the child or causing any form of pain, then I will personally hunt you down and kill you."

"I promise." She wiped away her tear. "What will you tell your husband? What are you going to do with Declan?"

Rolling my tube of lipstick up, I painted my lips with the red shade I had hidden away. "I'll handle it. That's all you need to know. If a man hurts you, then you owe him nothing."

CHAPTER
THIRTY-SEVEN

"BRADLEY, it is your job to obey me. I am, in fact, your boss now," I boasted confidently as I told him to bring Declan to me.

Bradley looked at me with confusion. "Declan Rothschild is expected to leave tonight with his wife."

"And he will eventually; I just need him to stay a bit longer." I had already asked Sarah and Marisha to get in touch with the resort's connections to the media. They would help me put together the elaborate story I would issue in a week.

"Alister is to not be stressed about anything regarding this."

"Demi..." Bradley walked over to me as I stood in my black lace robe on the balcony.

He put his hands around my waist and turned me around to face him.

"Don't," is all I said before trying to pull away.

"Do you want Declan to be the father of your child? He's sick. He puts his wife in a cage… What would he do to my…" I froze as Bradley looked at me sadly.

"I need your help. It's the only thing I can do for Layla. What she did for me… Bradley, I'd have been the one who was trapped having baby after baby and spending all my time in that cage. Please let me do this for this child. For your child." I stroked Bradley's cheek.

"There is no way Alister would let me keep the baby here. They are paying millions for your baby. But this is a way we know they can live a beautiful life with means and freedom, Bradley."

"What do you propose?" he asked.

"I need you to help me convince Alister that Declan has left the resort with Sage. There will be a boating accident in a few days that Declan will be on and it will make headlines. This will be somewhere else…in water that isn't anyone's to worry about. Then, Sage will send payment from the life insurance policy to Alister for the baby. We will go through with it all."

"You're going to kill Declan Rothschild?" Bradley asked me in a hushed whisper.

"Yes," I said with no hesitation.

Bradley ran his hand through his thick blonde hair. "Don't do this, Demilion." He pulled me into him.

"No, you don't do this." I pushed him off me, ignoring the pain I felt in my heart.

I guess there was something left inside me. All because of him. But he wasn't mine.

He'd never be mine, and I could never be his.

"Will you do this for me?"

Bradley sighed. "Yes, it'll be a piece of cake." He leaned in and planted a small kiss on my forehead.

"A piece of cake." I smiled.

"Demi, I will always love…"

Shaking my head, I put my hand up. "Bradley, I'm begging you to not say it. Please."

He nodded and began to leave, but I grabbed his hand from behind.

"Do you love my sister?"

I dropped my eyes as he looked over his shoulder.

"I think that…it's hard for me to not love her, too. But we've been forced to spend so much time together and have this baby together. Alister wants the pregnancy to go smoothly, so he has me caring for her. At first, I was faking it all, Demi; I was pretending to love her, and now…"

"Then why tell me that you love me?" I whimpered.

"Because I do love you, Demi. I love you by choice. But Layla, I love…because she and I are bonded over a trauma deeper than it all." Tears streamed from my eyes, and he wiped them away before tilting my head up.

"I wish more than anything that we could have had our chance. You always felt like you were my Cinderella—the shoes even fit." He was referring to the Nikes he bought me all that time ago.

"Yeah, me too, Bradley. But the thing is, Cinderella is dead." I turned away and gripped the banister of the balcony, staring at the ocean.

———————

Alister was out of town again, which was perfect timing since I had many moving parts to organize. I finally found his private office after walking in circles through the penthouse. I stood in front of the wall, where I found a similar painting hanging, that was already in another room. The shriveled lips with shades of red and nude brushed against them to give them life had my stomach churning. Squinting, I could see names scribbled beside each one in black lettering. These women must have tried to fight back, talk back, or simply tried to speak up for their rights. Gagging as I tried to read the names, I forced myself to turn away.

I brushed my hand against the golden knobs of Alister's desk. There were random papers and pens scattered throughout. It was disorderly compared to everything else in the penthouse. Fingering through the knick-knacks, I found a few badges. These were the ones I had seen Alister use.

A phone rang as soon as I lifted it up, causing me to fall back with my heart pounding against my chest.

Looking up at the desk, I saw the old-fashioned telephone and waited for it to stop. But it didn't. Shaking, I stood and lifted it to my ear.

"My beautiful raven, what ever are you doing in my office?"

My eyes scanned the ceiling, but there wasn't a visible camera. "Your ass looks so good from here." I flung around and looked at the wall of bones.

"Alister, I…" I needed to compose myself quickly. "Alister, I need to get to the nightingales. I want to check in and make sure everything is going well. Sage Rothschild also wanted to see…"

"Ah, I see. My wife is managing the business while I'm away. Oh, Demi, you don't know how happy this makes me. You can keep one of the badges, and I'll have a custom one made for you," he said.

I smiled, knowing he could see me, and then I knew what I could do to seal this all up. Sliding on his desk, but still facing the wall, I spread my legs, revealing the lace panties I had on under my dress.

His moan echoed into my ear.

"I'll be back in the morning. Stay in the bed for me, my love." He hung up and I kept the façade going, knowing he was watching me intently. Grabbing the badge, I pushed everything back together neatly before walking out of his office.

Internally, I was fighting myself. There was some sick version of myself who was enjoying this game of power and control. I hated that person inside me, and it was plaguing me completely. She was taking over. But perhaps that was the only way I could survive. I think I've come to realize what we do to survive can't be held against us. We are all just fighting to live, after all.

CHAPTER
THIRTY-EIGHT

"SAGE, I need you to look at me and tell me that you can do this," I whispered. It was evening, and the outdoor pool was empty and quiet as new guests checked in and were enjoying the indoor entertainment and dinner.

"My flight leaves in two hours." Sage looked around us anxiously.

"I know, but I need to get him out of here and back to his mother. The others…we don't know who they belong to, but we know his mother is some famous influencer who is actively looking for him. We can hide him on the plane, and then you'll leave without Declan."

I opened my arms and hugged Sage. "Listen to me. This is the moment that you have real purpose in your life. This is the moment you aren't the caged girl, the favorite girl, or any label that's been forced on you. You can save a child, yourself, and…"

"It's ready." His voice had me flinging around. Bradley was standing there with his hands behind his back.

"Thank you, Bradley." I nodded. "Sage, promise me you'll go through with this."

Sage looked at me with clear panic and fear radiating through her body. She was the woman that felt lost and walked into the wrong arms. She was trafficked and sold to a man almost triple her age to be an obedient wife to.

She looked down at the ground. "I can."

"The golf cart will take you to your private plane. I'll be there soon with…the package." I looked at Bradley.

"Please let me guide you to your ride, Mrs. Rothschild. I just need one moment with Mrs. Ivory."

Sage raced over to me once more and threw her arms around me. "Fuck the patriarchy," I whispered into her ear.

I could hear the smile when she replied, "I get to be a part of something that I want to be a part of, and I didn't realize how meaningful that is. I hope I can see you soon, Demi, and not through a cage or a glass box."

Pulling from me, I looked at her. "Goodbye, Sage." I

knew that would be the last time I saw her. My time here was going to dwindle away very quickly.

"Demi, I'm proud of you. I know that what you're trying to do is making a small difference in something so out of control. Mix this into Declan's drink. It's not the one I gave you all that time ago when you tried to kill me; this one will kill him in sixty seconds."

Bradley lifted a necklace with a pendant designed as a cake. It looked like a pink wedding cake.

"It'll be a piece of cake." He winked at me before wrapping me in a warm hug.

Nodding, I brushed my hands against the locket and opened it.

I saw a large white pill and smiled back at him. "It'll be a piece of cake."

Bradley and Sage walked away together into the darkness, where only the moonlight was their guide.

I quickly made my way back inside. Alister assumed I was going down to the Euphoria floor, but he didn't realize I was wearing all white. I had to find out where they were housing the children.

This gave me hope, knowing I still had parts of my own soul left. I wasn't evil, even with the thoughts racing through my mind. I could fight them and remember who I was. Who I am.

The resort was crowded, and I made my way to the half-moon, all-white marble bar. A man who looked almost plastic smiled at me with his blonde hair covered in gel and his green eyes glistening.

"Mrs. Ivory, we are serving coconut margaritas tonight. Would you care for one?" I looked around and noticed all the women, who must have checked in tonight, were excitedly chatting with one another and sipping the white concoction.

The stunning chandeliers hung all through the entrance of the resort and light classical music echoed throughout the space.

"Yes, please," I said, knowing I needed to create my own alibi. I smiled and grabbed the drink from the bartender, who had his name scribbled on his badge. "Thank you, Lionel." I took a sip and winced at how strong it was.

"What are your plans for the evening, Mrs. Ivory?" Lionel asked me.

"I'm going to drink this, grab some sushi, and then go back home for a nice soak in the tub. How about you, Lionel?" I leaned against the bar and grinned at him, causing him to blush.

"Mr. Ivory allows all employees one movie ticket every quarter, so I'd love to catch a live-action film."

A pit in my stomach grew. "Of course, as you should." I placed my glass down and yawned. "I'm off to have some food and me-time. Goodnight." I patted his hand and quickly turned away. I squinted at the sign with the resort map.

Shaking my head, I went back to the front desk and cleared my throat. "Marisha?" I looked at the girl who I knew was a nightingale, but she now had blonde hair and bleached eyebrows.

"I got promoted to come back up." She sounded relieved. "Thank you, Mrs. Ivory!" she sang out.

"But I didn't do anything…" I questioned.

"I'm just thankful, is all." She smiled again. "How can I help you?" she asked me and started to type on the laptop in front of her.

"Marisha, you know what? Actually, I didn't want to take credit, but it was because of me that you were relocated to this…well, safer position." I paused and glanced around me. "I need you to tell me where the inventory for the Life Center is kept. Alister, my husband, has asked me to check it since I was the one who did a restock. I'd like to make sure the products were delivered safely." It was terrifying how easily the lie came to me.

Marisha looked nervous as she glanced around us. "Okay, Mrs. Ivory. I'll give you the map, and I'm sure your badge has access since only Mr. Ivory and you were granted full access to the entire resort."

"Thank you, Marisha." I smiled as I took the paper from her and looked at the map.

"The inventory is kept on the top floor above the Life Center. If you scan your badge, you'll be able to enter immediately. If there is any security breach, then we can discharge our guards." She laced her fingers together and asked, "Do you need anything else, Mrs. Ivory?"

I sighed. "No, I'm ready to turn in for bed soon, so this is all." I quickly turned the corner, glancing at the map of La Gabbia. It was massive. Making my way toward the employee-only elevators, I picked up my pace, dodging guests and workers. I stood in front of the gold elevator and scanned my badge. The doors opened and I dragged my finger across the various buttons. There it was. The floor, below the penthouse. I closed my eyes for a moment as the elevator shot upward and the doors opened. Taking a step out, I turned and saw the signage to the Life Center with a massive stork, but instead, I went the other way to where a hospital symbol of a red cross was hanging above.

My heart was racing as I scanned my badge again, thinking there was no way I could get inside, but the doors slid open just as doubt plagued my mind.

It was quiet, cold, and eerily peaceful. I entered and saw nurses in old-fashioned uniforms with hats on.

The blinding fluorescent lights pained my eyes as I turned and began walking.

"Mrs. Ivory?" a soft voice repeated multiple times as I continued walking forward.

Pausing, I looked at the nurse who quickly cut me off.

"What is it?" I said sternly.

"Welcome to the birth center. We are honored by your visit." She bowed her head.

"I need to check inventory, and I'd like a tour of the facility." I knew I had to hurry since Sage was already boarding the private plane to go home.

"Absolutely, ma'am. I'll need to phone Mr. Ivory, if that's alright. All birth center and inventory-related visits must be approved by him."

I looked at my ring; it was enormous and reminded me that Alister chose me. I was the favorite girl and reminding myself that the title held more power than any others had confidence soaring through me.

"I am going to pretend you didn't just disrespect me in my own house. I don't need anyone's approval. My name is on the deed of this resort. Before I throw you into the cages and force you to learn basic manners in dark therapy, I will give you one last chance to show me where it is."

Her face turned bright red, which was a pleasant shift in color against the all-white.

"Yes, of course, Mrs. Ivory, my apologies."

She swiftly guided me away, and once we reached

the door, I looked at her. "That'll be all." I waved her away. She hesitated for a moment before bowing her head and leaving me. I stood in front of the hospital-like doors and took a deep breath before scanning my badge in front of the keypad.

"I can do this." I brushed my hand across the silly cake pendant. "It's a piece of cake." Part of me knew the pill inside wasn't just meant to kill Declan Roth-schild, but it was also in case I needed to kill myself. I knew Bradley understood the depravity of this situation. I was risking not only my life, but his and Layla's. I was quietly starting a war. The doors slid open, and I walked up and tugged the curtain back.

"Oh my god."

CHAPTER
THIRTY-NINE

IT WAS ANOTHER GLASS WINDOW, and behind the window were at least forty cots side-by-side. Each cot had a woman with a shaved head and bony face. But each one was also clearly pregnant.

The glass door slid open in front of me, and I stepped inside. One by one, their eyes began to open, and they all stared at me with piercing green eyes.

Tilting their heads, some smiled and some stared in awe. My chest was visibly rising and falling rapidly as the door slid shut behind me.

Licking my lips, I walked to the bed closest to me. I saw the chains wrapped around the woman's wrists and ankles. A strong odor of feces and urine stung my nose.

She smiled at me peacefully before closing her eyes again.

Why would these wealthy couples want to take babies from women who were in these conditions? Why would they...

Covering my mouth and nose, I turned away and slid my badge to open the door. I couldn't be here right now. I had to piece everything together and save at least one life tonight.

Looking over my shoulder, I ran straight into someone. "Oh!" I cried out and placed my hands between us.

"Conrad..." I could feel the blood in my body turn cold. Conrad Ivory, the son of Ian and Daphne Ivory. The man who raped me on our wedding night and wanted to continue the legacy. The man I thought I had killed. My first husband.

"Hello, my beautiful wife." Conrad brushed his hands across my shoulders and then tilted my chin up.

I was frozen in fear, in shock, and paralyzed by the fact that this was it. I'd never escape from them.

"It's funny that you were so foolish to think we'd give you poison pills. This was all such a wonderful test of loyalty, wasn't it?" Conrad dug his nails into my wrists as I tried to move back, but my body wouldn't let me.

"Conrad," I breathed out. "I'm not your wife; I am Alister Ivory's wife, and if you don't release me right now, I'll have you hung and bleeding out." I forced myself to sound confident, though fear pounded through me.

He let out a dry laugh. "You stupid bitch, I don't want you. You've been used by my entire family. At this point, you're just the Ivory family whore. I married a caged girl, which was what I should have done all along. You probably have met her…Kandi? She's quite the hair and makeup artist. We are just picking out a child since I had her uterus removed when she was acting hormonal and hysterical during her monthly bleeding."

Kandi was married to Conrad? My heart sank as I looked around. No one could be trusted; everyone was a part of this sick and twisted family.

"We are leaving soon and didn't want to wait for one of these hags to push out a baby, only to hear them crying and whining all day. I convinced Kandi we needed a trained child. I heard you chose some new inventory." His sinister smile had the air in my lungs dissipating.

"I guess you needed the right Ivory husband to set you straight, and honestly, Uncle Alister is the most insane of us all." He winked at me before abruptly wrapping his hands around my neck and speaking into my face, where splatters of saliva hit my cheeks.

"Conrad, I… You died in front of me…" I was in disbelief. They never died.

"How are you here?" I rasped as I stared at him with my eyes wide, scared to blink because then he'd disappear and I'd know I was unwell.

"You can't kill an Ivory. But truly, you were the best fuck; I'll miss you, Demilion." Slamming his lips and tongue against mine, I gagged and tried to push him off with no luck. Releasing me, I began coughing and hunched over.

I had no words or thoughts left in me. Every bit of my life and story had felt like a nightmare I couldn't wake up from.

"Bye, baby girl." I watched him go in the other direction, which had to be where the kidnapped children were being kept.

"Conrad!" I called out.

He stopped and spun around curiously. "Yes, my beloved?" he mocked.

"The new inventory I selected isn't there right now; they went to get their health screenings done. You'll have to head to the medical wing." *Please, please let him believe me.*

"Well, thank God. I hate going into that disgusting, smelly, whiny-filled space." Conrad shrugged and purposely rammed into me before leaving.

Breathing out, I waited for him to leave before I scanned my badge over the next door.

"It'll be okay, Demi. You're going to try your best," I

whispered to myself, but once the doors opened, the malodorous odor slapped me as I stepped into an empty space. The door shut behind me, and then the lights went off before a second door opened.

I walked into the darkness and bumped into something cold. Whimpering and heavy breathing haunted me as I squinted and dropped to my knees. "Hello?" I questioned but couldn't see. This had to be the dark therapy. But I thought Alister kept that specific therapy to the bottom levels?

Sticking my fingers through the cold steel bars, I whispered again, "Hello?"

A sharp sensation pierced through my fingers, causing me to cry out. With my other fingers I jammed at the small mouth that had latched on, biting me.

"I'm here to help," I wailed as I clutched my hand to my chest.

"Mommy, mommy!" A tearful plea shattered my heart.

"Please, Mommy." I clenched my eyes shut, forcing myself to be brave. I couldn't regress, but I also couldn't help thinking how their cries matched my own and Layla's. I could see my mother and father counting through the stack of bills after they handed us off.

Clutching my knees to my face, I began crying.

"Please, help us!" a little boy screamed.

It was the same voice. The little boy whose mother was intently searching for him and using her massive social media following to spread his face and videos.

"What is your name?" Multiple voices screamed different names, but I crawled toward his voice.

"Myles…" he sobbed.

I padded my hands across the bars. If I could save him, he'd tell his mother what happened. Then, she'd use her following, her presence in this day and age to shed light on Ivory Island. The other children had to be saved, too, but I couldn't smuggle multiple kids out without notice. They may have been trafficked or sold here. I had to choose someone who had a family who wouldn't let this go.

A thick padlock kept the crate closed. Patting my head, I tugged out the small bobby pin.

I used to pick locks back in India when we'd run away to find food. Shoving it in and missing because of the darkness had my palms sweaty.

"Shit," I hissed as I dropped the pin. Running my moist hands through my hair, I began to panic until I felt one last pin.

Myles began screaming at the top of his lungs. "Myles, I need you to calm down." I wasn't a mother, so I didn't realize telling a child to calm down meant they'd retaliate and do the opposite. His screams pierced my ears. I was sure this area was sound-proofed. "Myles, can you tell me your favorite movie?"

He sobbed, and chanted, "No."

I jammed the pin into the lock and tried to finagle it. "Mine is Titanic. It's about people on this big ship and a love story of sorts." I was rambling, but by some miracle, it was working.

The lock clicked and opened.

I slowly opened the door, and Myles flung forward into me. "Mommy!"

"No, sweet boy, but I'll get you to her. We must go, now." I couldn't see him but felt the stream of tears flooding his face.

"I need you to be calm, sweetie. I have to get you out." Guilt ran through me as I shut the crate and put the lock back on as the cries of the others swirled around me. I couldn't risk Conrad coming back or telling anyone he saw me here. Time was running out. I whispered my apologies to the children I'd have to leave behind for now.

I waved my badge, and we entered the first space before the door shut and the second opened. I flinched at the bright light and looked down at Myles, who was covering his eyes. He was wearing a small black gown and covered in dirt and feces. I couldn't parade him out of here like this. I began hurriedly looking around and pushed through a door. It was a hospital room.

Shutting the door behind us, I kneeled in front of Myles. "I'm going to clean you up, then drop you off to an airplane with a lady named Sage. She's going to find your mommy. I promise."

"I'm so hungry," he cried.

"The plane will have so much food." I stood and began looking through cabinets and drawers.

"Bone broth?" I looked at a small jar. "Here." I handed it to him and, without a second thought, he drank it.

Filling the empty jar with water, I offered it as he excitedly took it and drank it all. I wet a napkin and began wiping his small body. I didn't have time to coax him or make him feel comfortable; I had to get him out of here. I had to hope his mother would talk about this to the world.

"I need you to tell your mother everything, and tell her that Alister Ivory is running a resort called La Gabbia that has kids and women trapped." I nodded as he stared at me, probably not even able to comprehend what I was saying.

I found a small white gown stacked underneath the sink and swapped his black one for it. He kept squinting at me. The children must have been put through dark therapy to become obedient for their new families. How sick could Alister be? He used a child's natural fear of the dark to make them into the perfect addition to some wealthy couple.

"Myles, promise me you'll tell your mother." I placed my hands on his cheeks and whispered, "Can I give you a hug?" I fought back the tears in my eyes as he smiled.

"Yes." Hugging him tightly, I had to put all my hope in a child. He would have to be the messenger.

"Let's go." I pulled the map of La Gabbia out and glanced at it. There were employee elevators toward the back that could take me all the way down to the gardens, and then to the golf carts.

I just had to hope no one would see us.

"I hope you rest in peace." Myles looked up at me as I held his hand in mine, and we walked down the bright white hallway.

"What do you mean?" I asked, swiping my badge and getting into the elevator with him.

"I begged the others to let me out. They hurt us. But you...you must be an angel, and Mommy said angels are dead people. Are you a dead people?"

Nodding my head, I sighed as a tear rolled down my face. "Yes, Myles. I died a long time ago."

CHAPTER
FORTY

"GET INSIDE of this storage box for now, Myles, and then once you're in the air, Sage will let you out." He climbed into it. The Rothchilds' private plane was small but luxurious.

"Is the pilot employed through Declan or Alister?" I whispered to Sage, who kept staring at Myles in shock.

"Declan," she said quietly.

"I need you to find his mother. If you do a quick search, you'll find her. I can't look anything up without being detected, nor can you on Ivory Island."

"I'm going to give him snacks," Sage said calmly. "White rice and yogurt?" She was talking to herself as she stood and walked to the back of the plane.

Myles looked at me nervously. "Listen, you'll be okay. If she tries to keep you, I want you to bite her and run for your life once you're back in America. Run toward a busy area, okay?" I brushed my hands against his cheek.

"We just have white rice and plain yogurt..." Sage brought a crystal bowl out for Myles. "Declan likes for me to maintain the same diet."

"Sage, he's not going to be around to tell you what to do anymore."

"Mrs. Rothschild?" The pilots voice cut through the intercom.

"Bye, Myles." I felt sadness and relief as I shut the lid to the bench. "Let him out as soon as you're in the air."

"I've been notified by Mr. Bradley Ivory that Mr. Rothschild will be leaving Ivory Island by boat to explore nearby islands. We will be preparing for takeoff shortly."

Sage touched the cake pendant with a grin. "I like your necklace."

"Thanks, have a piece of cake for me when you get to freedom, will you? Preferably not vanilla..." I wiped away a tear and got off the plane.

For the very first time in my life, I felt a sliver of peace. I wasn't evil; I was still good.

———

I was exhausted, but my mind kept going back to the birth and Life Center. The pregnant women and the children in dog kennels.

I sat on the balcony of the penthouse and stared into the night sky, hoping Myles and Sage were already far away from the island of hell.

I took a bath, hid the necklace Bradley gave me, and put on a set of silk pajamas. Alister would come home at any time. I was already nervous about the possibility that he had cameras and had seen me.

The hours went by slowly, I paced around with no appetite, and I even had dark thoughts about swallowing the pill and killing myself.

But then I thought about my sister, Bradley, and the others.

"My gorgeous raven…"

"Alister." I was already shaking at his presence.

He immediately hugged and kissed me before tugging his tie off and throwing it to the side. "I've missed you, especially after seeing you on camera today…" he trailed, letting his hands trace my neck.

Swallowing the lump in my throat, I looked into his dark eyes. "Camera?" My heart was racing too fast.

He tilted his head and narrowed his eyes at me. "When you teased me from my office?"

"Oh yes, of course. I just missed you." I nuzzled my face into his neck, hoping he'd loosen the grip of his hands.

"I want to have my own fantasy come true tonight, my love," he whispered into my ear.

"Okay…" I shuddered at the thought of having any kind of intimacy with this sick man.

"If you do this for me with a smile on your face and no objections, I'll grant you a wish." Alister ran his fingers against my lips. "My very own princess Jasmine." He beamed at me. "I know you want something from me…"

This couldn't have been a coincidence. What did he know? "I'll do anything you want. I'll make your wildest fantasy come to life." I started as he looked at me. "Anything, my love."

"Let all the children that you kidnapped go back home."

Alister's eyes darkened. "Kidnapped? My raven, you don't understand. They weren't kidnapped; many of them were sold by their own parents, much like you and Layla. However, I distribute them to happy, wealthy homes…"

"The children I found in Miami and the rest of them... Are you planning on taking them all?"

Alister tossed his head back and laughed. "As much as I am the best all-inclusive resort with many services, there are a few others that do offer a few similar ones. No one has the Euphoria program, of course. No one has the white and dark therapies or intricacies I do..."

He was proving himself to be the best. There had to be other resorts that were selling children and trafficking women.

"So, no, those children are spoken for. Ask for something else."

"Let Bradley and Layla go."

Alister's breathing grew crass as he scratched his head and rolled his sleeves. "Look, my beautiful raven..."

More tattoos had been added to his forearm. My entire face covered a massive part, and then I was surrounded by a dove, a raven, and a nightingale.

"I love you, but no." Alister poured whiskey into his glass. "Choose one person."

I flinched. "You'll let one go?"

He lifted the glass to his lips and sipped the

caramel liquid. "Yes. If you promise me to do what I tell you tonight."

"I promise," I whispered.

"Who will it be? Layla or Bradley?"

My hands were shaking as I looked at Alister. "Bradley."

His forehead creased, and I continued, "Layla is pregnant with the Rothschilds' baby. We need her to be here and fulfill her duty. I don't want La Gabbia to lose money over a silly personal connection."

"I choose Bradley to leave. I'm honestly sick of having him lurking around. It's uncomfortable for me."

Alister started at me intently with amusement. "My loyal wife. Your wish is my command."

He tossed the rest of his whiskey back and then grabbed my hand. "Let's start our evening, shall we?"

———

Alister had me put on a winter coat before we went down. "Where are we going?" I asked.

"A buffet of sorts." Stepping inside, I stood in the middle of the black-and-white-checkered floors. There were rows and rows of drawers in alternating colors:

white and black. A ladder was put off to the side. The scent of formaldehyde and bleach floated around us, and the frigid temperature let me know we were inside the morgue.

An in-house morgue at the lavish La Gabbia resort.

"Choose our girl, Dem." Alister nudged me. "And then Bradley will taste his freedom."

"Choose her for what?" I sniffled.

"Each has a tag with her face, race, name, weight, height..."

I looked up at him. "Alister, choose her for what?"

"To spend a night in our bed. I have fantasies, too, Demi. It's unfair that all of these men come to my resort and make their desires come true, but now, as my wife, and all that I do for you, like let you breathe and survive...well, it means you must repay me."

I walked toward one wall. My eyes stung with tears as I saw the images from the hallways.

"Oh no..." I said quietly so he wouldn't hear. Brushing my fingers against them, I saw all the girls I had met here. Karina, Taylor, Sarah, Jamie, Anu... "Alister, they were amazing at their jobs. They were my..."

"It's a liability to have the same girls know all our

business, Demi. They serve while alive, and then they will serve a new purpose."

Shaking my head, I looked up. "No,"

"Demi, pick a girl and let's go." His voice shifted to anger. I knew I was risking Bradley's exit from this place if I didn't play by the rules. These girls, some who I considered my friends, were all dead now. I couldn't fight for them.

"Her." I pointed at a random girl I didn't know, and one I had never met.

"A good choice. She's been here for a while. I'll call someone to pick her up." I followed Alister out, but paused at the entrance. There were rows and rows of magazines. Lifting one up, I flipped through but dropped it.

The breath left my lungs. It was image after image with 'product information' listed below.

"You know our most high-paying clientele are the men who come here for these ladies. Necrophiliacs are shunned in the real-world, Demi. But truly, we are real men; we're the ones who have power and control far greater than life. The ones who can appreciate the beauty of a woman in all forms. I mean, you may think we are sick, but think of these women, the ones with all their fake hair extensions and wigs. Demi, the best ones are made from human hair. Do they truly think all those girls voluntarily shaved their heads? The wives who come here leave with top quality hair from these women. Then we have our fun." He spun around in the morgue proudly.

Please don't make me do this. It's what I wish I could say, but I didn't. Instead, I followed my husband back to the penthouse as grief overcame me. Because I knew if I didn't obey, I'd be stuffed into a freezer, too.

CHAPTER
FORTY-ONE

I STOOD in front of the corpse that was lying in our bed. She now wore a red-lace lingerie set and a white wig had been put on top of her head.

"You're going to fuck her and me. Then, I'll have you both."

A video recorder was set up in front of the bed. "Don't worry, my love, I only keep these films for my personal collection."

"Shall we?" He began to direct me to get on top of her.

"Kiss her." Stomach acid rose in my throat as I straddled the corpse. Closing my eyes, I started to think about Bradley. He'd get to leave, and maybe he'd get to change. Maybe therapy or something could help heal the childhood trauma that led him to this path, or maybe he'd just finally soak in the sun and live a real life.

I pressed my lips against the shriveled ones in front of me. "Open your eyes and use tongue." I turned and looked at Alister pleadingly as he stroked himself in bed.

"Do it, Demi!" he barked at me and then revealed a knife. "Do it well, or do it while bleeding." He waved it at me before I did as I was told.

He forced himself on me, brushing his naked body against mine as he kept telling me what to do. I hated myself and I hated him. I hated her for being here, even in death. My mind spiraled as he raped the corpse, and then choked me as he forced himself inside me.

I didn't see him, I didn't see her, I just let myself die inside.

I knew once he choked me hard enough, I'd lose consciousness. "Harder, Alister," I begged.

And just like that, everything went black.

————

I opened my eyes, and they immediately grew wider. I was staring straight at the corpse. Her lips were painted red. Did Alister put lipstick on her?

"She's beautiful, but you are far more gorgeous. I'll

have her lips added to my art. I can't believe I never did earlier." His arms tightened around me as he squeezed. "Last night was everything of my fantasy and more, my raven," he softly said into my ear.

I sat up and wiggled out of his grip full of disgust and remorse. "When is Bradley leaving?"

"Today. Although I didn't want to, but I think it'll provide you closure. He's requested that you come and say goodbye to him. I told you I'd make your wish come true."

I slid out of the bed from the end and turned to Alister, who was cradling the dead woman next to him. He kissed her lips and smiled back at me. "Don't be jealous." Red lipstick was smeared on his mouth.

"I'm going to shower and get dressed." Everything hurt inside, and I didn't want to even think about what Alister had done to my body after I fell unconscious.

"I love you, Demi," Alister called out to me. When I didn't return it, his voice changed. "Say it back." He warned.

. . .

I knew I had to stay strong. "I love you, Alister." Looking down, I added, "I'm just feeling very shy after our wild night."

A look of pleasure painted his face as he sank back under the covers. "Go on, my love. Bradley is leaving in thirty-minutes."

I scrubbed my body so hard that my skin felt raw. I brushed my teeth and gargled with mouthwash before crying into the sink just to cleanse and purge the death, torture, and pain I could feel seeping into my every crevice.

I quickly tugged on a black dress. I knew Bradley would be down below somewhere before he left.

Racing around, I left the penthouse and picked up my pace in fear I'd miss him, but as soon as I got to the garden, I stopped. It was a peony garden.

This is where all the girls who are brutally raped, beaten, used, and tortured eventually went to rest after their corpses were defiled and abused. And on top of their graves, beautiful peonies grew that guests were given to consume. Alister really did make himself out to be some kind of sick environmentalist with his recycle, reduce, and reuse mantra.

"Demi." Bradley came around and was dressed in a

black suit. "Why, Dem?" His voice broke as his eyes glistened. They weren't green; he took his contacts out.

"Why didn't you choose Layla? Alister told me he gave you a choice between us." He put his hands on my hips and hugged me.

"She's pregnant. Sage will need the baby in order to keep her quiet about Declan. But now, you can find a way into your baby's life." I smiled sadly.

"I need you to promise me you'll get out, too," he whispered into my ear. "Please, Demi. This can't be the end."

I pulled away and looked at him. "Go find your happily ever after, Bradley Ivory." Tears streamed down my face as I stood on my tiptoes and planted a kiss on his cheek.

But he turned my face and kissed me on my lips. "No." I shook my head. "You will always be Layla's, and until then, just be..." I stepped away as he stared at me.

"This is for you." He handed me a golden key. "It's not on the map. It was once used in the resort as Alister's in-house prison for the men who didn't follow his rules. But now it's empty. Declan is there, and however you choose to kill him, well…he'll never be found. You have to go down to the bottom floor, exit, and then take the secret elevator in the back corner past the janitorial closet. It's all hidden behind a tunnel, Demi."

I clutched the key to my chest. I was going to kill Declan Rothschild, protect Bradley and Layla's baby from having that sick bastard as their father, and get revenge for what he did to me and the others. I was making up for the fact that I once left girls like Sage behind and now she'd finally be free.

It was poetic in a way. "Go." I pointed to the golf cart.

"Come with me." Bradley gripped my wrist.

Taking one deep breath in, I wiped the tears from his face. "This time there isn't enough room for Rose… there's only enough room for Jack."

"I hate this sinking ship. It forced us to fight for our lives when all we wanted to do was sail. I'm sorry I was too much of a coward. I knew they'd find us all along, so I thought if you and I went here willingly, then we'd get to be together. I never thought Alister would change the course so much. I'll always love you, but please let her know I love her and I'm sorry."

One of the greatest gifts in life is realizing that it is not your job to fix something you didn't break. I didn't break any of this, but ultimately, only a few of us get to have the band-aid, and in that moment, we must decide to fix it or choose our own peace. I fixed something I didn't break, and I set him free from his cage.

"Promise me you'll leave here and meet me. I don't think I can leave knowing you're staying here, dying here..." He began to question everything, and I knew the feeling. Feeling like you should carry guilt for surviving. Feeling like you're a coward for taking the opportunity no one else has.

"I promise you I'll escape, too." Part of me knew I would escape, but the other part knew I would never go find him. When I escaped, I'd never want to be around any of them again. I'd need to just finally be set free from my own gilded cage, and that meant leaving them all behind.

"See you soon, Demi." And just like that, Bradley Ivory had left my life. This time forever.

CHAPTER
FORTY-TWO

STANDING in front of the oversized, gold mirror, I brushed my hands against my white lace dress. It was beautiful with a high, transparent neck and long lace sleeves. I put my short blonde wig on after neatly brushing my hair.

Alister had assigned a new girl to be my hair and makeup artist, but I declined. I wanted to dress myself the way I felt happiest, and this ensemble felt like a version of myself I knew the most.

Lifting the gold key in front of my face, I placed it alongside my tube of deep red lipstick.

I didn't care as I slid my feet into sky-high heels that I knew would never be permitted to walk around in. It was my small act of defiance.

I followed Bradley's intricate instructions and went back down to the Euphoria floor. It was risky wearing white on the otherwise dark floor, but I was the co-owner of this resort. I was no longer powerless; I was the queen.

Some of the nightingales greeted me, and some tried to offer me drinks or a seat for the live-action film, but I kept moving past them all.

There it was. The hidden elevator Bradley told me about. I slid my badge in front of it, but it didn't work. "No, no..." I pursed my lips and tried it again. The light turned red.

Looking closely at the keypad, I widened my eyes when I saw something scanning my face.

It turned green.

What was this? I glanced over my shoulder, but there was no one there and the doors slid open.

I took a step in and watched the gold chain door shut.

I watched as it went down through wiring and darkness while the temperature dropped rapidly. I knew I was going to where the dark therapy cages were—the cages the nightingales were housed in to make them become the subservient, obedient women who catered to a man's every need. They'd rather be able to face their monsters instead of fearing them in the darkness down here. The elevator jerked as it hit the floor, causing me to grab through the chains and hold myself up. The door opened, and I slid out and looked around. This entire resort was a maze.

This was a different floor. I could hear water drip through the crevices as I looked up. I was deeper underground. There was a musky odor as I stepped on stone and wet dirt. I was freezing cold and rubbed my arms as I made my way through the terrifying darkness that only held an orange haze from what looked like worn battery-powered lanterns.

The black brick was closing in on me as I continued down and heard the echo of sobs. Rolling my shoulders back, my heels clicked against the floor as I looked to the side and let my fingers brush against the emptied cages. Buckets, broken plates, and random black gowns were strewn throughout the small cage.

I stood in front of one that had a lock and broken dangling chain, and opened the door.

Stepping inside, I cringed at the odor. It wasn't the rotting feces, maggots, or urine-tinged ripped clothes.

No, it was the scent of death. I closed the door and shut my eyes; I could hear the cries and the pain of some innocent young girl who was flinching at every single sound, thinking that the grim reaper was coming for her.

What must they have told her she did to deserve a place in this hell? A girl goes running in a sports bra and fitted leggings, and is told she is setting herself up to be attacked. A woman meets the man she found on an online dating app, and she's raped, but told it had to be consensual since she was the one on an app. A college student walks across campus at night to go back to her dorm and is brutally murdered, but it was her fault for partying. It's always her fault. It's always our fault. The greatest fault we have as women is simply being alive.

Layla and I were trafficked by our parents, who saw us as financial burdens. A son would have been a blessing. We were sold to the highest bidder, and no one cared—not even the ones who gave us life.

What it must feel like to hold life in the palms of your hands.

I turned and traced my nails in the fingernail markings all over the brick walls. What she would have wanted me to do...

I pushed open the door to the cage and touched the cake pendant-locket with the pill inside.

I could force Declan Rothschild to take it—it would be better than this, of course. But as I walked down the rest of the hall, I began to count out loud.

"One...two...three...four..." My nails screeched against each cage door until I saw him.

Tilting my head, I looked at him. Bradley did a wonderful job. The cage was locked with a shiny, new gold padlock that I held the key to.

But the most beautiful part of La Gabbia was right here in this moment.

"Help," he cried, his voice gagged. His mouth and eyes were covered with silk ties, while his wrists and ankles were chained.

Declan Rothschild, the violent man who would have played dad to my niece or nephew, who would have continued to abuse his wife and countless other women, was in a cage and no one knew besides Bradley and me. I smiled and clutched the steel bars.

Tilting my head, I cleared my throat. "Hello, my precious little bird. You will make for the very first and perfect caged boy." Declan began sobbing, but I couldn't understand what I assumed were his pleas. I heard a puddle grow around him and scrunched my nose.

"Oh, you dirty little bird...you've pissed yourself. How embarrassing." I clicked my tongue and shook my head.

"Who are you?" I could finally make out as I silently watched him.

"I'm your keeper." I pushed the key into the lock and opened it slowly. Tapping the necklace around my neck, I knew this would be the start of something new. I had never felt so much happiness in my entire life. I had never felt as healed as I did in this moment.

This would heal me. This would be my retaliation.

Opening the Chanel purse I brought along with me, I lifted the knife out of it and twirled it in between my fingers.

Gripping Declan's arm, he tried to move but Bradley did an impeccable job having him tied up, probably assuming I was going to force a pill down his throat.

But instead, I lifted the knife and began carving her name into his forearm. "S-U-S-I-E" I spelled out as he screamed in agony.

"That's the girl you chose from the catalogue. The nightingale you paid extra to rape. The girl who cried and begged for her life, but you laughed and hurt her."

He was pleading through his disgusting saliva and snot draining down his pathetic face.

"All the money in the world, all the power and prestige that has come from the tears of others…and now here we are." I stepped on his fingers covered in blood with my Louboutin's and couldn't stop smiling as he screamed loudly.

"Oh, my precious little bird, we will have so much fun together…" I began choking him hard enough for his breathing to become shallow, but light enough for him to not lose consciousness. I had learned so much from the way Alister had choked me.

I tugged the blindfold off his eyes after releasing his neck. His eyes widened in shock as he looked at me. "I get it, I really do." I winked at him, referring to the fact that this same man strangled me, thinking I was another toy to play with.

Glancing down at his arm, he cried harder as the blood poured out and Susie's name was clearly engraved into his tender flesh.

"I'll be back soon. I'm going to have to recruit a nurse since there is no way I'm going to let you die." Wiping my hands on the blindfold, I threw it down at him. Tugging out a tube of red lipstick, I colored my lips before leaning down and placing a kiss on his forehead.

Turning away, I locked the door behind me as fear and panic painted across his pale face.

"It's time for you to really immerse yourself in dark therapy. I don't like all the noise you're making." I wiggled my finger at him before tucking my belongings back into my purse.

"Bye bye, birdie."

CHAPTER
FORTY-THREE

"MY BRIDE." I was in the bathtub with my head tilted back and the bubbles covering my body.

"Hello, husband," I whispered.

He came around to me and brushed his hand across my face. "You are glowing." His eyebrow lifted. "Perhaps a soon-to-be mother's glow?" He bit into his lower lip.

"You've come more inside corpses than you have in me, Alister. Perhaps we could leave the dead girls out of our bed?" I shot back. Something was changing inside me. I didn't just feel powerful; I *was* powerful. A man's life was in my hands, and I couldn't help but love the way revenge tasted.

Alister looked at me carefully. "Bradley leaving seems to have put you in the best mood…"

I nodded. "It's freeing knowing that parts of that

period of my time are gone, Alister. I'm just looking forward to this next journey; one where I take more control over the way we do things at La Gabbia," I said confidently. But I realized I had shown Alister Ivory that I was gaining too much confidence, and a confident woman was his trigger.

"How was your day?" I toned down the way I was speaking to him, but it was too late. He was taking off his belt, and I held my breath in hopes it was because he was undressing.

"Get out of the bath, Demi."

My heart raced as my lips quivered. "I'm all soapy. May I go rinse off in the shower?" I hated the way my voice sounded in front of him.

"Get out of the bath, Demi," he growled as he folded his leather belt. Forcing myself to stand and step out as soapsuds clung to my naked body, I began walking to the shower, but just as I turned my back to him, a loud crack that felt like heat blazed into my skin. I didn't feel the pain because the shock of it all delayed any form of a reaction...

"Alister," I cried. *Powerless.* That's what I was and would always be.

"Mocking my sexual preferences? Mocking my desires?" He didn't stop. I could smell the scent of leather meshing with my dampened skin.

"Please." I cried out.

The taste of blood intertwined with my saliva as I began coughing. "Please," I begged before he crouched behind me and splayed my legs apart, shoving himself inside me while grunting.

"No." Everything blurred as I rested my head on the cold tile.

"Shall I kill you now, Demi, so I can have you as a corpse?" he hissed in my ear.

I closed my eyes and let myself drift away into the ocean. I saw him. I saw Bradley. I wondered what he was doing at this very moment.

And with that, I smiled and didn't feel anything anymore.

———

The sun shimmered through the curtains, and I opened my eyes. "Marcie?" Her bright green eyes were staring down at me.

"Demi, you just can't behave..." She shook her head with disappointment.

"Did you know we are all microchipped?" She pointed to her shoulder blade.

"I thought the tattoo was just their identification?" I brushed my hand against the raven tattooed on my shoulder blade that no one else had here except for Layla.

Marcie let out a small laugh as she wrung out a washcloth and dabbed it over the bruise circling my eye.

"Alister drugs every single girl who is brought here. That cute, pink peony welcome drink?" Marcie placed antibiotic cream on the cuts as I winced from the burning.

"All laced. Then they insert microchips before putting a tattoo over it." She shrugged.

"Why are you telling me this?" I whispered.

"Because the woman you let go…Sage Rothschild? She's microchipped, too. All the former caged girls are. She was one of Ian Ivory's caged girls. That means the little boy, Myles, you sent with her will be found and dragged right back here as soon as they kill her. Now, my question is, where have you stashed Declan Rothschild?" Marcie sat back on the stool and squinted at me.

I took a moment and looked at her closely. "Marcie, you never did tell me how you came here to Ivory Island? Or why you never seem scared…"

She looked familiar.

Oddly familiar.

"Marcie…what's your last name?" I questioned my former roommate.

She smiled at me as she ran her fingers through her hair. "Ivory."

Standing, she moved her hair from her shoulder; only bloodline Ivorys get a pretty white bird.

"I'm Ian and Alister's younger sister." She stood proudly. "So that makes me your sister-in-law."

My jaw dropped as I looked at her and pushed myself upward. "Marcie..." Shaking my head, I didn't know how she knew everything about Sage, Myles, or Declan. She knew I was here hunting for answers and a way to end all of this.

"I was told to keep an extra close eye on you, and now I know why my brother asked. We can't have you going around killing off our bloodline, silly little girl." She booped my nose.

"Now, Alister has no idea what you've done with his product—the little boy that a very wealthy family is trying to purchase by the end of the week. We must remediate the situation because, if I tell him, then you'll be slaughtered, and I'll have to deal with Alister moping around over you dying."

"Marcie, please no." I clasped my hands together. "Kidnapping children and selling them to families? Trafficking young women to keep her as disposable toys for old, rich men? I mean, this cannot be what you think is…"

"Demi!" Marcie shouted at me. "Stop speaking and listen to me closely. You let Bradley leave his family and duty behind. Now, Alister has forced me to take over his duties while upholding mine, and that means managing inventory. If you don't help me convince Sage Rothschild to bring Myles back, then it's both of our lives on the line." Her jaw ticked as she stood.

"I have a proposition. You can tell Sage to come visit Layla…talk to her unborn child or whatever you'd like, and then tell her if she doesn't bring Myles back, the deal is done, and we kill Layla."

"Declan went on a boating trip. I didn't do anything to him." I pulled the blanket off and stood, immediately grabbing the headboard as my body ached from what Alister had done to me last night.

"Marcie, I'll handle it. Give me time."

"You better, Demi."

CHAPTER FORTY-FOUR

"MRS. ROTHSCHILD, this is Demi Ivory calling to check in on you and Mr. Rothschild." I sat in the new office space Alister had apparently created for me.

This was his way of saying 'I'm sorry I whipped you to near-death, then raped you while denying your request to stop having corpses in bed with us.'

He wanted me to be more involved, to show him that I cared about his business…his empire.

"Demi." She sounded relieved. "I'm doing well, thank you for checking in. And can you believe Declan went off on some fancy boat excursion right after we checked out of La Gabbia?" She cleared her throat.

"That's absolutely amazing." We both knew there was high chance this call was being monitored.

"So Sage, I know you ordered virgin hair extensions, but we were freshly out of blonde, so I checked in with our salon, and they are making some right away for you since we have new inventory."

"Did the package of…hair extensions you already bought here make it safely?" I was hoping she'd figure out what, or rather who, I was referring to. It would be risky for me to search for Myles's mother here with Alister watching my browser history.

The long pause had me worried, but then Sage sighed. "Everything I brought home made it safely, and I've put everything up where it belongs."

Myles was safe with his mother. I made a difference. I saved a child the way I had wished to be saved.

"Demi, I needed to tell you something… There's a beautiful boat that our friend is going to sail near Ivory Island tomorrow. I hope you'll go peek at it for me. Declan said he wanted to know if it was worth purchasing."

A pit in my stomach grew as I traced the grooves in my desk. "Will you check the boat for us?" she asked slowly.

It had to be Bradley. He was coming back for me.

"Of course, I will. You take good care, Mrs. Rothschild." I hung up the phone and turned around in my chair to look at the wall of shelves.

Neatly lined books, small golden décor, but then what I ignored and no longer couldn't were the glass canisters filled to the brim with eyelashes.

"Eyelashes are the dream catchers for tears." I jerked around as I faced Alister.

He was wearing all white.

"I can hear their cries as I look into these jars." He smiled as he made his way toward me. I stood and moved around the desk, fearful of the belt that snaked around his waist.

"Just like the caged girls, you are the most beautiful when you cry." He paused before reaching for one of the glass jars and bringing it to my desk.

"It's a bit funny, isn't it? Every single woman who has walked through the doors of La Gabbia are, in fact, all or have been, caged girls..." He began sprinkling the eyelashes all over my desk.

"Some of them were fortunate to be trained via Ian's white therapy and turned into pretty little wives, but my girls..." He laughed. "My girls all stayed beautiful, precious little birds. And birds so beautiful must stay in La Gabbia." He ran his hand across his facial hair.

"You do know what La Gabbia means, don't you, my wife?" He smiled at me.

"No, Alister, I do not." The shake in my voice was clear, but I made sure to speak respectfully.

"The cage, of course. This entire resort is one beautiful cage, isn't it?" He stood and began throwing the eyelashes all over us, like a sweet flower girl would on a wedding day with flower petals.

"Make a wish, my darling raven." He was laughing wildly as he spun around and kept tossing the eyelashes into the air.

"You do know making a wish on an eyelash is always granted!" he cheered as I watched Alister Ivory flip into yet another sick version of himself.

I waited for him to stop. His face was flushed, and he gripped my shoulders, dragging me closer to him. I could smell the strong scent of whiskey on his breath.

"One more wish." He lifted one finger up and pressed it between my eyebrows.

"Anything?" I asked lowly, terrified this was another game, another trap.

"Let Layla go..." I whispered. Alister's breathing was heavy, cutting through the chilly silence of the space.

"Demi, I cannot. Because once I kill you, I'll have to marry her—especially since you've sent her husband away." He grinned. "She is the perfect substitute. Besides, the official caged girl is never allowed to leave. She is my property. She let you be the favorite girl, and she gets to be the caged girl. Rules are rules." My heart crashed. He was going to murder me, then subject my sister to being his wife after she'd already been forced to go through hell and back.

I lowered my shoulders, hunched a bit, and let the moisture in my eyes build. I needed to look like a damsel in distress.

"One wish, Demi," he rushed out before stretching his arms above his head.

"Let me go…Layla is far better fit to being your obedient wife. I can work in Miami for you as the bridge to new inventory." I was a coward. I was the weakest link. I was selfish.

His eyebrow lifted as he stared at me curiously. "You really do hate it here, don't you?"

"No, Alister. I'm just not the wife I know you deserve, but my sister is. I could lure the children and women. I know you are looking for a new confidante. Let it be me." I nodded as I felt hope the way he was processing it all.

"Layla would be more willing to do…" I felt sick to my stomach, but I knew I was doing what had to be done.

"You have been defiant and truthfully, a boring hag in the bed. The corpses excite me more." He tapped his fingers across my desk erratically.

"Father always said the two women you must not

ever release from the cage are the favorite girl and the caged girl. The caged girl is the most obedient bird of them all. But the favorite girl is the one who is the best front. The best at a façade. You aren't much of anything, Demi. I suppose Layla and I could keep this baby for ourselves. It is an Ivory, after all." I didn't know if he was having some kind of manic episode, but I did know he was considering my request.

"I will grant you this wish, but not fully. You are still mine to keep. I just need you to go away for a bit as I do a trial with Layla, my other raven. I have been extremely stressed about inventory and need someone to go to Miami while I handle La Gabbia. You will be allotted one week away." He clasped his hands together and eyed me.

"I think that time apart will do us good, Alister. It's not that I don't appreciate you and our marriage; I just think I'd like to be in the field more, and then when I return, if you still want me to be your wife, I will. If Layla is more suited, well, I'll accept this heartache and serve La Gabbia to the best of my ability." I bowed my head and prayed he'd believe me.

"You can take one of the private planes. I'll be tracking you. I still love you and that pussy." He patted the tattoo on my shoulder before wrapping his hands around my neck and tightening them. "See you in a week, wife."

CHAPTER
FORTY-FIVE

"MARCIE, please let me see her one time before I leave. It's a dangerous job that I'll have. I've never gotten to even talk to her," I pleaded with her as she brushed her blonde locks. My shoulder was aching as I decided to play a game of operation with myself. I had a large band aid covering where my tattoo was.

"Fine. Only if you'll bring me back the new Louis Vuitton from Miami. I want the white with the colorful logo."

I nodded eagerly. "Of course. Alister is letting me take plenty of cash."

Squinting at me, she shrugged. "Let's go." I had tried everything to see Layla, but nothing worked. Alister had me on zero access to my sister.

I clutched the small tote bag to my chest. I was

wearing my favorite lace dress with the long sleeves and slight high neck.

"Why don't we have a quick drink? A toast?" I slid the two rosy champagne glasses between us.

Marcie paused as she held the white keycard in her hand. "You're being way too emotional, Demi."

"One last drink?" I nudged Marcie as she lifted it and swirled it around.

"You know I can't pass up the glass of this stuff. I mean, it's blended with the peonies that are grown on grounded up girls who were just too weak to survive heaven on earth. Imagine living at a resort and complaining?" She scoffed as she drank the champagne I had poured for her.

We chatted for a bit as I waited for the medication to dissolve. I didn't want to kill Marcie; I just needed to have her sleep for a bit.

And it worked. As soon as she stood, she grew dizzy and slurred her speech.

"What… Demi…what did you do?" She collapsed onto the floor, and I tugged the white card from her hand. I didn't have time. She'd be just fine, but for now, I had to see my sister and say my goodbyes.

. . .

The rush to get to Layla was one that went by in a blur. My white heels clicked against the cold floor as I kept looking over my shoulder and waiting for Alister or Marcie to magically appear.

But they didn't. I made it. I slid Marcie's badge over the keypad and waited for the door to slide open. It was the most deranged living situation. Alister Ivory was truly sick. Layla was asleep on a small cot in the middle of a life-sized bird cage. One small light flickered by her.

How afraid and alone she must have been all this time, being used to reproduce for elite couples and entertain the highest bidder as they gawked at her. I slid my heels off and walked barefoot against the cold, black marble. She was truly beautiful. Her long black hair hung over the pillow, and I watched her breathe softly. Tugging the cage door open after using the gold key I found in Marcie's pocket, I halted as the creaking echoed and woke her up.

She slowly opened her eyes and looked at me. Bruises covered her face. I'd have thought that Alister would keep her extra safe since she was pregnant, but I suppose he had allowed someone to have their turn with her for the right price.

"Demilion," she whispered as she blinked faster and stood slowly as I entered my sister's cage.

"Layla." I fought back the tears and closed my eyes.

I was taken back to the memories of us as little girls with big dreams. We thought we'd grow up and have a beautiful little shop on the beach, selling seashell jewelry. We thought we'd grow up and marry princes and buy homes next to each other. We thought we'd have a lifetime of memories being sisters.

"What are you doing here, my sister? I thought you went to Charlotte?" She glided over to me and lifted her hands, but didn't touch me. She froze mid-air.

Tears fell from my eyes as I questioned, "Why won't you hug me?"

She smiled with sorrow lining her lips. "Because I'm scared you're not real."

Throwing my arms around her, I squeezed my sister tightly.

"Why didn't you go to Charlotte? Why did you not let them keep you as the favorite girl?" I sobbed.

"You were born to soar, my Demilion. You weren't meant to be caged. Mama and Papa sold us…they tore us apart. I wanted to protect you, even though I knew it was the lesser of two evils."

"I miss you…" I cried, unable to compose myself the way my sister was. "How can you be so calm?" I clutched her even tighter.

"I've been kept in the darkness most of the time, but today, my light is finally here…my beautiful light. We appreciate the light so much more when we've been trapped in darkness for far too long." She held my face in between her palms and kissed my forehead.

"I'm sorry about Bradley. I didn't know, sister. I didn't know. I just obeyed Alister's demands, and Bradley..." Layla looked to the floor.

"He's a good man."

"A baby..." My hand brushed against my sister's stomach. "Do you love Bradley?" I asked her, knowing we didn't have much time left.

She offered a small smile. "I've only ever loved one person in my life, and that person has always been you. But with Bradley, I felt safe, and I suppose that feeling safe with someone is its own kind of love. I just didn't know you and Bradley had a love story of your own, so sister, I promise you this child will go to its rightful family, and I'll beg Mr. Ivory to seek a different man to breed with."

The way my sister was speaking crushed my soul. She had been brainwashed. "I don't love Bradley." I forced myself to say. "Layla, I need you to lay down and turn around for me and trust me." She looked at me curiously as I guided her to her small cot. Laying my tote bag out, I tugged the bottle of alcohol, a small sewing kit, and a knife.

She jerked away in fear. "Demilion!"

I covered her mouth and begged her to trust me. "Please, Layla. It'll hurt for only a moment." After a few minutes of pleading and explaining to her why I had to do this, she sobbed and held me in her arms, trying to change my mind.

I slid the blade carefully into my sister's shoulder blade, right under the matching raven tattoo. She began bleeding, and I calmly grabbed the gauze and dug around as she cried out in pain, but bit down on the makeshift gag I had stuffed into her mouth.

There it was. The fucking microchip that was what dogs have inserted into them. Stitching her wound up messily, I prayed she'd have a chance to be seen by a real doctor, but at least now we weren't two animals. We were two human beings.

"I love you." I held her in my arms and handed her the rest of the items in the bag.

Looking down into it, she pressed her forehead against mine. "I hope to see you soon."

Shaking my head, I knew I'd never get to see her again. This was it. I was going to be free.

CHAPTER
FORTY-SIX

BRADLEY DID SHOW UP. Of course, he did. I released a long breath and stood in front of him. "You just can't stay away," I mustered up the courage to say with my hands up as he grew closer to me, even though I just wanted him to wrap his arms around me.

Bradley opened his palm to me. "Let's go home, Demi."

"Home?" I laughed dryly as I looked at his hand.

"We can make one together, finally."

Nodding, I licked my lips and smiled. "Home," I repeated the simple word that meant nothing to me. How could it? I'd never had one. I had given up all hope for one. You can't possibly miss something that you've never had but some reason I did. I missed the idea of a place so happy and welcoming that I'd never want to leave it.

"Alister offered me the private plane to go back to Miami. Ditch the boat and come with me." I took his hand and led him to the plane.

"You look beautiful, Demi. I know he gave you a week, but I think we can make it out there on our own. I've already set up the fake IDs, the spot in Mexico, and money has been moved. We are going to leave this life once and for all." Bradley looked around nervously. I was scared too, thinking Alister would appear at any moment, or a camera was watching us. I had to keep moving.

"What about Layla and the baby?" I questioned.

Sadness grew across his face as he looked to the floor. "If there is one thing Alister won't let go of is his original captive. His caged girl. The sale of our baby will seal his future in custom-pro—"

I flinched. "Don't say products. Don't refer to your child as a product."

"How else can I survive knowing my own flesh and blood will be sold...the same way his or her mother and aunt were. Demi, sometimes disassociating from it all is the only way we can survive."

I brushed my hands against the white lace dress and tugged out the oversized white hat, placing it on my head before sliding my sunglasses on.

Bradley smiled as he watched me adjust it. "Your favorite hat."

"I forgot one thing, but I'll be right back." I gave Bradley a quick hug before climbing down the steps and hiding in the shadows.

The suitcases were being lifted onto the plane and the pilot who I had paid off with the help of Sage Rothschild agreed to keep Bradley hidden in the cockpit in case Alister boarded to see me.

I stood and looked at La Gabbia. From the outside, it truly was a gorgeous all-inclusive resort. It looked like the perfect escape, the perfect getaway. A stunning all-white exterior that was hugged by palm trees. But inside of it was where every nightmare was made true, even though most guests thought their dreams would be the ones granted. The wealthy were bored, and this luxury resort was their playground.

Goodbye, La Gabbia as we knew it. I had some revisions in mind.

———

BRADLEY

Demi was quiet as the plane took off. The oversized hat she always loved was covering her face, along with the sunglasses. She looked beautiful in the white lace dress, and it felt symbolic to where our story began. For the first time in my life, I'm not scared to forever leave the Ivory name behind, and it was all because of her. Demi has always fought to escape and survive. She's always wanted to live a life of her own choices. And because of her, we'd both get to. I let her have her time, but once we were long gone from Ivory Island and the plane was soaring through the clouds, I squeezed her hand.

"I'm glad we didn't take the boat; a plane always has room for Jack and Rose," I said playfully before tugging her hat off.

My lips parted as she turned to me and, even with her sunglasses on, I knew it wasn't her.

"Layla..." My voice cracked as she slid her sunglasses off. Tears flooded down her face as she cried for Demi.

"I'm sorry, Bradley, but she convinced me to take her spot. She said if I didn't, she'd kill herself. She did it for us and the baby," she rushed out as if I wouldn't give her time to explain.

I sank my head back and closed my eyes in a state of shock as tears rolled down my own face. Reaching over, I held her hand in mine.

"Demi..." I shook my head. She could have saved herself but instead, she sacrificed her life to save the three of ours.

Layla and I sat in our seats, crying silently. "He can track you...the baby..."

I felt panicked but she shook her head and lifted a small metal microchip. "Demi outsmarted everyone and gave me hers; she has mine. Alister said it was a rule that once a caged girl was chosen, she could never leave. The caged girl was the Ivory's property and losing her was a sign of failure. After rejection from his own brother and dad his entire life, he would have never let me go. I'm so sorry, Bradley, but I took her offer because..." She looked down at her stomach and I nodded.

"I know, I know..." I breathed out.

"It just hurts too much."

Alister was going to kill her and now, there was nothing any of us could do to save her.

CHAPTER
FORTY-SEVEN

DEMI - EIGHT MONTHS LATER...

As the elevator went down, I felt a surge of energy and a rush coursing through my veins as I took a step out and my Christian Louboutin's echoed against the black floor.

I was wearing my favorite, all-white lace dress with the hat I wore when I thought my new beginning was starting and put Layla in the same outfit. My lips were painted in my favorite shade of red, and I brushed my hand against the black brick wall.

Swiping my card against the keypad, I waited as it slid open and saw him. Declan Rothschild was sitting hunched over in a corner, sobbing.

I flicked my small flashlight on and smiled at him.

"An angel," he cried out, seeing me standing out against the darkness he'd been accustomed to for months.

"Oh, you silly, little man...I'm not an angel. An angel is who greets those who make it to heaven. I'm the caged girl. The one who will stay here with you for the rest of eternity and make sure you never die until it's meant to be. I want you to live through hell with me." I smiled at him. "It smells so terrible, Declan. So very terrible." I took a step back and rolled my shoulders as the chains he was bound by echoed.

Each cage was occupied now. Alister hadn't been down here yet. He trusted me with the new renovations I was instilling in La Gabbia after he found out I swapped spots with Layla. At first, he beat me until I passed out. Then he raped me and threatened to kill me. And finally, he kept me in the dark cage for four months, where I didn't see a sliver of light, I heard no voices, and I sat in my own piss, eating only darkened food that blended into the world around me. A girl would bring me beets, blackberries, and occasionally, strips of steak. I thought I'd die. I thought I'd kill myself by bashing my skull against the wall. But my dream was to be released and then make new developments. Give myself purpose to live.

Ultimately, Alister saw my little swap as a sign of dedication to him. He thought my love for him had me envious of his desire to switch me out for my sister. Now, I had a new set of clients coming in soon. Ladies who had all experienced a pain unlike any other. Therapy wasn't helping them; medications weren't soothing them. They felt rage and anger that never went away, and now, they could live out their wildest fantasies and desires.

If there has been anything that I have learned is that I do love being the favorite girl and being that to the most powerful man in the world has its perks. He may be the king, but I am the queen, and just like in a game of chess where everything is as simple as being white or black, Alister Ivory knows a queen protects the king. I will protect my king now that he's allowing me to play my own game. Just for a few more rounds, until I have him where I need him. He thinks we are on the same team, but we aren't, and there's nothing more deadly than an opposing queen against a weakened king. I was light and he was dark. And something else that I've come to learn is that light always finds a way to seep into the darkness. A storm can only last so long before the sun fights its way in.

I headed to the entrance of our resort and stood by the girls all dressed in white holding beautiful peony bouquets for each of our new guests. A beautiful white limo arrived and there they were.

One by one, they exited with tired eyes and weakened souls. They weren't all rich women, and they weren't all powerful. They've been stripped of everything by a man they trusted. Rather than seeking revenge and being caught in their own countries, here they can come and release their inner anger and rage. They can rest and heal. Some of us need to taste revenge to heal, and now that my inventory is well-stocked, I know I can help these women. I can help former girls that the Ivorys sold and trafficked or caged. I can help the women who were abused and who wished they could hold the power to attack without repercussion. I know I have the caged men ready to have a taste of their own medicine. My inventory is packed to the brim with Alister's former clients. I decided to lure them here with false pretenses of the Euphoria program, and instead cage them. Alister found it more amusing and lucrative than his former business. I convinced him by telling him that the more powerful and wealthy men we cage, the less there are competing with him. We take them from all over the world in order to keep it safe. We don't want hundreds of shady CEOs, corrupt businessmen, or questionable celebrities going missing from the same place. Many are assumed to have died by overdose or running from white collar crimes. Many times a missing, rich white man isn't as worrisome as I thought it'd be. Those in their lives were probably relieved an egomaniac was gone. I've strategized this with the help of all the women who once worked here as prisoners. It's my own form of rehabilitation for my girls. *They aren't his precious little birds anymore; they are my soldiers.*

"Welcome to La Gabbia, I'm Demi Ivory. My husband Alister started this exclusive resort years ago in hope he could rebuild marriages and expand families. But then when he married me, he realized he had it all wrong. The truth is, women are the focal point of our society, and if we hurt them, then everything will crash and burn. So now, we focus on your desires, fantasies, and healing. We focus on being set free from the gilded cage."

The girls began handing out welcome drinks and peony bouquets. The guests were staring at me with fascination. Even Marcie had decided that she wanted in on my new business plan and helped obtain my inventory.

"I will make sure you leave La Gabbia feeling relieved and happy. I will make sure you have the means to start fresh. You will be given an entirely new identity when you leave here to protect yourselves against your abusers. We've anonymously notified the police in your areas about the men who have led you here in the first place—they will assume these men killed themselves or ran away in fear of the law. Now, our beautiful team that we lovingly call our doves will hand out binders of exactly what your options are. You can choose your customized treatment plan, which can involve immersive rage release therapy or talking things through verbal therapy. You'll be given beautiful new clothes, along with all the perks: hair, nails, skin, etc. Our goal is for you to be a brand-new woman... one who recognizes her power."

Suddenly, a warm arm wrapped around me. Looking down, I saw his tattooed arm. It had my face on it. Looking up at him, I smiled. I knew I'd have to kill him for what he's done to me and the others, but right now, I may have some kind of affection toward him in some sick way. He was allowing me to create a new world something I couldn't do without him. We both were broken shards of glass that somehow thrived together with our sick desire to hurt. I still needed him around so I could slowly funnel his money into my accounts. I needed his connections and to learn more from him.

Sometimes we justify the scars because the person with the knife was someone we finally let ourselves love and trust. And for now, I knew, I would have to let the person holding the knife keep carving into my flesh so I could save others from bleeding out.

He kissed me, and I turned back to my new guests. I had one empty cage waiting for him that I'd fill soon enough. I had even hired a new physician. Dr. Serena

Indigo was beginning to perform penectomies and castrations on my captives. We'd give the choice to the ladies first, of course, if they'd like to do them. I already began filming some of her surgeries while the men were awake as part of our movie night selection. My husband once enjoyed collecting eyelashes in jars, and I had ordered the same crystal jars so I too, could store my new souvenirs.

Everyone was watching me as I spoke more about our program. Brushing my hands against my beautiful lace dress and slightly adjusting my hat, I smiled. Guiding them down to the darkness, I handed them each a whip, a knife, and a bag full of tools. Each cage was unlocked by the nightingales, who still preferred to stay down in the darkness. The cries of the men made me smile. The fear I could hear as they pleaded once my new guests entered filled my heart.

Deciding who I wanted to be meant deciding who I would never be again. I will forever live in an Ivory world; I'll never be set free from these walls. *The beauty of it all is sometimes the safest birds are the ones that are kept in the gilded cage.*

Perhaps, this wasn't a selfless heroic act, but rather one driven based on the notion that I am simply exhausted from being hunted, and now I just want to be safe. The truth is, there isn't always a happily ever after. Sometimes there's just a 'I will survive. I can survive. I survived,' and that has to be enough. Even when you know you deserved better. So much better. I want to make a difference. These men attacked, raped, abused, and tormented innocent women. They didn't deserve to get away unscathed; they deserved to feel the pain they inflicted.

Clearing my throat, I waved the ladies inside the darkness. "Now, my precious little birds, off you go... It's time I teach you how to fly and be free."

EPILOGUE

DEAR DEMI,

    I hope that this letter finds you well. There is not a day that goes by in which I do not think about you, or the sacrifices you made to set us free from the gilded cage my family always kept me bound inside.

    It pains me to use the word 'us,' knowing that simple word doesn't include you. Layla is ready for our son to be born. She's uncomfortable and doesn't speak much, and I know the guilt plagues her as well. It is our deepest desire for you to escape and join us, your family. We will wait for you forever.

    There are too many words I have left to say, but there is something I have to tell you in order to make peace with much of the evil I have participated in my life. As a soon-to-be father, I am hoping I will be able to heal, and my son's karma won't be impacted because of his father's sins. I also want you to know that Alister had Conrad killed. He saw the video of Conrad hurting you. He's gone, Demi. He is gone.

Ian and Alister Ivory had a younger sister; her name was Maggie. Maggie died of suicide—gruesome, at that. She hung herself from the chandelier above the Ivory family dinner table before one of their dinner parties. She killed herself because of what they had done to her. Maggie had fallen in love with one of Ian's butlers and became pregnant. As soon as Ian found out, he kept Maggie in a sensory deprivation cage. She spent her pregnancy locked up in an all-white space with no noise and nothing to eat beyond rice, yogurt, and egg whites. Once the child, a daughter, was born, her father forced the child and mother apart. Maggie never found her. It is to my understanding that Alister took the baby with him to La Gabbia, assuming this child would be the only Ivory girl birthed by a true Ivory woman.

Maggie left a journal detailing the horrors Ian had put her through and pleaded that anyone who found the journal should find the child and save her. Her dying wish was that the little girl be sent far away from the Ivory family, to be adopted by a normal family and live a normal life.

Demi, I know this is much to ask for, but if there is an Ivory daughter caged in the resort, I know you will find her. I dug through some of the blueprints and folders Alister gave me when I worked for him and saw there were sensory depri-

vation cages all across the underbelly of the resort, where he kept the children he had kidnapped. There has to be a cage we missed.

I looked away from Bradley's letter and watched the ocean waves crash into the beautiful white sand. I pursed my lips and took a deep breath, watching as the sun set.

Alister had assured me there were no children left here. He had promised that if I stayed with him, we could amend some of the rules and business practices he was once adamant about. He craved a family of his own and a wife that would love him. I knew that he was in love with me after I survived everything that he thought would kill me.

Folding the letter, I slid it into my pocket and tugged my white suit jacket closed. Brushing my hands against my dress pants, I spun around on my heels and made my way to the medical wing of La Gabbia. I didn't have time to waste if there were secrets; I knew I had to uncover them and be one step ahead of my husband at all times.

My heels echoed against the beautiful marble floors, and I waved my badge against each door, picking up my pace until I cut through the mostly empty medical wing. The eerie silence and lack of people had me glancing over my shoulder.

Swallowing, I turned toward the hidden space where Alister once kept the children he intended to sell to our wealthy guests. The doors opened with my badge, but the cages were empty. Walking into the room, I flinched as I could hear their cries and smell the scent of feces and urine, even though they were no longer here.

Looking around, I padded my palms against the wall until I began waving my badge across it aimlessly. And just like his brother, Ian, I knew how much Alister loved secret rooms and spaces. The wall slid open and revealed a glass room.

I stumbled back as my lips parted with my heart-beat picking up. "Oh my God," I breathed out. She walked closer to the glass and pressed her palms against it. Tilting her head, her bright green eyes stared back at me curiously.

Her long, curly blonde hair fell over her shoulders and looked strangely fuller compared to her tiny frame covered in a small white gown.

I placed my palms on the glass, matching her hands to mine. The glass slid open. My fingerprints alone could open anything in La Gabbia.

The little girl walked backward as she kept her eyes fixed on mine.

She stopped as I drew closer to her, and I dropped to my knees to be at eye-level with her. "Hello there,

I'm Demi. I'm here to help you, little bird. What's your name?"

She smiled at me blankly, lifted her hands, and cupped my face into her palms. "I'm the favorite child," she whispered.

AUTHOR'S NOTE

Dear readers,

Thank you so much for reading The Caged Girl. It is truly the biggest honor to know you spent your time escaping reality in my deranged world. The Favorite Girl and The Caged Girl are so very special to me, and I'm thankful beyond words that you read Demi's story. As always, each of my thrillers are based around something happening in the world around us. Human trafficking and sex trafficking are massive global issues, and unfortunately, get hidden away easily.

Examples of many topics in this novel happening around the world and right here in the United States- violence against women is not outlawed in all countries, there are countries that allow rapists to marry their women to avoid punishment, children account for nearly one-third of identi-

fied trafficking victims globally, 'Epstein island' and famous celebrities who used their power to victimize young women along with trafficking them. Men have been able to abuse women time after time with no repercussion.

Power and wealth are abused, and lives are stolen from them. Secret worlds may seem fictional, but they truly happen around us. A simple google search alone yields horrors of the world and the dark depths people will go to just for power and wealth. Demi is a symbol of resilience and sacrifice and knowing that although the world can be a scary place for many, we deserve to fight for a life we want. Demi is seeking revenge from all the men that have hurt women time after time because she knows no one else will punish them.

If you find me on social media you'll see all of the updates on the next books and what is to come in the Ivory world. If you saw the mention of the book mentioned in The Caged Girl with the main character, Mila that is a shoutout to the next thriller that will be less dark, more twisted and nostalgic thriller set in 2006 / present day.

If you enjoyed The Caged Girl, it would be such a gift if you could take a moment to leave a review on Amazon, Goodreads or anywhere else books are loved.

I am so grateful for you and wish you all the love, happiness, and light in the world!

XO,

Monica

ACKNOWLEDGMENTS

Thank you never seems like enough to say to those who make this dream of mine a reality, but here goes.

Thank you to my family, of course who have clapped so loudly for me I never noticed anyone who didn't. My beautiful children, Mila and Ari, who are the reason I find the strength to write. I love you both more than anything in this world, and I am so honored I get the front seat in your stories. Mila, you are forever my favorite girl and Ari, you are forever my favorite little boy.

Thank you to my husband, who has stood by my side since we were kids. We've built this life from literally the ground up, and I am so proud of us. I love you forever and always. Thank you for being nothing like the villains in my books but everything like the swoon-worthy book boyfriends I promise to write more of.

To my parents who are the epitome of sacrifice and hard work. I'm so thankful you never restricted me from dreaming big even when those dreams didn't include being a doctor.

To my sister, Paige I don't even have to write it out

because I know you already know how much you mean to me. I love you to the moon and to Saturn. Thank you so much for being there through it all even when *it all* isn't always pretty and easy.

To my Joss, sharing the ups and downs with you without an ounce of judgment but only understanding is a gift I'll forever be thankful for. Whether it's unlimited podcasts or reunions with you my heart is full! I love you always!

To my Marcie, you believed in me from the very beginning of this wild ride with my books but you also have a beautiful heart.You just get me. I love you my fellow, unhinged blonde twinnie.

To the ladies in my life – Jackie, Silvia, Marisha, Kealey, Allyson, Lauren, Taylor, Kandi, Kori, Sarah, Lacey, Mary, Jessica, Kelly, Katie, Amanda, Sammie and Erin. I'm beyond words, thankful for each of you. Your support and friendship is what every girl deserves.

To my incredible, amazing, and wonderful ARC team, you all have always had my back and my books. Thank you for celebrating each of my books with me and cheering for each success or pulling me up through each heartache. I am so grateful for you all.

To my Facebook reader group members and moderators (Monica Arya's Misfits) you all make my heart so full and happy. Seeing the posts, reviews, conversations and support is one I'll never take for granted.

And of course, thank you to the most FABULOUS readers a girl could have. Without you, there'd be no author in me. Thank you for your kindness and support.

ABOUT THE AUTHOR

Monica Arya is an Amazon Top 35 bestselling author of multiple novels. She is a multi-genre author but focuses mostly on thrillers. Monica resides in North Carolina with her husband, two beautiful children and golden doodle. She loves to connect with readers on social media @monicaaryaauthor or in her Facebook reader group Monica Arya's Misfits.

ALSO BY MONICA ARYA

Thrillers :

Girl in the Reflection

Shades of Her

The Next Mrs. Wimberly

Navy Lies

Don't Believe Him

The Favorite Girl

The Arranged Marriage

The Caged Girl

Romance :

Saved by You

Misfit

When Love Breaks Us

Stay in the loop for all upcoming books and behind the scenes by joining Monica Arya's Misfits my exclusive Facebook reader group or following me on social media (Instagram, TikTok) @monicaaryaauthor